On the table he placed a short, polished horn. It was stout enough to balance upright; the thick end was encased in a leather grip, studded around the rim, while the tip was smooth and waxy yellow. 'In time, all pleasures shall be experienced, all avenues explored . . . but now, your hand, Sianon – use it gently.' Her left hand remained tethered; her right hand hung down. 'Go on,' he whispered.

By the same author:

THE SLAVE OF LIDIR
THE DUNGEONS OF LIDIR
THE FOREST OF BONDAGE
PLEASURE ISLAND
CHOOSING LOVERS FOR JUSTINE
CITADEL OF SERVITUDE

Other Nexus Classics:

THE IMAGE
CHOOSING LOVERS FOR JUSTINE
OBSESSION   July
HIS MISTRESS'S VOICE   August
CITADEL OF SERVITUDE   September

A NEXUS CLASSIC

THE
HANDMAIDENS

Aran Ashe

This book is a work of fiction.
In real life, make sure you practise safe sex.

First published in 1995 by
Nexus
Thames Wharf Studios
Rainville Road
London W6 9HT

This Nexus Classic edition 1999

Typeset by TW Typesetting, Plymouth, Devon

Printed and bound by
Caledonian International Book Manufacturing Ltd,
Glasgow

ISBN 0 352 33282 4

Contents

1

The Twisted Cross

He was an unwary traveller in an unfamiliar land. To him, it seemed simple: they were young women in distress; they needed help. But he did not understand the rules.

Josef Stenner stood beside his horse at one end of the small wooden bridge and watched the peculiar convoy crossing. Cayu, his guide, hung back, pretending to repack his panniers but throwing furtive glances. The two companions had earlier passed the convoy on the road; Cayu had wanted to avoid this second encounter, but Stenner had overruled him. So now, the young traveller stood his ground alone as the first team of horses thundered onto the bridge. The heavy carriages looked ancient, even for this land. Their doors were emblazoned with a strange symbol in gold – resembling a cross but with its arms ascendant instead of horizontal. And the drivers, uniformly hooded and clad in charcoal grey, looked like monks.

Because the bridge was narrow, the carriages were forced to slow, and for the first time Josef could clearly see the occupants he had previously only glimpsed – young women, all of them, their faces pallid, their expressions dream-like, beautiful. Then the whips cracked, the dust rose and the pale sweet faces were gone. But that fleeting vision was fixed in Josef's mind.

A peasant was waiting to cross the bridge. Josef asked Cayu to find out what he knew. The local spoke so quickly that the traveller could understand very little of it, but when he had finished, Cayu's face was grim. 'They are from the abbey at Servulan,' he said. 'The women are being taken there.' Then he added hesitantly, 'It is a place of training.'

His tone made Josef ask, 'But they go of their own free will?'

Cayu again began attending nervously to his panniers.

Josef took him by the shoulders and faced him, until Cayu at last shook his heavy head in sighing resignation. 'These women have been chosen, Mr Stenner. Free will does not apply. The men with them – they are Tormunites. You saw the twisted cross? That is their mark.'

The peasant muttered, 'Evil . . .'

The young man turned again to his guide. 'Cayu – is it true what he says?'

'Please – I only know this: you must stay away from them. It is not our business.'

'Not our business!'

Cayu had started to walk away.

'But those women!' Josef shouted after him. 'Did you not see them – that look on their faces!' The guide winced under the reproach but kept moving. 'What fate awaits *them* – in this evil place?' And Cayu stopped in his tracks.

The traveller squinted down the dirt road; the procession was already a receding speck. 'Must we stand by and do nothing?' But the accusation in his tone was wavering. 'There must be something, Cayu . . . ?'

The old guide turned back slowly, staring at him, shaking his head, then finally putting his hand on Josef's arm. His thick, soft voice was unsteady as he spoke: 'It is not in our power to interfere – you must believe me. Those people are dangerous. Even by standing on the bridge, you took a risk.'

'The abbey – how far is it?'

'Mr Stenner – I beg you to heed this – it is not on our route.'

Two days later, continuing east, they were about to descend into a valley in order to reach the village at its head when they met a solitary horseman coming the opposite way on a black mare. From the cut of his clothing, he might have been judged an official. There was an aloofness about him, and when Josef shouted a greeting, the man stared back coldly, then finally raised his hat without replying. It was then that Josef saw the twisted cross motif upon his sleeve. Cayu threw a warning glance.

'You saw it?' Josef asked excitedly as soon as the rider was out of earshot.

'Yes,' Cayu answered through his teeth.

Josef watched the horseman turn off into the driveway of a large black and white, half-timbered hall. Then he tried again. 'And did you see his eyes – the way he looked at me because I spoke?' But the guide refused to be drawn and relapsed into his moody silence of the last two days.

It was early afternoon when they reached the inn. No one was about. There were sleepy dogs chained in the shadow of the wall. Cayu left Josef in the yard and went inside. Eventually, he emerged with a thickset man in an apron and they began talking in subdued tones. The man appeared to be the landlord, although there seemed to be none of the usual welcome forthcoming. Then Cayu walked over to Josef, took the reins of his horse and confided, 'It is wiser that we leave. Look . . .' Josef glanced behind. There, on a hillock behind the village, stood a large bronze Tormunite cross.

Before Cayu had finished speaking, a young woman dressed like a serving maid hurried out of the inn and across the yard in front of them. Josef saw that she was crying. As she passed him, she looked up at him pleadingly. He had never seen a face more beautiful and he had never seen eyes so sad.

'Cayu,' he whispered firmly, 'we stay the night. Arrange it.'

2

The Postulant

Sianon had glimpsed the darkly clad stranger in the court-yard of the hall. She saw him dismount from his horse, ascend the steps, then enter without knocking, as the master might have done. His confidence made her uneasy. She returned to the milking, but could not keep her attention on her work. After a few minutes, the message came – the mistress wished to see her. Sianon, pale now, nervous, almost shaking, put aside her apron and fastened back her auburn hair.

The stranger's mare was still tethered in the yard; her bridle was ornate and her coat glossy black. Skirting a wide circle round her, Sianon hurried into the house and up the stairs. The stranger was waiting with the mistress in the parlour.

'Commissioner Fevrun –' began the mistress, but the stranger dismissively waved his hand.

' "Warden",' he corrected. 'That is the style we now prefer – a truer reflection of our duties.' He gazed at Sianon. 'Put her at her ease,' he said, moving away and placing his broad grey hat upon a chair. And there he waited, watching Sianon with patient interest.

'Sianon – you know that we love you, your master and I?' Sianon's wide brown eyes turned to her mistress, sitting stiffly forwards, her hands clasped tightly, her thin voice labouring faintly against the frailty wrought by pain. 'We love you, Sianon ... but we cannot keep you – you are special.'

As Sianon watched her mistress's earnest face, and listened to those words repeated, then looked again at the stranger dressed in dark brown leathers, she felt the butterfly break free inside her breast. Though she was surrounded by the love of which her mistress spoke, still she felt the wing-beats of the butterfly tapping nervously at her heart.

'Sianon – do not be frightened. I have told our new . . . our new Warden . . . I have told him about you, and all that he has heard has pleased him. He has made this journey to see you and to speak to you, Sianon, and I know that, whatever he decides for you, you will be strong.'

The Warden moved to the bow-window. He was tall and straight, not crooked like the mistress. His age was hard to judge – he had the quickness of youth but his face was thin and his skin had a pallor. His sandy hair was straight and reached his collar.

Suddenly he turned, putting himself against the light. 'Do not seek to study too closely.' The warning, though whispered, seemed to echo round Sianon. She glanced at him, against the light, unsure that he had even spoken. She looked at her mistress, whose weak, pained expression had not changed. Then, on the floor in front of him, she saw the hassock. The whisper came again: 'Come over here,' and she felt the wing-beats of the butterfly fighting up into her throat.

Head bowed, Sianon moved in slow, uncertain steps towards the hassock, until she was standing in the full light from the window. The Warden waited. Sianon knelt unsteadily upon the thick, firm cushion. Her long hair lay in clear brown drifts against the pure white of her blouse. 'Lift your head,' he said. 'Let us look at you, Sianon.' Her anxious eyes met his, then slid away. She was bare beneath her blouse; its criss-cross lacing stretched between her swelling breasts. She did not whisper or resist.

He spoke gently to her as he unknotted the lacing. Her hands hung limply, but not calmly, by her sides, her shoulders and her arms were shaking.

'You know why I am here?' He tilted back Sianon's chin. She felt her breasts expand against the tightness of the lacing, each pull drumming through the stretched material, her nipples responding, filling quickly, pushing through her taut breast-skin.

5

'Yes, sir . . .' she whispered.

'You may call me "Master", Sianon, for that is what I shall certainly be to you until your future is arranged. Let your head fall back – there – I should not have to keep directing. You should understand my simple wishes in these things.'

She could not suppress her murmur as the lacing broke away. Before the front of her blouse was fully open, her breasts burst through the gap. 'So full, so young, so strong . . . Exquisite. Let them spill,' he whispered. And Sianon gasped gently, holding back while he drew the remains of the lacing free and spread her blouse asunder.

'Master . . .' Her breasts were fully out, their nipples large and firm and he would see what had been done there. But he pushed her arms away, warning her:

'This reluctance is becoming tiresome.' Trembling, understanding fully now, Sianon closed her eyes, thrust her shoulders tightly back and arched her body up. She felt the weight of her breasts slide out, then swing; she heard him murmur: 'Oh . . .' And he had seen it.

'Master, please,' she blurted out, 'I love my mistress and I do not wish to go.'

'Sianon . . .' Her mistress had forced herself onto her feet. The Warden threw a glance at her and she was silenced. But Sianon's blouse was already open to the midriff and its lace was on the floor. And there was no denying what had been done to her.

He pushed the blouse back from her shoulders and over her arms, trapping them. And for the first time, she felt his open hand against her naked skin. 'Madam – her breasts – you use a whip?'

'I use a rope.'

Sianon shivered.

He lifted them up and touched the short, curved lengths of darkness that crowded the skin on the undersides, then the newer, raised pink narrow welts that grazed the bulging nipples.

'And during this purging – for I take it to be so – you restrain her?'

Sianon's mistress drew herself up; she was shaking. 'It is neither purge nor punishment – ask her.' Her stiff, angular fingers reached out and tried to smooth Sianon's hair but succeeded only in dishevelling it, the long shiny strands catching on her twisted nails and cracked dry skin.

'And what of her excitement? You assist her in such things?'

Her mistress chose to move away and turn to the window rather than reply. The Warden simply lifted up Sianon's face and read the answers in her eyes.

But with her eyes, she tried to tell him this: that she would never betray her mistress by any word she uttered, neither would she betray her master, and she would never betray the one to the other.

The Warden had stepped back, and it made Sianon feel good inside, knowing that she had faced him.

When she looked at him again, she saw in his fingers a small piece of parchment that he was shaping into a trough. He opened a phial and began tapping its contents into the trough. Then he came towards her. 'Open.' Sianon was afraid, but she knew this was a test she must not question. The powder stuck to her tongue; its dust caught against the back of her throat. Then it melted: like a hammer-blow, it struck Sianon breathless. It was as though her body was propelled on a giant invisible hand, out through the window and up into the air and she could see everything – the farm, the hall, the black mare in the yard – and she could feel behind it all a presence that, in this soaring, she shared, a presence that was both terrible and sweet. The vision lasted but a second then she was back in the room, gasping, and he was supporting her as she swooned. When she opened her eyes, the room looked brighter and the aftermath of the sweetness was a dizziness in her blood. The butterflies inside her breast were teeming; between her legs was the first gentle throb of warm peculiar feelings. Then she saw the wrist-tether draped across his arm.

He drew her blouse over her head, touching her breasts while they were shaking. He made her stand up and drop her skirt; she wore no knickers, because the master of the

7

house had decreed that it was better she went bare. Then the Warden made her take off her boots and walk nude across the room. He put the tether round her left wrist, stood her with her back to the wall and fastened her hand to the lamp bracket a few inches above her head. Her balance was upset, her right arm dangling loosely down, her left breast lifted. The cheeks of her buttocks brushed against the heavy paper on the wall. She could see her reflection in the mirror opposite. Her body looked long, her hips exaggeratedly angular because of her stance, and her belly projected palely in the light. She saw that the figure in the mirror stood with one knee slightly open; that the man was approaching – then the breathless feeling struck again and Sianon closed her eyes.

It was as if she were floating just below the smoky brown panelled ceiling and looking down – upon the rich red-carpeted floor; the mistress on her chair again; the man in leather poised before the naked figure fastened to the wall. A figure whose legs were slightly open with arousal, whose quickened breathing was the only movement in the room, scratched breasts swiftly lifting then descending, breasts that were full, were aching. She saw the man reach, she felt him test her pulse through the leather restraint. Then her eyes were fully open again and she was there against the wall.

The Warden placed a stool next to her. Then he lifted her right foot on to it. Sianon felt the warmth of her aroused sex against the coolness of his hand. 'The potion is working – she's running,' he whispered. She could feel it down her leg – the warmth, the tickle. The stool creaked gently. 'Let it flow,' he murmured, and Sianon's open belly gently pushed, her foot arched on its toes, her soft sex glutted on his fingers.

Her mistress suggested the use of the breast-rope. 'She must use her hand,' the Warden said. The mistress protested that this was forbidden, that Sianon was a good girl, that she would not understand. He listened patiently before replying: 'But the denial can never bite unless the pleasure has been tasted.' Then he studied Sianon's eyes. 'And the

8

spark is there – I see it. The powder can but free what is already within.'

On the table he placed a short, polished horn. It was stout enough to balance upright; the thick end was encased in a leather grip, studded round the rim, the tip was smooth and waxy yellow. 'In time, all pleasures shall be experienced, all avenues explored . . . But now, your hand, Sianon – use it gently.' Her left hand remained tethered; her right hand hung down. 'Go on,' he whispered.

When she saw the longing in his eyes, the excitement came, and her fingers gently reached between her legs and moved. She shuddered when she touched herself, because the feeling came so strongly, with him watching. She looked down – at the wetted hairs, the muscles tightening in her leg, her toes upon the stool, her fingers circling, pulling away, squeezing, teasing, slipping up inside her, causing trembles in her knees.

'Gently . . .' Sianon heard him whisper. He was polishing the horn in a soft cloth. Then he put the cloth against her ankle on the stool. Her breathing caught. 'Do not stop – never stop – just keep it gently at bay.' He made her hold her pubic lips apart. 'Touch the knob. Rub it.'

Gasping softly, Sianon stroked it with a single slippy finger. When her breasts began to shake and her head moved back against the wall, he took away the stool and cloth and stood her upright. Her inner lips were swollen. He lifted her under the arms to keep her body stretched, to keep the pressure there, between her legs, which dangled, pressed together, gently squeezing out her wet.

Small escaped droplets clung to her shiny brown pubic hairs. He lowered her again, her hand still fastened, and made her open out her legs. He made her try to sit upon the stool, which he placed away from the wall so that only the backs of her thighs were supported. Her legs stayed open and her swollen sex pushed down into the gap. She hung from that one hand, from that broad wrist-tether. She wanted to be touched between the legs while she hung in that position, her bulging, sweetly aching sex exposed between her legs.

'Look down,' he whispered. Wet drops darkened the carpet beneath her. She had never had it come like this. 'Squeeze it with your fingers. Make it drip.' She was gasping in arousal, hanging by her arm; the sweet throb of congestion was down below her belly, so deep the pleasure hurt her. 'Gently . . .' The lips between her legs felt large and wet and hot and slippy. A falling droplet caught upon her little finger. 'Drink it.' Sianon sucked her finger, then her hand. While she sucked, he took her legs and held them wide apart and rubbed her small knob with the polished horn then held her belly steady while she whimpered. He made her pull her nipples while he twisted the waxy yellow tip against her knob. When she shuddered, he took the stool away again and made her stand.

He turned her round, so her left arm wrapped across her face and her knees and nipples rubbed the stiff, ridged paper on the wall. Then he asked her to continue very slowly with her hand. He said this slowness was important. She heard again the sound of the cloth being rubbed against the horn. She felt each gentle squeeze between her legs intensely; her fingertips were running wet. The feeling of wanting to come was overpowering. Each time her legs went stiff, he made her take away her hand and stretch it out in the same place, palm against the wall. The wetted paper had softened round the imprint of her first two fingers and thumb, which could not stay at rest but gently rubbed away the paper. Her round, tight buttocks stood out from the wall, moving slowly and separately because her legs had bowed apart.

Again he was beside her. 'Hold it open.' She thought he meant her sex. 'Your bottom,' he said gently and the fingers of that one hand, slickly wetted, attempted to comply. 'Hold it still.' Sianon moaned. 'Do not fight it; never grip. Let it slide and it shall take it to the studs. Shh . . . oh, yes . . . shhh . . . Now let me lift you up. I shall support you. Use your hand where it is needed . . . use your fingers. Rub it. There . . . so sweetly, can you feel it?' Her buttocks pushed into his hands; her feet were off the floor, her sex was weeping.

10

When he put her down, she could hardly stand. Her wetness was running like tears of pleasure down the insides of her legs. But again, he made her stretch the soft lips open and rub the burning tip. Then he took her by the buttocks again and lifted her, with the horn still in her bottom, until her breasts and belly touched the wall. The forbidden, drowning feeling started coming to Sianon. He drew her back and asked her to keep still. She tried. The feeling ebbed. Her legs hung limply open in the air. 'Play with it,' he whispered.

He kept her that way and made her do it. Her sex shed its tears of pleasure through her fingers. The tightness of her bottom came in waves against the horn. Easing her down, he twisted the horn very slowly; he said he wanted no tightness in her bottom, that all the movement must be free. When her toes cramped up he lifted her body gently to the wall. Her breasts and belly rubbed against the paper as she breathed. Then he made her play with herself again. Twice more he made her suffer this – the playing, the drawing away, the slow twisting of the horn inside her, then the gentle renewal of the pressure of her breasts against the wall. And that was where it happened – through her nipples. This time the feeling would not stop. It tumbled. It came right through her nipples as they brushed against the wall, then it surged between her legs and up between her buttocks, then burst deep inside her, below the belly of the horn. Sianon shuddered and cried out; her tongue pushed out and licked the stiff ridged paper and her bottom pulsed about the wax-smooth horn.

When she had finished and he had put her down and turned her, with her hand still tethered, and he had taken out the horn and begun polishing it, the Warden said to Sianon's mistress: 'Now show me the rope – how it is applied – since we shall need to understand her present usage.'

And when this was done and the marks upon her breasts were rendered fresh and livid, and by this means – an approved means, this time – the tiny bulb between her legs was restored to hardness, the visitor said, 'You are a

11

worthy teacher, madam. I had not anticipated that her breasts would prove so responsive to the tether. You may take comfort from the fact that we shall put them to good use.' And he requested that Sianon be kept that way – erect in nipples and clitoris – as a preparation. Then he made her kneel while he fitted round her neck a soft black leather choker with a blue cabochon in the centre. He said that this choker should be worn henceforth, whenever she was used for sex, whenever she was naked, and that, whenever she was on the verge of climax, the choker should be touched in some way, the skin beside it should be kissed or licked, or a finger should be slipped beneath the choker and the choker lightly held. Then he took his leave with these words: 'Bring her to the village tomorrow and leave her at the inn.'

Throughout that final night, her mistress remained with Sianon, attending to her preparation, and when the master of the house returned next day, Sianon was already taken.

3

First Night at the Inn

After supper Cayu went to check the horses and Josef retired upstairs, on the pretext of attending to his journal, but in truth his mind was on the girl. He could not forget the sadness in her eyes.

When he took hold of the bellcord, his grip, normally firm, was suddenly unsteady. His fingers slipped and he became convinced that the pull had never registered, and soon he tried again. When the knock came at his door, he was acutely aware of the waver in his voice, but he could not tell whether she had sensed any of his agitation. He knew only that he found her guileless.

'I need wood for my fire,' he managed.

She glanced across. 'Of course, sir.' Then she curtsied and waited. She had hair that fell in soft blonde ringlets round her cheeks. She didn't move but waited, her arms naked below her elbows, her beautiful, sad blue eyes upon him, sending shivers to his soul. 'Will that be all, sir?' And the tone in which she whispered made him wonder even then. Her gaze slid away in shyness, but her lips, so full and soft, stayed open, invitingly it seemed to him, making him want to reach out and touch them.

Suddenly there was a knock at the door; a gruff voice sounded and the girl fell to her knees in front of Josef. Before he could gather his wits the landlord strode in. 'I heard the bell,' he declared, staring at the girl, who trembled as his surly voice growled across the room.

'Oh . . . yes. I rang twice . . . an error.' Yet Josef found himself drawing himself up to confront the stare of suspicion moving round to him. The landlord stood, arms akimbo, his thick hands on his apron.

'Iroise –' he nodded his head abruptly towards the girl,

'she is to your satisfaction?' Josef must have hesitated – thinking of her name, perhaps, which he had not previously known, and thinking how it suited – because the landlord said more loudly, 'There is no problem with her?'

'No,' though taken aback by the uncouthness, Josef answered quickly, 'None. I simply . . .' Then he decided it was better to say nothing about the dearth of wood. 'No – none.' But he could tell from the landlord's square-set, jutting jaw that the man did not believe him. He stared at Josef then marched over to Iroise. She cowered as he raised his hand. Josef jerked forwards to intercept it, then stopped himself in time. All that the landlord did was to take hold of her ringlets on one side and draw them back from her cheek – but repeatedly, sliding his thick fingers through the silky curls while her head slowly tilted up and away, exposing the delicate tracery of her ear and the smooth paleness of her neck. 'If there are any complaints, Mr Stenner, you have only to call . . .' He turned her face towards him. She swallowed and her lips stayed open. 'And she will be dealt with.' Then his heavy hands released her gentle face; he moved back, looked once round the room and left.

Iroise remained kneeling on the floor in front of Josef and now he knew not what to do or say. He needed ink – the stand on the desk was dry – but he did not dare ask for that now, lest its omission be taken by the landlord as some further failing on her part. 'Please – you must get up,' he whispered, extending his arms as if to help her, then letting them drop ineffectually to his sides. Her eyes looked up at him again and seemed to smile through the sadness. She clambered to her feet. 'I will bring it –'

'No!'

She stared at him strangely. 'The wood, sir, that you wanted for the fire?'

Josef bit his lip and nodded. She curtsied and retreated quietly. And when she was gone, he sank down into the chair and closed his eyes.

He thought again about the scene that they had witnessed in the stable when they had arrived – the two grooms and a girl. Whether she belonged to the inn or to

14

the village, he could not say, but it was certain that there was no shame on her part at the interruption, just that look, the same guileless, guiltless look that he had seen in Iroise's eyes. That incident was the spark that had set his emotions smouldering. But before supper, something had taken place on the stairs and it had inflamed his passions to burning: he had heard scoldings above him – the landlord, he soon discovered – and soft pleadings, then smacking. Venturing a step or two higher and looking up, he had seen Iroise spread-eagled against the wall, and the landlord's broad hand smacking across her naked thighs. To witness a young woman used in such a way was terrible enough, but looking on – evidently overseeing her punishment – was the very same official they had met on the road above the village. He was back here at the inn. He had stood with arms folded and not a glimmer of emotion on his face.

Perhaps Josef should have interceded. If it had happened now, he knew he would have. But at that stage, all he had was the single pleading glance she had offered him in the yard. He knew not what was done with her thereafter; she was still being spanked when he crept away. Yet when she had come to his room just now he had seen nothing of the incident in her eyes – until the fear when the landlord arrived.

Fancying that he heard something, Josef got up and looked out of the window. Everywhere was dark, but he remained there and, while he listened, he looked about his room. It was well-furnished for these parts and much in excess of his needs, for he always travelled light, finding it simpler to purchase what was needed as it was required and to dispose of it when it became a burden. Chattels meant little to him; he had left all that behind at home. Besides, it was safer to restrict the accoutrements to the essentials, to shun the unusual, and not to draw attention. But his main problem was gold – pretending he had little and keeping it secure. Without it he would be lost: there were no banks or agents here. He knew no one but Cayu in this land. Hiding gold was the traveller's main preoccupation. Josef had three caches in this room. His purse, containing the smallest, was kept in the cabinet nearest the bed. The others were well hidden.

Moving over to the desk, Josef took out his journal and stared at the calfskin cover, new but already battered from their travels. He opened it at the inscription on the flyleaf: *To Josef – God speed you on your journey – Elisabeth.* And he thought again of those who had not wanted him to go. Then he unwrapped his pens and knife and the small ink-bottle that he so jealously guarded. But he left it unopened and went back to the window. He was concerned about the girl – this girl he had not met before this afternoon and had spoken but a handful of words to. Her effect upon him was a drug. His journal stood open on the table with its pages staring in blank emptiness up to the ceiling.

Seeing no sign of anyone, Josef turned from the window. Then he heard a crash in the passageway below, between the two wings of the inn. Immediately, a curtain opened opposite: someone else's attention had been attracted by the noise. Josef moved back from the light and snuffed the nearer candle.

Because the other room was at a slightly lower level, he had a clear view inside. What he beheld there made him gasp. There was a girl with flame-red hair, naked in a deep armchair. He knew her: she was Kynne – a serving maid. There was a man behind her, fully dressed and holding her arms up, holding her wrists together. But she was looking forwards, at someone who was out of view. Josef heard this someone shout an order, and Kynne's leg lifted. She was wearing something there, between her legs. Her ankle came to rest on the arm of the chair. But it seemed this display was insufficient; the muffled shout came again and her foot began moving back along the arm until she was straining, lifting, pushing forward, with her heel almost touching her belly. Josef could not make out exactly what was between her legs. Then the man behind her bent down, bared his arm, slid it under her breasts and lifted them. Josef saw her belly bulge, saw her small mount lift – there was something fastened there – then the speaker moved across and blocked his view. And again it was the same man, the one who had overseen Iroise's punishment.

At that moment, Josef was seized by jealous hatred of him. There was no sign that any harm might come to Kynne, but the feeling of detestation was overpowering. Suddenly, it was as if this very thought had taken flight as a cry, because the man turned and stared at Josef – across the gap and through two windows. How could he have seen him, from a lighted room? Josef retreated, shaken.

When he ventured another look, the curtain was already closed. He opened his window and listened: all he could hear were the street noises and the waves of laughter from the alerooms at the front, and the thumping of his heartbeat in his ears. But still the scene and sounds behind that curtain unfolded in his mind. Two men; Kynne belly-naked, something there between her open legs; and pleasure being taken even through the constraint. He had seen it in the way she offered herself, in the way she had responded when her breasts were gathered on the man's bared forearm. He thought of her taking pleasure with the man in leather and he thought of that same man giving such pleasures to Iroise – Iroise, whom Josef could have no demands upon. Logic told him this, but the waves of jealous arousal struck again, just as they had struck him on the stairs. They kept coming, and he could not stop them. He thought of Iroise, smacked and naked, moist with her arousal, in another's arms.

Josef remained over long at that window; he was still there when the door-latch lifted, startling him. It was Iroise returning, laden with the wood. The desire in him was undiminished, but the jealousy was replaced by guilt. He closed the window quickly. Pretending the candle had blown out, he relit it with a taper from the fire. It was when he put the candle on the desk that he saw she had been crying. She tried to hide the fact, kneeling and keeping her head down and mending the fire. His emotions were in tatters – so many feelings coming quickly – what was he to do?

Crouching beside her, he said as gently as he could; 'Please – do not be upset. Are you hurt?' She didn't say

17

anything and the tears kept welling. Josef tried again. 'If I can help in any way, pray tell me.'

She bit her lip. 'No. It is nothing . . . a cold in my eye – the night air – nothing more. I am quite well sir, thank you kindly.' She poked the iron into the old wood, making the sparks billow upwards. Embarrassed now to have intruded, Josef retreated to his desk. Shyness in the face of women's unhappiness is a bad gift in a man. But he sat and made out that he was intent upon his work, whilst he watched her from the corner of his eye.

When she had done with the fire, she turned down the bed, then began tidying round the room. Whenever she drew close by him, he bent across his writing. Then all went quiet. At last he turned – and she was standing there, her hands crossed on her belly, just watching him. She seemed so peaceful and so beautiful. There was no sign of the tears now, but her cheeks were flushed. He moved his hand away from the page. 'Here – you may read it if you like,' he whispered, offering the book. Her eyes grew wide and her mouth opened, her lips hesitating before she answered, 'I cannot read.'

'Oh . . . It is just my record of the journey.'

She took it, turning the pages slowly back then stopping at the flyleaf. 'What does it say? This part here?' She looked at him. She had picked out the inscription. Josef read it out loud, just as it was written. Then he felt compelled to add, 'Elisabeth is my sister.'

Iroise said nothing for a while, but stared at the page, then said, 'Josef . . .' softly, not to him, but to the page, then: 'They say you come from over the mountains.'

'Who says it?' His heart was soaring.

'My master.'

Josef nodded. 'He seems very harsh with you – your master.' When she didn't respond, he stoppered the ink bottle quietly and carefully and put his pen away.

Her face had turned away, towards the fire and he could see again her fine pale eyelashes and the fullness of her lips in profile. They were still trembling. Her arms, bare below the elbows, were very lightly freckled. Then she spoke.

18

'You mean – on the stairs?' She looked at him, and now she made him ashamed by saying, 'I saw you. I thought that you were with Warden Fevrun, and were waiting.' It was like a hammer-blow.

'With him?' he croaked, 'No.' And though the denial was now superfluous, she nodded softly. Then her gaze dropped.

'He is expecting others.' Again she waited. 'He has me ... he has me spanked first.' She was looking at him again but her eyes had taken on a strange and distant expression.

'First?' His heart was pounding in his ears; his throat was dry, so tight. The scene through the window crowded his mind.

'Before he uses me for his pleasure,' she whispered. Her eyes had refocused on him, suffocating him so gently and so softly with their gaze. Josef, dizzy now, looked towards the bed that she had turned down and he froze: there on the wall above it were leather shackles. How he had missed seeing them before, he knew not. When he finally moved, he saw that she was looking there too and his guilt at being caught out was unbounded.

'I would not have minded,' she said.

He couldn't speak, but could only stare as the meaning of her words became apparent.

'If you had been there with him. Sometimes, there are two. Truly, I would not have minded. In the yard, I saw it in your eyes – your kindness. I like you very much.'

He jumped up, surging past her to the door because he trusted himself no longer with her innocence – and she was innocent, whatever she might have been made to do. Her nature was innocent; her eyes were pure, he knew it. But in his gallant haste he spoke too tersely.

'You have to go now.' And he opened the door. She did not move, but it was as if she had been struck. Her upper lip trembled and the tears fell quickly down her cheeks.

'I do not please you?' She collapsed to her knees. Then she looked at him so plaintively that his heart shivered as if it already lay in those trembling hands that reached out in beseechment.

Josef shut the door and ran to her, putting his arms around her. 'Iroise – I would not hurt you, please believe me.' He could feel her body shuddering with silent sobs beneath her breathing. But as he lifted the ringlets from her cheek, and his fingertips were wetted by the tear-marks on her skin, the feeling came that comes to men. Then her face turned to him and her lips, hot, salty, soft and open, brushed against the corner of his mouth as if there were a drop of nectar there that she would take. He felt the sweet warmth of her breath against him as she whispered: 'Then if you would not have me hurt, I beg you – let me please you?' From that moment, he was lost, and his eyes gave the lie to all the noble words he had uttered.

Slumped in the chair, Josef watched her in her shy obedi-ence – kneeling up, untying the sleeves of her dress, unbuttoning it at her breast then lifting it from the hem and pulling it over her head. Her breasts shook once and she was naked but for the pale, meagre undergarment that sheathed the cheeks of her buttocks and the small pubic bulge so ineffectively. All that she had worn was the dress and these paper-thin linen knickers. She wore no shoes, but her toes were neither callused nor discoloured; she must have taken her shoes off before entering his room. When her shoulders moved back, her small pink nipples lifted. Her thumbs slipped into the linen round her hips and she rolled the hem over and drew it up: the paper-thin material tightened, and in the pubic bulge was now a notch. Josef did not move; Iroise stretched towards him and he could see the tight, dark shadow of that other split, between her buttocks, and in his mind he saw again the vision of their smacking and of the stranger she had called 'The Warden' standing there, watching. Who was he? Why had he had her smacked? Josef closed his eyes for a second and pic-tured him with her on the bed. She had said that he had used her. She was so compliant – how had so cruel a per-son used so sweetly soft a creature?

Iroise slid, sylph-like across the floor until she reached

his chair. She leant her back against it but did not attempt to raise herself. Instead she put one arm behind her back. It seemed to increase her vulnerability; it made that one breast more exposed. Then she allowed one leg to slide out across the floor, leaving one knee raised. When Josef still did not move, she opened the lifted knee and pushed her head back against his leg; then she took hold of his hand and pulled it forward over her shoulder and let it hang so that his fingers touched her breast, his fingertips against its small pink nipple.

As she leant back, he could see all the way down her body to the sparse hair visible through her knickers as pressed-down, curving lines. The bulge of her sex, faintly coated in the flimsy linen, pressed its double pout against the floor. He thought of the stranger touching it, using it, and more. Those thoughts excited him.

Her head moved back and her mouth opened, then he felt her nipple tighten through his fingers – which were squeezing it, though he had not known it – and Iroise made a sound, a soft deep-throated murmur. It was a sound that he would come to know, in time, and it would come to haunt his dreams when she was gone. It was this sound that Iroise – head back, and gasping – would call out repeatedly when the pleasure became too much for her to bear. For him, it would come to be the most delicious sound that he had heard.

He bent across her face and kissed her upturned, open lips and pinched the hard balls of her nipples between his fingers. When he drew her up on to his lap, her shoulders sank back, her belly arched out and her breasts lifted as if she had taken a gulp of breath and held it. He could see her ribs pushing through her skin, and he could feel her buttocks sliding across his leg, the soft linen unrolling, exposing the round nudity of her belly and forming a twisted string above which peeped her soft, blonde pubic curls. Then he could feel her back pressing against him, and her breasts sinking down against his arms as she relaxed. She turned her head and kissed him and took his hand again but slid it down across her linen string, across her silken tuft of hair until the tips of his fingers slipped against the roundness of her linen-covered split.

Then the leg that lay bent and open writhed gently, its slim muscles standing against the light, her pubes pushed out, undulating, offering her knickered sex into his palm. Her head arched back again and she made that soft deep-throated sound. Her ribs stood out and her breasts seemed constrained within the tightness of her skin. It was as if they were being pumped up, the pressure forcing the sur-rounds of her nipples into cones which he brushed now very gently with fingertips that, even through the cloth, had acquired the scent of her arousal. When he touched her between the legs again, her knee tightened and he felt her pubic lips split open inside the linen in his hand. The tip of his finger moved inside her. She felt like a succulent fruit which had been slit, so flat and smoothly perfect were the clinging linen surfaces, which exuded a film of moisture that felt like oil.

Josef lifted Iroise and carried her to his bed; her body rolled on to the counterpane and she immediately moved upwards and placed herself on one side, her wrists pressed together in front of her face. He realised she had positioned herself by the shackles. So he drew her body down again, to the middle of the bed. Unsure, she looked at him, and he found that expression so beguiling. She lay on her back, breathing quickly, one leg slightly lifted, the twisted knickers clinging against her, split by a seeping line of wet-ness; and the aroma of her sex was on his fingers. Her scent was strong, even beneath her arms. When he undressed and lay beside her, she turned on to her face, not to turn away, it seemed, but to offer him the entirety of her back and her legs. They moved open, like her arms, but for one hand which held her hair up and away from her neck, to bare this too, to leave a slim and curving expanse of un-blemished skin from her hairline to the thinly rolled linen line halfway down the split cheeks of her buttocks.

He kissed her neck and she shivered; then he slid her knickers fully down. They felt like gossamer, his fingers pushing through them, threatening to tear them like moistened paper. He took them to the backs of her knees; then they did tear, one leg breaking free, and he pulled away the remainder. Iroise lay very still. He could hear her breathing; he wanted her legs more open but, with her last protection gone, it was as if she were afraid. But Josef touched her. He ran his fingertips across her buttocks and again she shivered; the skin seemed sensitive. He was thinking of the way she had been spanked. It had left no lasting mark; the cheeks were round and taut and flawless. When he opened them, she stopped breathing. The skin within the groove was pale fawn velvet and there was a dark magenta recessed eye. Josef waited: still she did not breathe. Then he very gently stretched the skin around this eye and held it thus between thumb and finger. Her toes tightened. He held the small eye stretched. He kept it thus and ran the fingers of his other hand slowly to the top of her inner thigh. Then he touched the small stretched eye with the soft bulb of his little finger and her face pushed sideways into the bed, her breathing burst, and the small magenta eye contracted like lips against his fingertip. When he slipped his hand beneath her, he found her pubic split was sealed but gently leaking.

He opened it to make an almond slit whose lips bulged round his fingers when they entered her to stretch the deeper surfaces within, which were softer and more wrinkled. Her body looked so small and frail but her sex was used to men. When the deep moan came again, it felt as if a soft mouth was taking suck upon his fingers. The junction of her pubic lips had swelled to make a small cone. Josef slid his fingers out of her and squeezed it, and through the cone slipped the nipple of her clitoris, which he rubbed until she gasped and pulled away and lay there trembling. She was used to men but she seemed unused to this. Josef reached for it again; again she pulled away. 'Keep still,' he said gently and, trembling, she obeyed him. She did not seem to want him to touch this nipple though its touching clearly brought her such intensity of pleasure. But he could not resist: at the thought that she might have been denied such things, the urge to bring her pleasure was

23

so strong. She had turned onto her back and she was shaking.

'Please . . .' she begged him. 'Please . . . I must not.'

'Must not what?' He touched her even more gently and she shuddered. The nipple between her legs was standing hard.

'I must not. Please, it is forbidden!'

Josef frowned. 'Forbidden?' he asked softly. 'Who forbids it?'

But Iroise turned her head away and closed her eyes tightly. 'The pleasure – its consummation . . . Please! Not this way. I must not. It is wrong.'

He made her face him. She must have seen in his eyes, that he would do it. 'No,' she begged him, *please . . . ?*'

'Shhh . . .' To him it seemed so right. Iroise swallowed, making him want to kiss her. He moved above her; she gave her lips freely now, but when he touched that place again, her body froze. 'Open your legs,' he whispered. He had to open them out himself, and when he again caressed her soft wet pubic lips, she gave that tender, deep-throated moan and her fingertips reached to touch his wrist beseechingly.

'Sir, take pity?'

The only pity that he took was selfish; yet Iroise seemed to prefer it that way and to want only to please him. She pushed herself against him as he lay behind her. His naked penis sprang between her legs; she took it in her hand and trapped it between her thighs. Then she turned and kissed him, open-mouthed, with a kiss so full of sensuality and wanting; as she twisted, he could feel the warm wet of her sex sliding against the upper side of his penis. There was no penetration. Her sex was kissing him; her movements showed she was experienced. She pushed her tongue into his mouth; she began rubbing him with her fingertips and moving her bottom from side to side. When he gasped she opened out her legs fully; he felt her take the head and squeeze it. Then she wetted it with her liquid and moved against it more slowly, arching her back now, thrusting her bottom back against his belly. He felt the small protrusion of her clitoris touch the upper side of his penis at the base and again he heard her moan. He began thrusting, slowly, while he held her leg lifted, with her sex becoming wetter and her belly rotating forwards, throwing her vulva down and making this hardening ball of her clitoris rub against his shaft.

Suddenly her feet cramped, one in the air, the other on the bed; her pubic lips spread wide about his shaft and sucked its upper side; her body froze. He was on the verge of pleasure at witnessing her in this state; he could feel the muscle of her anus pulsing; she groaned as she fended off the pleasure and the pulsations gradually slowed. Pulling herself off him, she flung herself face down and began moaning. Her hands came round behind her and pulled her legs wide open. 'Smack me, smack me please?'

'Shhh . . .' He rubbed the flat of his hand up her back, while she writhed and pleaded with him:

'Smack me – smack it, *please*?' But he gently rubbed her buttocks near the split itself and opened out the small magenta pulsing eye. He wetted it with his finger to make it slippy and toyed with this tight round slippiness while the skin was stretched. Then he turned her over.

'No,' she whispered, 'please . . .' He opened her legs. Her thighs felt soft. He kissed them, allowing the kisses to progress slowly towards the blonde-fringed wetness, feeling the muscles of her thighs begin to tighten. And once again she began to beg him not to touch her there. He ignored her words and paid attention to her body. Her pubic lips were swollen; they shone, they oozed a clear, salt glaze which was warm to his tongue as it pushed against the soft cone with the nipple, before sliding all the way down to lick the tight magenta well. Iroise gently moaned and her resistance seemed to melt; her belly lifted, her bottom opened to his tongue.

Then he drew her up, facing him, on to his thighs and very gradually fed his penis into her sex, which began a rhythmic, slowly pumping contraction round the bulb. And when he started to shudder, her body stilled. Then slowly, she took his hands and spread them round her buttocks; she led the tips of his fingers into the cleft. Then she looked at him pleadingly. She trembled and her mouth fell open as his thumb and finger found the rim. With that hand, he kept her bottom stretched, leaving the fingers of the other free – to lift the soft pink pouch of her sex back and expose the small protrusion that she seemed so afraid of, to wet it and to hold it, while her nipples tightened and she tried to keep still. But everything was too far gone now, and with a soft, deep helpless moan, she came on so wetly that her clitoris slipped through his fingers. The mouth of her bottom opened; she took his fingertip inside, and the contractions of her sex brought on his climax, sucking upon his penis like a mouth about a teat.

Suddenly, her eyes turned panic-stricken as she realised what had happened. 'No! Oh, no!' she cried. She wriggled off him even before her contractions had ceased. Josef could not hold her; in truth, he was dumbfounded. Iroise jumped off the bed and stood shivering in the middle of the room, until a noise from outside startled her. She stared in terror at the door.

'Iroise – what is it? What have I done?' When Josef spoke, she looked at him as if he had appeared from nowhere. He kept repeating the same entreaty, but she did not seem to hear him any more. But every time she heard a noise from outside, she jumped. Then she became distraught with tears, tearing her dress in her attempt to put it on. When he tried to approach her, she ran, leaving the door wide open.

For a moment, Josef stood there almost as stunned as she had done, before he had the wit to act. He shut the door and dressed feverishly, expecting the alarm to be raised, even a hue and cry, but the landlord certainly, the militia perhaps – and at the very least, impossible explanations to a people whom, it was now certain, he did not understand. Then he just sat in the chair, racked with guilt at his behaviour.

But as the minutes passed and nobody came hammering at his door, his guilt was gradually tempered by the facts. He had not forced Iroise; she had seemed to want it. But what had made her so frightened? Was it that he had spent inside her, or was it that other fear, her fear of being brought to pleasure? And then there was that singular request – she had begged him to smack her while she was excited.

Josef looked across and saw her thin, torn knickers on the bed. When he lifted them, they felt so light. The only weight they had was Iroise's living moisture. He breathed upon them and, with the warmth, her scent took flight again and the feelings returned – not guilt this time, but hot desire.

4

On the Stairs

At breakfast Josef found himself avoiding the landlord's
eyes. The man said nothing to indicate whether he knew
what had befallen; he remained his surly self. But it was a
different maid at table: there was no sign of Iroise or the
man he had seen with her the previous day. Josef ate sparingly of the cold meats, bread and ale he was brought.
When he plucked up the courage to question the serving
maid, her answer was polite but evasive. 'She is still here,
sir,' she said, then seeing the landlord watching her, began
to hurry away. Josef caught her by the wrist. He had seen
a fleeting sympathy in her eyes.

'Still here? You mean she might be leaving?'

'Sir ... *Please?*' She waited until he had relinquished his
grip. Then, pretending to brush away crumbs from the
table, and not looking at him now, she whispered: 'There
is a visitor expected today. Iroise might be taken ...' She
did not finish before the landlord called her away and,
after that, she would not be drawn further. Josef could see
she was frightened. He left breakfast unfinished and went
in search of Cayu.

His horse was missing. Josef questioned the stable-hand.
It seemed his guide, having discovered a split hoof, had
taken him to the farrier. Cayu was a good man, strong but
kindly. He made friends easily. By now, he would know
much of what there was to know about this district and its
people, and there were many things the traveller needed to
ask him. So, having obtained directions for the farrier's,
Josef ventured onto the streets.

The place was very different from the villages of home –
the cobbled streets were narrower and more crooked, with
the crowding of an old town. But everywhere here seemed

so much cleaner. The air was fresher. The people he met smiled and passed a friendly greeting. There were tiny shops with dangling signs – he passed a bakery, a small tavern, a cobbler's and a merchant's. Goods were being brought into the village on packhorses and carts. There appeared to be a market being set up. As he moved on, he noticed that the dwellings were decorated with baskets and tubs of bright summer flowers. Josef was cheered by what he saw, and began to wonder if the ill-starred events of the previous night were not simply a function of his having chosen that particular inn, with its insolent landlord and strange clientele, and whether he should have followed Cayu's advice and stayed elsewhere. But where was the farrier's?

Josef turned uphill, resolving to walk to the end of the row. Then he saw the cross. It sent a shiver through him. Fashioned of burnished bronze, it stood, large and imposing, on a mound at the end of the village. Even from a distance, its nature was clear: its arms curved skywards. As he climbed guardedly towards it, he could make out broken stones in the surrounding grass – as if some other monument had been torn down and replaced. Josef picked his way across the moss-covered debris and stood below the sculpture, looking up at its upraised massive arms. It faced the morning sun – towards the east. The metalwork looked new; there was almost no patina. It felt sun-warmed to the touch. The surface was hammered and the edges were rounded. He examined the other side; it was identical, the cross had neither front nor back, this side would face the setting sun. And everywhere below him were the dwellings: the Tormunite symbol would be visible from every household, dominating the prospect overlooking the village.

It was while Josef was still at the cross that the riders appeared. From a distance, the only remarkable thing about them was their number – five people on horseback entering the village from the east. The three leading riders were cloaked and wore tall, wide-brimmed black hats of a kind long out of fashion in his country. They were closely followed by a monk, very long-limbed, with a beard, then at a distance, by a much younger man who might have been a groom. But the rider in the centre of the three looked like a woman – if so, she was very unusual because she was riding astride, like a man, and because she was dressed almost identically to her male companions, although in black instead of brown. Yet as she drew closer, this first impression became a certainty, on account of the slightness of her figure, and the small, unlined unshadowed, almost childish face, pure white below the black brim of the hat. The members of the group carried themselves well; their horses were immaculately groomed and not one of the leading riders so much as glanced at the traveller as the horses cantered past. But as this singular troop moved into the village, stooping beneath the crooked overhanging buildings, the street gradually filled with people, pointing and watching, but in silence. Abandoning his search for Cayu, Josef followed the newcomers beyond the inn to the centre of the village, where they disappeared through the gateway of a large, walled manse overlooking the market-place. None of the bystanders would admit to knowing who the riders were.

On returning to the inn, Josef came upon an argument being enacted between the landlord's wife – a red-faced, portly woman – and a lanky man in a dark coat. It appeared to be over a girl whom the man had brought to the inn. The woman had her by the arm and was dragging her away, with the man pursuing them, raising a bony fist and shouting. The girl was clearly very upset. Josef strode forwards, intending at least to ask what they were doing, but when the landlord suddenly appeared, his courage melted and he backed away. His conscience still pricked him sorely about last night: perhaps the man did, after all, know what had happened and was only awaiting an excuse to use that knowledge against Josef.

'You like the look of her?' The smooth voice, coming so abruptly from behind him, caught Josef completely unawares.

'No . . .' Josef turned to ask the speaker what was going

on. Then his blood ran cold; he regretted even answering. Facing him was the person he had seen on the stairs with Iroise. From a distance, this man had seemed a fitting adversary – older than Josef, a man of the world perhaps, but a tolerably handsome one, and a man whom women might admire – but now it made the skin crawl even to be near him. There was a sneer upon his thin lips; his flesh looked waxy and pimpled, and around his collar were loose hairs that he had not brushed away. Josef shivered to think of such a creature touching Iroise.

'Mr Stenner, my name is Fevrun. I am the Warden for this district.'

'You know my name?'

'Of course.' And having declared his advantage over the traveller, the man extended a thin hand. Josef was forced to take it; it was cold, colder than he had expected of a man of only moderate years, but the grip was sure and strong. 'I was sorry to hear of your misfortune.'

'What misfortune?' Again, Josef had been forced to the defensive.

'You have not heard? The route to the north is blocked – an avalanche. The road is swept away. You will have to turn back.'

'There is no other road?'

'Only east – but I understand your companion will not –'

'You seem to know a great deal about my business.'

'Only what I am told, Mr Stenner. But I admit to an interest – other lands, other cultures, I find them fascinating. There is much that one people can learn from another – as I am sure you have become aware ...' Pausing, he glanced obliquely at Josef through half-closed eyes, before smiling thinly, 'How goes the saying? "We may be severed by our customs, but we are bound by the needs of flesh and blood." Perhaps we two should talk, Mr Stenner – perhaps I can help you in what you seek.'

'I seek to travel – that is all.'

'But can your quest achieve fulfilment in hills and trees and stones? Believe me, we need to speak together – soon.'

'Sir – I have matters to attend to. Now, if you will excuse

me . . .' But Fevrun made no attempt to move aside and, in the end, Josef was obliged to squeeze past him to get into the inn.

There was a second shock awaiting him: she was there, on the stairs. She must have been listening. And the dreadful suspicion in Josef's mind now crystallised to a certainty: that all of the veiled references the Warden had made were to do with Iroise. Josef glanced back to make sure the man was gone; then he looked at her again and every other thought was blotted from his mind.

'Iroise . . .' he whispered when he reached her.

She backed against the wall. 'Sir – I beg you, please, do not come near me.' Yet she said it protectively, as though she were tainted and was afraid for him. And she looked so beautiful – her eyes, her gentle blue eyes that looked as if she had been crying; all those feelings of love and desire surged inside him. 'Please – just leave me?' But in her intonation was the question, and it spurred him on.

'I love you!'

'No! Such things, they cannot be – between us.' But the softly pleading expression in her eyes gave a very different message, and her hand had reached and touched him as she spoke.

Her body tensed as he pressed closer. Her eyes darted towards the doorway. 'What is it?' he said, moving back. 'What frightens you? Is it him – Fevrun?' When he took her shoulders in his hands she was trembling. In the light from the tall window, her body was illuminated through the thinness of her dress; she was naked underneath it. He could feel her warmth against his hands and he could smell her; she had been aroused – he could smell it in her skin. And though she murmured her protests, her body was responding even now. He had never known a woman so sexual. He had to have her, even in her fear, he had to touch her naked skin.

'Josef . . .' Her lips whisper-kissed his name against his neck; her fingertips brushed his cheek and chin. When he took her leg and gently lifted it, she did not stop him. The dress rode up her thighs, and she was naked even there; she had stayed so. Her torn undergarment still lay on his bed. She murmured when he stroked her skin. He moved back to look at her. Her breasts were wreathed in the crumpled dress; her perfect belly was exposed in the shaft of sunlight sloping across the stairway. And between her legs she was burning against his hand and her soft pubic curls were wet. She gasped and opened to him – her slim thighs round his hand, moving together, pressing, squeezing, her lips about his tongue now, her warm breasts touching him through the crumpled, soft material. It was desire that he felt, a more intense desire than he had known – it was love and lust and jealousy combined. He was jealous of that other man, of all other men who had ever touched her, and he was jealous of the way that, even in lust, there was some secret fear that she harboured, that was keeping them apart.

There was a noise of footsteps up above them. 'Come to my room tonight?' he said in desperation.

'I cannot.'

And he could not accept this contradiction – why she seemed to want him, but was afraid. On a sudden impulse he said: 'Then come with me, Iroise – away from here. Come with me?' She shook her head, but her eyes were shining and she was swallowing her tears as he begged again: 'I love you and I could not bear to leave you – please?'

'Shhh . . .' she whispered, putting her fingertip across his lips, 'Shhh . . .' Then glancing over her shoulder, she took his hand and led him upstairs.

The room looked as if it had not been occupied for some time. Iroise closed the door and drew the curtains shut. And then she was upon him, kissing him deeply, hungry for his lips, inflaming his desire. The ringlets of her hair brushed like springy satin against his neck and face. Her tongue was hot inside his mouth; her hands were searching, coolly searching – Josef gasped into her mouth. She unfastened him; he pulled her dress up; her bare breasts touched his belly; she put her legs about his right thigh. He felt her naked sex against him – it was open – he could feel the lips,

33

pressing separately against his skin, and the warm, damp, hollow mouth between them, and he could smell her scent again, the scent of sex and breasts and underarms; the arousal that it drove him to was more than he could bear.

He kicked his trousers off and turned her round to face the wall; he pushed her dress right up her back, which hollowed so deeply that her small round buttocks pushed out from the wall and he could see her sex between them, pouting open, its wetted curls flat back against her skin. His penis was so hard it hurt him; the scent of her sex and bottom was overpowering; he wanted to kiss them as she leant there, gently swaying. He touched her sex lips; they were hard and swollen and smooth. He touched inside where she was moist; he touched her bottom and she moaned; he kissed her naked shoulders. Beneath her arms was wetness. When his penis touched her back, she arched and lifted on to her toes. He felt the head sliding down the groove between her buttocks, kissing her anus, mouth to tip, then sliding underneath, between the open lips, against the scented hotness, then catching. Iroise gasped; it entered her; her body sucked it; Josef thrust. Suddenly she cried out – after only an inch or two, the head had touched some object inside her.

He pushed again; she whimpered. There was an obstruction in her sex – something had been put there; it filled her, blocking off the deep part of her vagina. It felt impenetrably firm, yet soft enough to mould against him. It felt strange as it began to move with him – like an extension to his penis. She wanted to continue: she opened her legs, but he could not penetrate her any deeper. 'Hold me,' she moaned, and again the excitement overtook him. He pressed his lips against her ear and cheek; she twisted round and kissed him – while her sweet, round buttocks rubbed against his belly and his balls shook with every squeeze she gave him; while he pinched her rigid nipple that was like a small hard ball trapped under her skin. When he tried to touch her sex, she pleaded, 'No . . .' and spread her buttocks with her hands. 'There . . .' she whispered, 'Please? Your finger – please, like last night . . . ? Put it in my mouth first – let me wet it.' As she coated it and sucked it, he felt her body squeezing the bulb of his penis wetly, steadily pumping, making her liquid trickle warmly down to his balls, which shook against the smooth bare skin of her inside leg.

When he put his middle finger into her bottom, Josef almost came – the squeeze about his cock was so intense, her nipple between his fingers was so firm, her moan so deep, so sexual. She took his hand from her nipple, drew his forearm up between her breasts and sucked his fingers as she pushed against the wall. His finger inside her bottom rubbed the buried, round obstruction through the separating wall of skin; the bulb of his penis pushed it from the other side. She gasped, her legs wide open – then suddenly she wrapped them round behind him, forcing him to take her weight. And he was trapped, his hand inside her mouth, his finger in her bottom, the head of his cock inside her and all the weight – her body, his pushing, their joint arousal – was squeezed into that one place deep inside him, like a ball pumped up with liquid, full, but the pumping still continuing until he burst. When his first spurt came, she bit his hand and squeezed the finger that was in her bottom. Through the force of his thrust, she was lifted on the plug inside her and her breasts were flattened to the wall. The bulb of his cock, still pumping, was expelled by her first contraction. She grasped it in the fingers of two hands; it slipped; she caught it; she kept milking it with the eye stretched open and the flow kept coming through her fingers.

She let his hand fall from her mouth so she could lick her fingers clean; then she took his finger from her bottom and put it to his mouth. Josef took it. Iroise smiled and kissed him, with the finger still in his mouth. She wiped his semen from between her legs and on to his belly and played with him until it dried. When he was erect again, she kissed it. Then she turned him and gently rubbed him between the cheeks. His penis swayed; his balls were tight; his penis hurt him. His erection did not subside until he was dressed. When she kissed him, it came on again.

'I love you, Iroise,' he whispered. She put her finger to his lips; he could smell his dried semen on her hand; again she kissed him. But when he looked at her again, her expression had unaccountably changed. It was as if a cloud had now descended and all the brightness in her eyes had gone. Then there were footsteps outside, moving up the stairs, and the last of the magic was broken.

'Please . . . I have to go now, Josef. Please let me?' She was at the open door; he tried to hold her but she pulled away and ran upstairs towards the footsteps.

Maybe it was by chance that she ran in that direction, perhaps she was only hurrying about her duties, but the traveller's jealousy was fired again. After she had given him so much pleasure and had asked for nothing in return, all Josef felt was jealousy. In his heart he wanted to pursue her, but the fear was there, that if he did so now, he might succeed only in destroying what he strove to nurture. And suddenly Fevrun's words came back to Josef, with the poignancy of a prediction by the minute coming true. She was what he sought – he now knew that – but he could not have her, and that hurt. Love – desirous love – is greedy; it takes everything; it is relentless and it allows no cure.

At the foot of the stairs he met Cayu. 'We must stay another night, sir.'

The guide's words were quite redundant; Josef had no intention of leaving without her. But he asked him: 'Your horse – is he lame?'

'No, he is fine now, Mr Stenner. But no one may leave: the Perquisitor is here.'

Josef stared at him blankly. 'Who is he?'

Cayu shook his head. 'Not he, sir – she: Quislan. The locals say they have never known a woman hold such office – and that she carries the seal of Tormunil itself.'

5

The Perquisitor's Men

On the afternoon of her arrival at the inn, Sianon was made ready, as Warden Fevrun had requested. The landlady took her to the rear wing, where it was quieter. While Sianon was still being bathed, the Warden returned with a group of men: she glimpsed three leather-clad soldiers striding purposefully up the stairs where the other girls had been taken. And there was a man she took to be a monk, in a grey-blue cowl, who paused at the foot of the stairs to look at her. He was even taller than the Warden. He had a black, pointed beard that was flecked with grey, but she could not see his eyes below the shadow of his cowl. On his left hand was a thick ruby ring. The Warden was showing him the jewelled choker.

'Put it on her,' said the monk. His voice was almost gentle. He now advanced, drawing back his cowl. Sianon saw that he had dark eyes; there was a calmness in his countenance. 'The Warden is right – your gaze is too inquisitive – Sianon,' he whispered. 'Have you not yet learned your place?' Her eyelids lowered; her grip upon the towel loosened.

'We would be honoured, Dom Enken, if you would instruct her,' said the Warden.

'Then first, the collar.' Before it could be done, one of the maids hurried down the stairs and whispered something to the landlady.

'It is Iroise,' the woman said anxiously.

The Warden frowned. 'I am sorry – would you excuse me, Dom Enken? One of the postulants is proving difficult.'

The monk bowed graciously and the Warden started up the stairs. As the maid turned to follow, Dom Enken called to her: 'A moment. In my saddlebag – the left one – you will find a small canvas pouch. Bring it here to me directly. Madam,' he handed the choker to the landlady, 'shall we proceed?'

When the maid returned, Sianon was already gasping, naked before the mirror in a small side room. Her belly sagged; her legs were open; her nipples were distended, her fingers clenched; her cheek and wrists and forearms were pressed against the glass. The blue cabochon choker was around her neck, and poised between Dom Enken's finger-tips was the shiny wet ruby ring.

And now that he had stopped the stimulation before her climax was effected, he took the choker off her and put it in her hand. Then he moved her from the mirror and made her sit on a chair. Her naked skin was prickling with excitement. Her nipples were on stalks. 'Put your feet up on the table,' he whispered in that same soft steady voice he had used upon her all the while that she was being masturbated. He pushed a cushion down behind her. Then he partly emptied the bag that the maid had brought. Sianon saw steel rings, a tiny bottle and a piece of leather shaped like a tongue. He selected the tongue and put it between her legs, between her pubic lips. Her naked feet were on the table; her naked thighs lay open. Then he began touching her between the legs, where her moist pubic lips clung to this wafer of leather that projected as a ridge. Her arousal came on very quickly. Her head fell back. Her swollen breasts thrust out. The choker slipped through her fingers to the floor. He picked it up and placed it on the table, between her feet. Then he massaged her nipples with his fingers. So deep and thorough was the stimulation that Sianon almost came. Then he used both hands between her legs, asking her to keep her knees relaxed and open. She started to shudder. He drew her body upright, with her feet still on the table, until the ridge of leather touched the chair and she was gasping on the verge of coming. Then he put the choker on her and held her very still, running his fingers slowly down her breasts, transferring the pressure of pleasure back to the nipples. Again, the feeling started coming. 'Stay still . . .' He eased her backwards against the cushion, and pushed her legs outwards across the table till it hurt. The small, wafer-like tongue of leather stood out between her pulsing pubic lips.

'Let her rest a little while,' he said, removing her choker. 'Then she may put her dress on.' And he moved away from Sianon to talk quietly with the landlady.

Later, when she was dressed, she could still feel the leather between her legs, protruding from between her labia like an extra lip. Dom Enken tested it, then said: 'You had a master, Sianon?'

She bit her lip. 'The Warden is my master.' And she glanced up to see whether she had answered correctly.

'Yes, but at the farm – besides your mistress – you had a master there?'

She nodded.

'And he was attentive to you?'

She felt a tiny jump between her legs, like a pull on the protruding tongue of leather. 'Yes . . .' she whispered.

'Hmmm . . . Madam – you may take her upstairs.' He handed the woman the canvas pouch. 'Take this with you. There is a matter I must attend to.'

Barefoot, with the wafer of leather between her legs and the choker in her hand, Sianon was led into a room where the air was laced with sweetly scented tobacco smoke. She heard a soft moan, then she saw Warden Fevrun sitting on a bed on which a blonde girl lay naked. His arm made a bridge over her body as he leant across and spoke to her. Her skin looked flushed with warmth and she was sobbing softly into her pillow. The landlady put the canvas bag beside a jug on the table then left.

The three soldiers were there. On the opposite side of the girl was the youngest one, sitting propped against the head of the bed. Beyond them, on a very large padded stool which had a spiral wooden post through its centre, was the fair-haired soldier, locked in an embrace with a second naked girl. She had long, orange-red hair, which was fine but heavy, so it clung to her body wherever it touched.

And in the background, by the fireplace, was the largest and oldest of the three, a powerful-looking man in a sleeveless blue woollen shirt. There was a glass in his hand and a long black cigar between his lips. He was the only one in the room who seemed to have noticed Sianon's presence. He put his glass down on the fireplace, walked to the table, examined the bag, then moved over to the wall next to the bed, leant back with one foot perched against the wall, and studied Sianon. His gaze moved down to the choker she held loosely in her hand. He half-folded his arms and took a puff at his cigar. The sweet smoke drifted across.

Without looking up, the Warden said: 'Her name is Sianon, Captain Kellor; but she is not available to the military – and that goes for you too, Valrenn.'

'And how is that?' demanded the blond man.

'You must ask Dom Enken. But come, come, Valrenn – you have Kynne, at least. And surely you do not find her disappointing?' Valrenn glared at the Warden. The redheaded girl looked anxiously from one to the other. Then the captain said casually:

'But he will not have her for long.'

'Oh?' Valrenn's defiant gaze now turned on him.

'Indeed – our Perquisitor will choose the redhead for herself.'

'You think it, Kellor?'

'I know it, my young sir – and, "*Captain*", if you please.' Valrenn was silenced. The captain tilted his cigar at the girl. 'Lift her up. Turn her round.'

Everyone was watching – the Warden, the young man on the bed; even the blonde girl beside him had stopped crying – as the subdued Valrenn followed the captain's instruction and stood Kynne on the heavy stool. She was beautiful, very slim-bodied. Her small fingers clasped the fluted post; her fine red hair sagged heavily to her shoulders then fell straight down her back. Captain Kellor walked across. 'Look at her, Valrenn. Lift her hair out of the way ... Now – the narrow hips, the small buttocks – more boyish than Petruk, here,' he called over his shoulder, and the young soldier on the bed shifted uneasily. 'And so

40

– Kynne? Are you not a good match for our Perquisitor?'
But Valrenn turned her sideways and pointed out her
breasts.

'Not boyish here.'

'And she shall pay for that.' Shaking his head, Captain
Kellor touched them gently as he spoke to her. 'For Quislan will choose you, I assure you. And Valrenn here had
best make the most of you while he can.' Then he moved
back to the fireplace to take up his glass.

'Oh, you may be sure that I intend to.' Valrenn's eyes
narrowed as he opened out a coil of leather. Sianon saw it
was a fetter of some sort, but too wide for the wrists or
ankles. It had two loops joined by three chain links. While
Valrenn sat by Kynne's feet on the stool and examined it,
her legs were trembling and her fingertips were moving agitatedly in the flutings of the post. But as the joining chain
clinked open and the loops separated from each other,
Kynne's hands slid up the post and closed around the
smooth knob at the end, and – in a gesture that disturbed
and yet aroused Sianon – Kynne bowed forward, bent her
left knee and slowly rubbed it against the post. Then her
hands unsheathed the wooden knob, her lips reached forward and she kissed it. Her lips remained there, just
pouting against the shiny round knob at the end of the
post, while Valrenn fastened the looped belt shackles
round the tops of her thighs. He left the joining links un-
connected, so her thighs could still move. And when he
moved away, there were two narrow constraining bands of
black below her buttocks, two collars for her upper thighs,
and the hanging links were shaking. Her labia were already
visible from behind, pale against the redness of her pubic
hair. Valrenn moved forward and tugged her small, pale
pubic lips. Then he tightened the belts. Again, he tugged
her pubic lips. Her legs were trembling, making the chain
links sway; above them, her inner lips now projected slightly open, as a notch. Valrenn then sat down again and
began removing his boots.

Sianon had watched all this; she had not heard Dom
Enken enter the room. Then she turned, and his quizzical

gaze was upon her. 'The pupils of the eyes grow wide,' he murmured. 'It is one of the signals.' Sianon's guilty dark eyes slid away, but fell again upon Kynne, her lips pressed moistly to the knob of the fluted pole, her labia being gently opened. And Sianon felt the wafer of leather softly pulse between her legs.

'You said you advised the stool?' Dom Enken said more loudly. Sianon's frightened eyes darted to the Warden.

'At some stage – yes,' he answered.

Her breathing quickened. Dom Enken's eyes were again upon her, searching. The sweet cigar smoke drifted across the room; she did not open her mouth, but her nostrils flared as she breathed it in.

'And what of you, Sianon? What do you want? Come close and let me see.' He stared down at her. 'Oh, but you are beautiful,' he whispered. 'My journey has been long, for such as you, but I may tell you, it was worth it. Even for one lesson, even for this short, sweet taste.'

She glanced up at his wrinkled face, his beard, groomed smooth and shiny, each hair neatly in place. As he lifted back her hair, she glimpsed the blood-red ruby ring. He put it to her mouth. 'Kiss it.' Because it had been used between her legs, she became excited by the thought of taking it between her lips. 'Go on . . .' Her lips sealed round it, gently pressing, and between her legs, the tongue of leather moved as she became erect. His fingertips, drifting down her naked neck and arm, came to rest upon the jewelled choker in her hand. Sianon's head dropped back; her lips opened; Dom Enken's eyes were heavy-lidded, almost closed. 'Would that it were within my remit to implement the full rigours of your training. Would that I could have you for a week.' He sighed. 'But for now, stand here,' he put her with her back to the wall, 'for you may learn as much by watching, to begin with.' And he placed himself upon the couch and leant back, one arm along its back.

The bed was beside Sianon. The sheets had been shed to the floor, where they lay in a tousled heap under the Warden's booted feet. The blonde girl on the bed was completely naked, one leg drawn up, one inner thigh exposed, her cheek against the pillow. Her lips were still swollen from her crying. 'Iroise,' the Warden coaxed, 'our guests have been very patient.' Her head turned and her blue eyes gazed at the captain across the room. The Warden drew the ringlets from her cheek. Then he put his hand against her breastbone and pressed, making her small, full breasts push stiffly outwards. 'I can feel it beating, but an inch below my hand.' His fingers curled. 'Iroise – sometimes, I want to reach inside and take you, thus, while you are beating.' His hand slid across, closing about her right breast, squeezing. Iroise moaned gently and softly, the skin of her breast stretched, polished and the nipple turned and lifted like a small blind worm.

'Sit up,' he whispered. 'We must examine you.'

At these words there came a warmth beneath Sianon's arms and a gentle pulling in her belly. Iroise started to sob softly. 'Shhh ... Sit up.' The Warden helped her; he was so gently persuasive and she was half crying and looking at him imploringly, but her body, her will, had no resistance.

The Warden rolled back his sleeve. His arm was densely clothed with hairs. Sianon remembered the way that they had brushed inside her thighs while he had played with her and put the horn inside her. And the feeling was still there in Sianon's mind – of her bottom slipping open, of the entrance being gently stretched – as she watched the girl's small, tight breasts hang forwards and her naked nipples brush against his arm.

'What of the traveller?' he asked her quietly. Her sobs redoubled. Taking her by the chin, he whispered: 'Iroise? Your fate is decided – you know this and accept it. Now, what happened with our traveller friend?'

'My lord – please, he means no harm,' she sobbed.

His teeth clenched; his fingers pressed into her cheek. 'Am I not your master?' he cried.

'Yes ... Yes!' Her tears were flooding.

'Iroise ... Oh, Iroise – what have you done?' His grip suddenly relaxed and she collapsed to the pillow, where the

43

young soldier moved up beside her and began stroking her hair.

The Warden turned on Sianon: 'You are trembling.' He stood up and Sianon backed along the wall. She looked pleadingly at Dom Enken: he was watching her absorbedly but did not move. The Warden's quick eyes danced about the room. 'The stool ...' he said to Sianon. 'Bring it – quickly!' She stumbled; he grasped her arm. 'Get it!' The captain casually moved aside. When she came back with the stool, the Warden pushed her to the wall. 'Now get on it. No – lift your dress first. Wait – what's this?' He touched the protruding leather.

Dom Enken answered: 'It is to assist her. And I wish it kept in place – she shall take care how she sits.'

The Warden nodded, then manoeuvred her buttocks forwards and apart, and lowered her. She murmured when her naked bottom pressed against the seat. But her pubic lips remained closed, projecting, stiffly swollen and adhering to the tongue of leather. 'Stay there.' The young soldier moved out of the way as the Warden returned to the bed.

'Dom Enken is quite right, Sianon,' the Warden said. 'There is much that you can learn from Iroise, here. We keep her always in arousal; we permit her no release. And oh, how sweetly difficult she finds it ... But now she has fallen in love.'

He lifted her shuddering body onto its side, eased her leg up gently, and a clear liquid leaked from inside her and ran across her thigh. 'Open ...' He turned her onto her back and her shoulders sank into the pillow. His hand slid up inside her thigh. 'Open ... Gently.' She murmured, frightened, her belly lifting and distending. One leg pushed out sideways, tucked up, the other stayed straight. She turned her face away as his hand continued its slow progression.

'Anhh!' she gasped.

He waited until her head was back on the pillow. 'Iroise – you must relax. Petruk – hold her still.' The young soldier pinned her by the shoulders. Her belly bulged; she gasped again; the Warden's hand withdrew. Pinched between his retreating fingers was a sticky ball of cloth, drenched in a viscid coating.

'He gives good, our Mr Stenner,' the Warden said. Iroise burst into tears. He took a dry towel to her legs, then bent across her and whispered softly: 'It is not wrong. Arousal is not wrong – giving yourself that way when I have asked you ➤it is proper.' He sat up. 'Petruk – hold her wrists – but gently.'

As Iroise murmured and her body twisted, the Warden carefully introduced the folded towel inside her oozing sex and slowly twisted it. 'Desire is good, but Iroise – fulfilment is forbidden . . . Shh . . . Oh, shhhh . . . She moves so sweetly. Kiss her.' Petruk bent over her face; Iroise sighed as the kiss developed; her open thighs swayed gently; the twisted towel slid out. 'See, how she has softened.' The Warden touched her between the legs. She moaned in pleasure. 'This is how it must always be – good feelings, coming stronger, all the while. Open your mouth, Iroise.' He had a phial like the one he had used on Sianon. Iroise shuddered, open-legged, as the potion was administered. 'I want you to feel the need so strongly that it hurts you.' Her eyes were closed and her legs wide open. He wasn't touching her but she was moaning and pushing herself as if she were mating. Sianon had not seen a woman so aroused. The Warden took something from the bedside drawer; it was in a cloth. Sianon shivered; it was the horn.

'Iroise, turn over. Captain Kellor – she is ready. You may care to use my belt.' The captain cast his cigar into the fire and came over to the bed where Petruk was now undressing.

'Sianon . . .' Dom Enken called. She could hardly breathe. To the right was Valrenn with the other girl, Kynne. The shackles on her thighs had been linked together and she was being slotted against the post – her tucked-up body was lifted high; the round wooden knob thrust between the tops of her legs and the chain connecting her shackles, then it slid up her belly, pushed between her breasts and spread them. When her knees reached the cushion, Valrenn used a cord to fasten her elbows round the post.

'Sianon . . .' She was shaking. Dom Enken lifted her from her stool and turned her to face the door but, looking back, she saw the Warden holding Iroise down on the bed, her breasts pressed into the covers, and Petruk selecting a pillow to be placed beneath her hips. And she saw the captain poised with the leather belt above Iroise's naked bottom.

A shiver went through Sianon's limbs as Dom Enken touched her. He unbuttoned her dress and slid his hand inside and gently squeezed her nipple.

Iroise moaned as the horn was put inside her; Sianon shivered again. The first smack struck, then the next. The rhythm was set, and the fingers inside Sianon's dress moved from one nipple to the other, gently squeezing, with each smack. Her nipples swelled against the fingers. Between her legs, the arousal hurt. She thought of the horn, the stretching – Iroise being spanked with it inside her – as she listened to the sounds Iroise was making, the extended moans of pleasure that came between the spankings. For Iroise was also being played with. That was why the pillow had been used under her belly – to keep her sex lifted and available for touching.

Dom Enken kept Sianon facing the door until her arousal came so strongly that she gasped and had the urge to crouch. He allowed her to sink to the floor. He never touched the leather between her legs, but constantly massaged and pinched her nipples and her breasts.

When Iroise's spanking was finished, Sianon's back and breasts were wet with sweat. She looked up and saw the Warden buckling his belt. 'I am leaving,' he said. 'Iroise is now more favourably disposed. But there is this – shall you need it?' Between his fingers was the horn.

'Give it here.' Dom Enken eased Sianon's shoulders back. 'Hold her breasts ... Head back, Sianon. Mouth open. Shhh ...' Sianon's lips slid round its smoothness; it was still warm from Iroise's body; its scent was strong, but there was no taste. It was the very act of taking it into her mouth that aroused her, because of where it had been and what it had done to Iroise.

Sianon's legs were moved apart. The tongue of leather was stroked. She almost climaxed. 'Get her to the couch,' said the Warden. They stretched her out on her back, with her legs open, and the horn still in her mouth, then Petruk was called to hold her ankles down. The Warden knelt beside her and played with her sex. She couldn't set the pace; she couldn't close her legs around his hand; she couldn't move them. Her partly open dress was pulled down from her shoulders. Her breasts were turning harder, and her labia softer and more moist against the leather leaf. Her belly writhed as he kept toying with her. Her nipples gathered; he slapped them, then he spread her labia back and gently tugged the leather tongue. Her body arched up, then collapsed again. 'Shall I make you sit up?' he whispered. Sianon moaned against the horn as his finger rubbed a soft slow circle round her clitoris, then drew away again. Her belly tried to follow it. He smacked her nipples with his fingers. Her breasts had balled-up; her throat was distended; her skin was running wet. The gentle tugging came again between her legs; the finger stroked her clitoris, then drew wetly away. She groaned; her taut body angled from the waist as her belly tried to seek the touch. He pushed her down; her lips sucked distractedly upon the horn; he held her sex and smacked it lightly and repeatedly until the bumping of the leather tongue against her clitoris made the pleasure start. Sianon's belly, seeking satiation, hauled her body upwards from the waist. But the Warden caught her and held her firmly, so her belly could not fully move to meet the feeling. Her throbbing sex pushed down into the surface of the couch, her nipples squeezed out through his fingers.

When her stifled moans had subsided, and the horn was taken from her lips, the Warden said: 'Re-arousal should be quick and easy. I shall leave her with you.'

There was to be no respite. Before the Warden had even closed the door, she was gathered in Dom Enken's arms and carried to the sideboard. When he put her down, her hands fell to her sides and the choker, she had held all this while, slipped through her fingers. Her knees moved together and to one side. He removed his ruby ring. 'I shall put you to the question.' He took her limp hand, pushed

47

the wide ring loosely over her thumb and closed her fist up. 'Keep it safe,' he whispered, 'for when we need it.'

He completed the unbuttoning of her dress. 'Breasts first,' he whispered, and it began again, with the swell of pleasure making her nipples hurt. He spoke of the density and smoothness of her eyebrows; the wantonness he said he saw within her dark brown eyes. He pinched her nipples slowly and touched the marks. Where her legs had come together she felt wet. From the corner of her eye, she could see the two men naked on the bed with Iroise. Sianon had never seen a woman taken by a man.

'They will try to make the pleasure come – you understand? She must not let it happen.' Sianon understood. She could see the red stripes across Iroise's bottom. She watched until she shivered with the feelings. Dom Enken made her open her knees. The tongue of leather was oily wet. 'Spread wider,' he whispered. The leather pulsed and, when he pulled it, slipped. When it came out of her, her pubic lips stayed slightly open, then collapsed against each other moistly and warmly, and the sensation was sweet.

He pulled her dress down to her hips, then slid it off her. She was fully naked. Then he put the choker on her, and the bareness, followed so quickly by the restraint, made the deep feeling start to come. It was as if she were already being touched again between the legs. He asked her to rest her shoulders against the wall.

There was a small dish on the sideboard; into this he dropped three steel rings which he took from the canvas bag. They looked like earrings, except that one was very much larger than the others. Apprehensively, Sianon turned to watch what he was doing; as her shoulder sank, she felt the weight of her breast rolling to one side. She saw him staring at them until they stopped moving. Then she felt his arm beneath her back, pulling her forwards, making her breasts push out. Her head lolled back. He slipped his thumb into her mouth and Sianon sucked it. He called Valrenn away from Kynne to witness it – the choker and the thumb and the breasts – this girl so inexperienced, naked, sitting spread-kneed upon the sideboard, her eyes

48

closed, her nipples swollen, her soft lips sucking round the base of his thumb. Then he had Sianon tongue-kiss Valrenn, and Valrenn's naked penis, curving, still glistening with Kynne's saliva, touched Sianon's belly. When he let go of her, she sank back against the wall, her breasts heaving, her eyelids heavy, her lips still open from the kissing, slightly swollen from the sucking, moist. 'Truly, she is special,' said Valrenn.

Even after the soldier had returned to Kynne, Sianon was still breathless, thinking of his words; thinking of the wet warm shaft that had grazed between her legs; thinking of the passion in his kissing. Dom Enken's eyes were searching Sianon's face. Suddenly, she lifted up the ring on her thumb, pushed the ruby to her lips and kissed it. Then she licked it with the point of her tongue. She wanted to be given to Valrenn.

But when she looked again at the monk, she saw that he was displeased with her outburst. He took the ring away from her. 'Kneel up,' he said abruptly. 'We shall resume the lesson.' He spread her knees. He pressed his finger against her and the skin of her labia clung to it because she had been wet and had started to dry. His finger was large; it probed Sianon as she knelt there; it found the place where her stickiness turned fully liquid and it slid inside. 'The truth now – have you had a man?'

She shook her head but her eyes moved uneasily away.

He stared sidelong at her. 'But there is a memory there which excites you.' He shook his head. 'I cannot fathom you: your breasts, your eyes – the darkness there, a sweet blackness in your soul; the way you shudder when I touch your belly; the way you look upon Valrenn. I have never seen a creature more wanton. Here ...' He brought a hand-mirror. 'Look – look upon yourself, look into it.' Sianon saw her own eyes. And she felt the power, the dizziness. The excitement was within her. Then she heard a sweet moan from the bed and she turned to look but he caught her by the chin and held her face. 'You know that you are beautiful.' He kissed her, with her knees still open, his hand deep down between her legs, his finger lightly pressed against the entrance to her bottom. Her tongue slid into his mouth and wriggled. When he pulled away, her tongue was still protruding, moving wetly.

'Kneel straight!' She had unnerved him. 'Your breasts are very large.' His voice was almost shaking. 'Look at me. Answer.'

'Yes,' she whispered.

'Lift your arms. I hear your mistress used to work your breasts – to make them bigger?'

'Yes.'

'Lean back again,' he whispered agitatedly, 'shoulders to the wall. You have been chosen for your breasts. Have they given milk?'

Her eyes widened. She shook her head in disbelief. 'No – how could they?' And when he smiled, she became frightened.

He nodded slowly. 'In time, we shall arrange it. For your training is begun, Sianon. Soon, you will belong.'

He made her kneel forward, so she was balanced on the edge of the sideboard, her knees projecting sideways. 'Push . . .' her belly filled out; her sex hung down, its lips moistening and swelling. He touched her breasts, lifting their heavy weights gently, letting them drop, arousing them slowly. 'You shall be milked while you are pleasured . . . Push.' He nipped her teats; she moaned. Her belly thrust into his hand; her pubic lips split open. 'Keep it open.' Two fingers went inside her; her legs began to tremble; she felt her arm being swept upwards and his lips against her skin, sucking her underarm, drinking gently, making the warm sensations trickle heavily down into her breast and fill it to the nipple.

And over on the bed, she saw Iroise reclining on the captain's lap, him holding her gently, directing her face, reopening her lips in readiness as Petruk's gangly figure crouched beside her, straining, his thick penis still pulsing, the skin upon it tight from the suction, wet from her repeated kisses.

The feeling surged in Sianon's nipple. Dom Enken wetted it then played with it and squeezed it. He slapped it gently with his fingers, then put the wetted fingers into her again and Sianon nearly came.

He went over to the table, filled a bowl with water and brought it back together with some wadding, which he moistened and wiped inside her labia. He rolled a larger ball and pushed it in to keep her open. Then he touched the open walls of Sianon's sex; he showed her the sensations at the front, and at the sides then at the back. He used the mirror frequently; he let Sianon kiss it with her open sex; its coldness left her inner skin excited. Then he began fitting the steel rings to her. He attached the first one under her nipple, leaving the nipple itself pushed-up and hard. The rings were clamps; small adjustments could be made once they were set in place. They had sleeves which could be twisted to effect the desired degree of tightening. Her flesh was nipped between two small balls. He demonstrated the tightening. Sianon moaned; he held her breast and the ring stood out stiffly below her polished nipple.

He put the second small ring between her legs, to nip one pubic lip. Then he made her sit. Her sex was kept open by the wadding; she felt as if her lip was pinned. He took it in his fingers and lifted it open with the ring, then sucked the ring below her nipple. Both nipples stood as hard as one another though only one was ringed. She felt her clitoris pushing out between her legs. There was still one ring left – much thicker than the others – and she did not know where he would use it.

Then she heard a moan; she witnessed Kynne being entered from behind by the curving penis that Sianon wanted. When she looked again, she saw Dom Enken unscrewing the jaws of the heavy ring.

'Put your legs up,' he whispered. 'Up in the air.' He put it into her only briefly, but that was enough. It was the simultaneous penetration of her sex and bottom, the coldness, the smoothness, back and front. She climaxed when he tightened it.

And she was still gasping when he took it out: she had scarcely come to her senses when he lifted her off the sideboard. She was wearing nothing but the choker and the two small rings.

He carried her back across the room then lowered her into the centre of the couch. The feeling came between her legs as her labial ring touched the cushion and she was made to sit. He teased the lip open. 'Sit forwards.' The couch was opposite the bed and she could see everything that was happening there: Iroise breathing shallowly, her cheeks cloaked by her blonde curls, and the men, so close, so naked, writhing slowly, both of them trying to take her. And on the other side, Kynne was fastened to the padded stool; she was kneeling up as best she could and Valrenn was in her. He was playing with her breasts, pushed apart by the post and trapped beneath her tied-together elbows.

Dom Enken drew Sianon up on to a loose square of chamois leather, like a thin loincloth, that he had placed on his lap. Its soft side was against her naked sex and buttocks. There were no fastenings for the cloth. He made her open her legs. Her sex was already open, held so by the wadding; and now its lips pressed down into the chamois. He put his hand beneath her from the back and pressed the leather gently into her opening. While he smoothed it into place, he rubbed the ring clipped to her pubic lip and touched it where it nipped inside her. He asked her if she liked these feelings. When she opened her mouth to whisper her reply, he kissed her, and she pushed her tongue inside and rubbed its tip against his, to show him that she wanted such feelings to persist. Then he kissed her nipple and licked the ring.

Soft sighing sounds of Iroise's pleasure drifted over from the bed. The young man, Petruk, was arched above her, directing his penis steadily down between her lips. Her feet were being fitted into a conical leather pouch resembling a holster. 'It will keep her legs open for the smacking,' Dom Enken whispered. It had a hole at one end for her toes and a short loop of a handle at the other, and it kept her feet securely pressed together at the soles. When the handle was drawn upwards, her thighs splayed open and she could not move. While the penis slid into her mouth, the captain spread apart her pubic lips and played with her until she started gasping. Then he turned her on to her front, with her head in Petruk's lap and his penis still between her lips. In the marks across her bottom was the pattern of the eyelets in the Warden's leather belt. The captain this time used his hand. She lay, legs splayed, toes projecting through the leather pouch, while her buttocks bounced beneath the spanks. Then she was eased on to her back again and played with, while Petruk's penis slid in slow deep strokes in and out of her mouth, and his balls descended wetly to her nose.

Sianon looked across to see Kynne being penetrated at the post. Kynne's fingers were clasped about the boss of wood, and Valrenn was behind her, balancing, knees bent, on his toes, his penis being steadily introduced between the cheeks of her buttocks. She saw the chain drawn tight between Kynne's thighs as she was lifted. Then her mouth opened, her hands unsheathed the boss and her lips pushed hungrily about the polished wood.

Dom Enken turned Sianon to face him. He asked if she would like smacking. He said that he would like to smack her sex, with its lips held open by the wadding. He touched inside it and she gasped; when he spread back its soft lips, she trickled freely onto the leather.

'Lift up,' he said. Her wet had soaked through to make a dark stain on the blue-grey of his habit. It was still running from her. He caught some on his finger and put his finger to her bottom, which opened and stayed so while the finger slipped inside. While she watched Kÿnne taken in that way, the finger gently moved inside Sianon; it caused a feeling there that hurt her since the pleasure was so strong while it could not know fruition. He put his thumb inside her open sex and squeezed against the finger in her bottom. Sianon moaned; her mouth fell open and she turned and kissed him. While her tongue moved in his mouth, her bottom went into a contraction. He warned her that she must learn to control this: even though her contraction might be a sign of the pleasure she was feeling, still, she must not squeeze until her master had expressed this as his wish, for it was a closure, and her master must always be allowed to explore inside her body freely.

He took his finger out of her and asked again about the smacking but was distracted by Petruk's choking gasp. The young soldier's penis slid out of Iroise's mouth and pulsed above her. Her lips reached up to try to reclaim it; her fingertip was still inside him. He pulled away and her finger came out. His glistening penis touched her neck; she turned and took the cap into her mouth and gently held it. Her feet were still restrained in the pouch; her sex was wide open; her clitoris projected red. The captain wetted his fingers and began to rub it slowly; Iroise groaned and began clutching her belly; the penis fell from her mouth. Then they turned her on to her front and spanked her, with her feet tucked up, her buttocks open, the mouth of her bottom pulsing.

As this was taking place, Dom Enken drew back his sleeve and reached from the front, between Sianon's legs and deep beneath her. The tips of his fingers touched the middle of her back, with the soft crook of the inside of his elbow between her legs, against her sex and, while he tickled her, her clitoris made a wet line on the muscle of his arm.

'Over – get over, quickly!' He turned Sianon on to her belly, with his finger in her bottom again and now a thumb inside her mouth. Her breasts overhung the arm of the couch. The ring below her nipple stood stiffly. Then he took his finger out and began touching her clitoris to make it tremble, and gently dabbing her with the chamois, then putting the finger back into her bottom. He asked her not to tighten and not to gasp, but to breathe evenly. When she came close to climax, he stopped and slid the finger slowly out and rubbed it in a small wet circle on her back. Then he started again, the touching, the dabbing with the wet chamois, the sliding of his finger up inside her. When she started to lose control, he slowed the stimulation and held the choker gently. He asked her to breathe more deeply. He touched her breasts as they hung down, pulling the ring below her nipple and the ring between her legs, then he played with her clitoris again until her breathing stopped.

'Turn over. Breathe,' he whispered gently. He took hold

of her clitoris. The pleasure was again so strong it hurt. Then he made her put her head back so her belly was arched across his lap, and then take the horn slowly into her mouth. 'More slowly,' he whispered. She was drowning with the feelings. 'Hold your sex more open – use your fingers.' Then he started again to play with the ring between her legs, the ring below her nipple. 'Breathe gently, through your nose.'

His finger, underneath the choker, slipped gently back and forth against her naked skin. She was drifting, drowning in the sweetness of the feelings. 'Hold it open; hold it tight.' Her gasps of pleasure were muffled by the soft wet pressure of her lips about the horn. Then he tightened the ring between her legs and she shuddered so strongly that he had to hold her legs apart to prevent her coming. He slowly withdrew the horn from her mouth and pushed the tip of it between her legs, into the open mouth of her sex, which pulsed and tried to grip it.

'Stand up,' he said quickly. The soft wet leather fell away from her thighs. Her legs were still shaking. She was on the verge of coming. He made her crouch, then stand up again and put her legs together, then open them and walk around the room.

'Go over to the corner. Face the wall.' The feeling stayed strong through the continual movement.

'Lift your arms up,' Dom Enken said. 'Hold them up . . . Keep them like that.' Her breasts touched the wall, then her knees touched. 'Keep pushing forward. Now stay there.'

She felt warm between her legs; thick saliva welled inside her mouth. Her eyes moved upwards, looking for a place where she might be fastened. She heard another gasp from the bed. 'Keep your arms up – high.' Her breasts rubbed against the wall; her knees turned inwards. 'Stand up on your toes. Push closer.' Her back was arched, her belly pushed into the corner, her breasts moulded to the angle of the wall. 'Stay on your toes.' Her legs were trembling. She heard him bring a chair across and sit upon it and wait. The muscles in her feet and calves were aching. 'Keep still – *obedience*, Sianon.' She began to sob. He didn't respond. Her legs were cramping. 'Up higher – closer to the wall.' She couldn't breathe. Her feet started giving way – she could feel her nipples turning up as her breasts slid down the wall. Then she collapsed in tears; but he caught her, and turned her naked body round. She went limp; she hung across his arm, her breasts like heavy melons. He smeared the tears across her cheeks. 'Good,' he whispered keenly. 'Good ...' And he seemed pleased that she was crying. He put his hand between her legs and checked the place where she was open. When he touched the ring there, the pleasure stung, and the tears came quickly.

He carried her back to the sideboard, where he made her sit. Then he opened a tiny bottle and put some drops of liquid on her sex. 'One drop inside each lip – gently – let it seep into the skin. Can you feel it, Sianon? Can you bear it still?' He would not let her close her legs, but made her kneel up. She sobbed and moaned and pleaded; her nipples thrust between his fingers; she wanted him to take her pubes in his hand, but all he did was to watch them swelling until the lips projected more open and more hard than they had ever done before. Then he lifted her down and made her stand with legs apart. 'Walk,' he said. 'Like that – go on.' And when she moved, the sensations came upon her so acutely that she stopped and gasped, and leant against the wall.

'Open your legs, Sianon – I asked you to keep them apart.' Her vulva felt so warm and swollen; she wanted him to take it in his hand and seal the lips together and squeeze the sweet arousal out of it, so the feeling filled her to the belly.

He brought the stool. He made her lift one foot on to it then bend across it and put her hands behind her head. Her breasts fell forwards; he swept them open, letting them swing. He asked her: had her mistress ever spanked her buttocks? She told him, no. And what if he should choose to spank her? She would take it. Would she like it? Yes. 'Bend forwards. Arch this foot.' And she was straining, one foot on the stool. Her dangling breast touched the inside of her knee. He ran his fingers along her leg and caught the nipple. 'Squeeze.' He supported her while he pulled the nipple. 'Squeeze, between your legs, keep squeezing.' She felt the wadding slip inside her; her pubic lips were still swelling; he worked her nipple as if she could give milk. She could feel the pleasure coming on. He warned her he would spank her if it happened. She was gasping with the feelings. He gathered her throbbing vulva gently in his hand, so its labial ring slipped between his fingers. Then he made her stand up while he held it. His hand was becoming wet; he was squeezing the wet out of her; she buckled, her sex pushing down into his hand.

'Stand up – legs open. Keep your hands behind your head.' Her sex lips stretched; the ring was nipping where he squeezed it; Sianon moaned again; he squeezed; her sex lips slipped through his fingers. He took the leather cloth and wiped her. Then he sat her on the stool and kissed her with her legs wide open and her vulva hot against his hand. Again he brought the tincture and dripped it on her vulva. She moaned; he made her stand again and try to walk. Her nipples were as hard as stones; her pubic lips were bursting; she tried to close her legs. When he stopped her from doing it, she fell to her knees, with the labial ring pushing out behind her. She crawled the last few yards to the couch with her legs half-pressed together, sliding on her knees across the slippy floor, then dragging the loose rug into folds.

'Kneel over. Head down. No, not to the seat – to the floor.' Her tears were flowing freely, her cheek was on the crumpled rug, and the weight of her breasts sank down. He pushed his outspread hands up her back and her nipples touched the polished floor. She heard Iroise being spanked again. 'Spread your knees out – wider.' Sianon's sex was burning; she felt the lips distending as she opened. He put his fingers into her and the feeling of distension deepened. He touched her nipples where they brushed against the floor, then turned them down and trapped them under his fingers. 'Shall I spank them?' he whispered. 'We have a rope.' She shuddered. He took all of her breast under his hand and pressed it to the floor. 'And, of course, we have the horn. Keep open . . .' She gasped as the waxy tip was pressed against her bottom. 'So smooth you are, inside – this place, this part of you – so smooth.' Her breathing came in shudders. 'There – let it slip. You are learning, coming good, Sianon.'

Once it had stretched her bottom fully, he slid it slowly out. She collapsed sideways, her legs tucked up, her sex pushed out behind her. It was open; she could feel it thus, its lips against the air, not touching, spread by the wadding and the feelings from inside her. 'We shall train your anus to the various means of love and pleasure.' Then he lifted her onto the couch. He told her not to move; he made her sit forward but lean back against the cushions and let her legs fall open – so he could see her sex, he said, and judge its state. On the table beside her, he placed three things – the horn, the tincture and a small wooden paddle. He said the paddle was for her breasts and nipples.

She could see Iroise lying between the two soldiers. The captain was behind her, gently stimulating her clitoris, and her labia were split about his shaft. Petruk's penis was in her mouth again, stifling her moans. When he shuddered and pulled away, her mouth stayed open, her upper lip still connected to him by a thread of spittle. She tried to lick him, then she groaned as the captain held her leg up in the air and gently pinched her labia where they gripped him.

Dom Enken turned Sianon on to her side; he held the leather cloth against her sex and smacked her nipples with the paddle. Then he asked her did she like it? Did it bring her on? And Sianon, open-mouthed, swooning gently, closed her eyes.

'Bring her over here,' the captain called.

They smacked her nipples on the bed, then played with her again until she was gasping with the sweet arousal. 'Here . . .' She felt the captain's hands about her head, pulling her down to where he was lodged in Iroise's belly. 'Yes . . . Oh! Unnhhh . . .' Sianon sucked his liquid coated balls and the slick tight skin of his penis; her tongue pushed up inside the soft flesh where he entered Iroise; she tasted all the female wetness leaking out. She took Iroise's sex lips in her mouth and Iroise turned rigid. Petruk pulled Sianon away; she felt his long cock reaching for her mouth. She took it, deep inside her throat, and kept it there, though she was gagging. Her lips, pushing up, touched his balls; she felt his shudder. When other hands pulled her off the cock, she took it in her fingers and tried to pump it. And again she was pushed between Iroise's legs to suck her while the captain's cock slipped and slid by turns from Iroise's open sex into Sianon's mouth. Sianon shuddered and sucked; her fingers squeezed. She heard the captain moan; then she tasted his hot sharp stickiness bubbling on to Iroise's sex, and Petruk's warm semen began pumping down her arm.

From the corner of her eye she saw the ring – the big one; she felt her legs being lifted open; then she felt it sliding up inside her, front and back. The deep searching pleasure came as it was tightened.

'Keep her legs open. Sit her up.' And she was gasping with these feelings. Her wrists were held behind her and the heavy ring between her legs was pinned down to the bed while she was played with. When she started to come, she was lifted and held, open-legged, knees sagging, the weight of the ring hanging free. Then she was gently lowered until the pressure came again so acutely that she had to be lifted up again. They dripped the tincture between her legs and into the groove between her buttocks, then gently worked it into her through tiny movements of the ring. 'Look at her nipples – so hard . . . Hold her up.' They spanked them with the paddle, then touched her between the legs until she felt faint with pleasure. But they would not let it fully take her and they would not put her down.

Her head lolled to the side. She saw Valrenn. He had been watching her.

'Let me take her out,' he said; she saw his penis bobbing stiffly as he spoke; she had the overwhelming desire to take it into her mouth.

'Give her to him,' Dom Enken said dispassionately.

Valrenn dragged Sianon across the floor, with the thick ring still fixed inside her. He pulled his trousers on but left her naked. Then he untied Kynne and took them, one on each arm, from the room and down the stairs into the smoky bar-room. Kynne was given to the men and passed around. But he kept a close hold on Sianon. Her heart was beating wildly as she watched. He threatened that he would smack her; he stood her shivering with her back to the wall and her legs wide open. He kept looking from her to Kynne, who was lain across the small round table between the two men, on her back, her legs spread, her head stretched back and hanging down. The two cocks entered her. Sianon felt Valrenn's hand between her legs, and she opened – wide – she wanted him to pull the ring. He tightened it; she gasped and fell to her knees. He pulled her up and made her watch Kynne's body arch between the two sets of thrusting buttocks. Then he took Sianon across, and made her touch the warm balls hanging down above Kynne's face. He made her close her hand around them and squeeze them. A peculiar feeling came to Sianon, in between her legs, when she heard the man's moan. She watched his buttocks pulsing. She could smell his sweat. Valrenn made her kneel and take the very balls inside her mouth. When she sucked them in, they filled her mouth, and she felt his pleasure coming. As the muscles of the ball-sac tugged against her squeezing lips, the sweet, peculiar feeling came to her again. With the balls still in her mouth, Valrenn opened her thighs and touched her from behind and pressed the ring against her body.

Then he took Kynne out into the yard and spanked her with his belt. He made her stand and spread out naked against the wall while Sianon watched with legs apart and leaking moisture running down the heavy ring, which was cold in the air, a smoothly curving prong inside her, holding the wall of flesh nipped tightly, like an ice-cold hand that entered her and gripped.

The captain then appeared beside Sianon. 'He will spank you next – and you would like that?' Sianon looked across. Kynne's hair flowed down her back to where her small buttocks were still thrust out, darkened with the stripes from the belt. Her legs were splayed as she leant against the wall. Valrenn stopped spanking her and began masturbating her from behind. Her legs started shaking; he whispered to her; her legs straightened. He began playing with her again. She groaned and began sinking down the wall. Then he made her walk, half-crouching into the stables. Sianon again heard the sharp cracks of his leather belt, then Kynne's sobbing gasps as she was played with.

'Go on,' said the captain. He took Sianon through the doorway. Kynne was on her knees, open-legged and shaking. Valrenn pulled her on to her belly on the straw. Her legs stayed open, the pouch of her sex protruding back between her thighs. Valrenn smacked it – the sex itself – from behind, taking high wide sweeps with the leather. After each few smacks, he stopped, crouched down and masturbated her.

The captain led Sianon to the wall. He made her spread her legs; the heavy ring hung down between them and her clitoris was out; he rubbed it with the small ring taken from below her nipple. He tried to fasten it to her clitoris. Her legs buckled; he allowed her to squat, her bulging breasts thrust outwards while he touched them.

Kynne was still being smacked between the legs; Valrenn was relentless as he brought the belt to bear.

Sianon was made to stand, and the balls of the small steel ring were again put gently against her clitoris and rubbed. Her liquid was running thickly down the captain's hand. 'You will be punished more severely should you come,' he whispered. He tried to tighten the ring. She gasped in exquisite pleasure; he let her squat again; she crouched so deeply that the thick ring touched the floor. Her clitoris was pulsing between her open pubic lips. He rubbed it with the ring while she was squatting; she cried out. He slipped his finger quickly through the choker and before he could stand her up again, Sianon did come, her breasts supported on his forearm, the cup of one breast in his hand, his fingers squeezing the nipple. And with her clitoris pumping like a tiny penis, her ankles gave way so she was kneeling, gasping, open-legged on the floor. He then took both hands to her nipples, pumped them very

61

slowly and her climax came again. And with each stabbing contraction, the thick steel ring between her legs lifted up then tapped upon the floor.

'Valrenn!' It was a woman's voice above her. Sianon looked up; she caught a glimpse of black hair, of a pure white countenance, of a slender hand which briefly touched her skin.

The woman strode across and stared at Kynne, sobbing softly on the straw. 'Valrenn – you are impetuous.' Taking her gauntlet off, the woman crouched. 'I have an errand for you – some more of these creatures to be collected. They are at the cross. Take Petruk with you. When their initiation is complete bring them to the manse.'

Her pale small fingers traced the marks on Kynne's buttocks, then moved up to touch her hair. 'Girl – come here. Come closer.' The woman turned Kynne's head, her slender hand reaching round to hold it. Her small body seemed even smaller as she bent to take Kynne's lips, administering a very slow and seemingly gentle kiss. But Kynne began moaning. The kiss continued, deepening; feeble moist cries escaped Kynne's lips; the fingertips softly squeezed her hair. When the face above her finally moved away, a thick dark trickle of blood was running from Kynne's protruding lower lip.

The woman's eyes smouldered. 'Kellor ...' she said. 'It seems there is a stranger in the inn. He has been asking questions. Before we leave, we had better see that they are answered.'

6

Quislan

Josef could not sleep that night for thinking of Iroise and of the mysterious place – Tormunil – that seemed to control everything that happened in this land.

'Have you seen it, Cayu?' Josef had asked him on the stairs.

'No, Mr Stenner, and I pray to God I never will – it is the eye of evil; Servulan is the hand.'

'The abbey – is that where those carriages were bound?' Cayu nodded grimly.

'And this woman,' Josef said, 'Quislan – why is she here?'

'It is the time they call "The Reaping": Tormunil requires handmaidens; the Perquisitor has come for them.'

'Iroise?'

'And many others – the village must give up more than twenty.'

'We must stop them!'

'Shhh . . . Calm down, I beg you . . . Stop the moon, Mr Stenner, stop it in the sky – it would be easier. No one can stop them.'

Josef gave a short derisive laugh, but Cayu, moving quickly, grasped his arm and held it in a vice-like grip. 'I am your guide. This is what you pay me for. Now you must listen to what I have to say: these creatures feed on innocence and on fervour – they can twist these virtues to their own evil ends. In your eyes, I see fervour, burning so intensely now because of your concern. Beware that these creatures never see it.'

Josef broke free, but Cayu's message had struck home despite the superstition in his talk. And then he offered Josef a ray of hope: 'We must bide our time. Wait till morning. Stay in your room.'

'But . . .?'

'We cannot hope to leave until their business is complete.'

'By then it may be too late.'

'Be ready in the morning.'

Cayu had not disclosed his plan; but neither had Josef risked telling Cayu of his own hope – that Iroise might come to his room that very night. If she did, then Josef would attempt an escape from the village – but would she come with him? Or would she be too frightened? Perhaps he should simply take her, if the chance arose?

He found that, as the night advanced and the noises from the inn and the alley-way grew less, their effect upon him became more telling. He had waited long for Iroise. The fire was dying and the air was growing cold. Only one candle still burned. He got up and lit another and began pacing the floor.

Then he noticed a lightening of the sky over the roof-tops, yet it was far too soon for sunrise; it had to be a fire. He hurried to the window, and faintly, on the breeze, he could make out voices chanting.

The knock at his door came unexpectedly. For a second, he could not move; then he rushed across. But he opened the door to a shock: standing before him, and clad in a leather tunic, was one of the riders he had seen that morning. The man would have had to stoop to clear the doorway, but he did not attempt to come in.

'Mr Stenner?' He spoke incisively. 'Come with me.' He stepped to one side and waited. The landlord's hovering anxiously behind the visitor put Josef doubly on his guard.

'What is it?' Josef asked weakly. But the man in leather seemed to think further explanation unnecessary and simply beckoned. Everything about his manner made a refusal impossible. Josef locked the room; the landlord remained at his door; people moved aside, averting their eyes as the rider passed. Everybody's reaction told Josef that here was a man to be feared. There had been no restraint or coercion, but as he was marched along to the steady thump of those booted feet he felt like a wrongdoer who had now been apprehended. He thought again about what had befallen the previous night – and he went like a lamb to the slaughter.

He was taken down the stairs and out through the stable yard then into the street, where for the first time the rider hesitated. Josef glanced up the hill – and there was the fire. The large bronze cross was backlit by it; there were tiers of figures crowded on the grassy mound. Some ceremony was in progress. The rider smiled, then turned and strode up the hill. Josef was too afraid to do anything but follow lamely. When he got to the base of the final slope, Josef stopped. The blood drained from his face. Peculiar feelings came inside him. He had never seen young women naked in a group; he had never witnessed ritual sexuality.

They wore long boots – only boots, nothing more; their arms were folded behind their backs and they were kneeling. They seemed in a trance; some were murmuring; some were swinging their breasts and buttocks. One moaned, then collapsed forwards, knees wide, breasts against the grass. She was lifted and revived by the monks attending the group. All around were spectators – villagers. Some of these were chanting. Two hooded men, naked again but for boots, moved among the girls; both sported thick erections. One carried a spouted jug shaped like a penis, which the girls were given to drink from; the other wore a thin tight glove over one hand, and the fingers glistened.

Each girl in turn was being opened from behind, the thumb entering quite separately from the fingers. The peculiar feeling came again to Josef as he watched this deep examination – the intimacy, and the pleasure it so visibly created. He thought again of the shackles above the bed in his room; and he thought again of Iroise's sexual desires linked so closely to submission. Looking round, he could not see her, but he was frightened she might be here.

As one girl's moans of pleasure increased, the chanting fell to a hush; he could hear the soft moist sounds of the glove inside her. There were girls in the background being prepared in some way – thin belts being put around their naked waists; others were watching and waiting. The one being played with suddenly lurched forward, collapsing in gasping struggling shudders – she had been brought to climax with the gloved hand still inside her, smoothly following every gyration of her body, all the way to the grass. She never pulled away from it, but twisted on to her back and drank thirstily from the offered penis-shaped spout of the cup.

A small group of young women were being led away. Josef's guard spoke to one of the monks, asking for someone named Valrenn. The monk pointed down the street in the direction they had come, and Josef was taken by the arm and led back, following the group of captives until they came to the large house near the centre of the village. Even before the gates were opened, he could hear shouts. There were soldiers in the grounds, busily unhitching a team of horses from a heavy carriage marked with the Tormunite cross. As he was being led up the steps of the house, he heard a second carriage rumble into the yard and turned to see more monks dismounting.

In the entrance hall, the group of frightened young women had now been put with others clustered in one corner; he recognised their guards as being another two of the riders he had seen that morning. His own guard spoke to one of them briefly then hurried him up the stone stairway to the top floor, where they entered an ornately decorated vestibule and then an extensive suite of rooms. He could hear a woman's voice beyond a carved inner door. When he was ushered through, his guard remained behind him and closed the door.

Then he saw her – Iroise, kneeling on the polished wooden floor in an attitude of prayer or supplication. In that first instant, he had eyes for no one else. But the surge of relief at seeing her unharmed was quickly killed by the anxiety written on her tear-stained face. Josef looked at the cause of her distress. Standing above her but half turned away was the woman in black – Quislan – clearly annoyed by the interruption caused by his arrival.

The bearded monk he had seen that morning with the riders sat silently in a chair near a curtained window. Opposite him sat the landlady and beside him stood the same brown-haired girl who had been at the centre of the argument in the yard; she too looked as if she had been crying.

There were two others in the room: the girl Kynne, sitting on the bed, and Fevrun, standing beside her, with his hand on her shoulder. When Josef's eyes met his, Fevrun's thin lips lifted in a smile, as if to say: 'Perhaps he is free to speak to us now.' But even Fevrun did not open his mouth.

Josef looked again at the woman who was clearly the leader. But here, at close quarters, she did not seem so menacing as Cayu's story had suggested, and Josef's original impression – not of youth exactly, but of a childish face and a pale complexion – now seemed reinforced in the soft light of the many candles in the room. She was of only average height for a woman – if anything, she looked smaller, the tightness of her leather suit accentuating her slimness. Joseph relaxed a little – and fell victim to deception.

Quislan suddenly turned squarely on him; she raised a black-gloved hand, the middle finger pointing at his heart.

'Is this the one?'

The silence was as profound as the aftermath of a gunshot in a confined room. Josef couldn't move. His eyes locked onto the line of the finger. Slowly they followed it back, up the arm, to the narrow shoulders, the slim, smooth neck and the small, triangular, sharp-cheeked face, its straight black hair cut like a long helmet about her ears. Her skin was the colour of alabaster, her lips were a pale rose-madder. Then he saw her eyes – properly, fully. And then the feeling took him, engulfing him like a wave: a cool numbness sheathing his body, a softness as of laudanum, a weight of tiredness. It lasted only while her eyes were directly upon him. Her irises were as black as her hair, as black as her eyebrows; in the pure whites of her eyes were these soot-black discs; he could not distinguish her pupils and could not read her mood.

'Is this the one?' This time she said it softly. Her gaze moved down and Josef breathed again; the charm was broken. Iroise, looking up at her, bit her lip and nodded.

There was a pause then, step by slowly clicking step, Quislan walked over to the traveller.

'Madam,' said he, not daring to look again into her face lest all words fail him, 'I demand to know –' Suddenly, the man guarding him grabbed Josef's raised arm in a crushing grip. Josef struggled, only making it worse. 'For God's sake, man!' he cried as his arm was twisted. His assailant was too powerful: when Josef continued to resist, the man jabbed his knee up sharply and brought him gasping to the floor.

He heard Iroise cry, 'No! Do not hurt him!' then scream as the heavy fist punched into his back. All he could see were Quislan's boots in front of his face, lifting then clicking back down to the polished floor, agitatedly, as though, stimulated by the guard's attack, the booted feet were impatient to finish him. Yet the woman's voice was subdued and steady.

'For God's sake, is it? Or for thine, Mr Stenner?' And he could tell now from the timbre of her voice that she was older than she looked. She stooped. Her black-gauntleted hand lifted him by the hair until he was looking up at her chalk-white face, rigidly supported on its high black collar. He had never been truly afraid of a woman until that moment. Her eyes were like slits; above the small, pointed chin, the mouth looked tiny, its lips sealed tightly. They opened to a twisted snarl: 'Answer me!' And again, the voice belied her looks; her teeth – unblemished, wet, polished pearls – looked as perfect as if they had just erupted. The guard moved forward again; Josef flinched. 'No . . . Thank you, Kellor – it is all right,' she whispered graciously, and the man immediately retreated to the other side of the room.

Josef did not see the boot lift until it was too late. He heard Iroise scream again, then he was sprawled on the floor, a searing pain from his jaw-line to his temple. Before he could lift his head he was choking under the heel of Quislan's boot pressing into the side of his neck. 'For whose sake?' the woman kept saying over and over, against the background of Iroise's frantic entreaties, until he choked the word out:

'Mine!'

Then the foot released him, Quislan moved back and Iroise was upon him, kissing him, wetting his face with her tears, pleading with them to spare him. When he finally managed to haul himself partly up, Quislan was already sitting in a high-backed wooden chair, her cynical gaze upon them, relishing their defeat.

Josef's hands were shaking but he stroked his lover's neck – she was his lover; if he had doubted it before, he knew it then. He kissed her gentle lips and hugged her. She was still crying. His body was bruised, but he felt content because she was in his arms. 'Have they hurt you?' Josef whispered.

'They make a pretty pair, Commissioner, do they not?'

It was Fevrun who answered: 'Perquisitor – you propose to take them both?'

The woman laughed, then stood up. 'And yet,' she waved a finger, 'it is a temptation – there could be uses for him.' Iroise's arms closed tighter round him. 'You see. It could be interesting.' Quislan came closer. 'Get back over there, child.' She jerked her thumb and Iroise slipped from Josef's arms and scurried away. Then Quislan said abruptly:

'Why were you trying to spirit her away? You knew we were coming?'

Before he could phrase a reply, the landlady joined the attack: 'Kynne overheard them plotting on the stairs. Ask him. He said that –'

Quislan's raised palm cut the woman short. When Josef still didn't answer, she bent over him. He saw her hand lift again. But he didn't flinch; he stared at her, determined to face her. Her eyes widened to blackness; he felt the wave of tiredness touch him. Her gloved hand descended softly, pressing coolly against the side of his burning face. Her lips looked fuller; her voice was almost gentle. 'You do not understand: she is not free to go.'

He said: 'I would pay the landlady compensation for her loss. I would pay off the indenture.'

The Perquisitor smiled at him as if he were an amusing

child. 'But there is a prior claim upon her – a claim more permanent than any gold.' She stood above him, slowly shaking her head and running her gloved hand across his cheek and neck. 'Traveller – do you still not understand? You are far beyond your depth.' Her eyes met his fully. 'You cannot swim.' And again the feeling came, the sleepy numbness and the weight. The hand rubbed the muscles of his neck slowly and sensually. He could not move until she suddenly clicked her fingers. 'Kellor!'

The guard flicked a gold piece through the air; Quislan caught it in her gloved hand, then held it up between her fingers. She moved back, closer to the centre of the room and removed the glove from her right hand. The hand looked small and delicate and, with no rings to adorn it, curiously bare. Into this delicate hand, against the youthful palm, the gloved hand placed the coin. The hand was now lowered open, that everyone might see. For a few seconds, nothing happened. Josef looked at the other women – they watched expectantly. He looked at the men; everyone's gaze was fixed upon the hand, excepting the monk's, which was on him. And when Josef looked again at the hand, it happened – the gold coin seemed to tremble for an instant, then it melted.

Josef believed it not, but that was what he saw. The landlady crossed herself and swooned; the girls fell to their knees; the men did not move; the monk remained unsearchably serene; and the room was deathly silent.

'What trick . . .?' Josef whispered weakly. The Perquisitor turned, her eyes falling not on him but on the shaking women one by one. She singled out Kynne.

'Hold out your hand,' she said in such a way that Josef now regretted having spoken. The girl had begun to whimper, but her trembling hand stretched out obediently.

'No . . .' Josef whispered. The hairs on the back of his neck stood on end.

Quislan surveyed the room. There was a noise, a faint sizzling noise; it was coming from her hand. Every eye was upon that hand as it slowly tilted and the bright, tiny droplets of molten metal cascaded into the offered palm. The girl's scream was cut off abruptly as she collapsed in a faint; the last drops of gold bounced on the polished wooden floor and disappeared into the cracks between the boards.

Quislan knelt down and raised Kynne's head. 'You are worthy,' she pronounced and kissed her. The girl's entire body trembled as Quislan touched it. She lifted up the dress to the shoulders and Kynne was naked underneath it; the tips of her breasts were tight. Quislan drew her backwards until she leant against the bed. Her dress had fallen down; it was lifted up again, above her breasts, while the Perquisitor now unclenched Kynne's hand. It had a red, angry mark in the centre. Next to it, she held her own hand open. It was unblemished. And on the wooden floor were tiny black marks where the molten metal had dripped.

If it were trickery, Josef could not see how it could have been done. But it must have been trickery.

'These women belong to Tormunil,' the Perquisitor then declared solemnly. 'In every portion of their flesh, every drop of their blood, they are bespoken. I, Quislan, am here to claim them. Remember well what you have seen.'

She turned to Josef. 'You are free to go now, traveller. No one shall impede you.'

He was so shaken by what had befallen that her words had no immediate effect. Then as the meaning dawned, he looked at Iroise, whose arms were wrapped about herself, cradling her trembling body. Her gentle eyes peered out from the shelter of her soft blonde eyebrows; he wanted to kiss her even then. But it almost seemed she could not see him. Her eyes were fixed imploringly upon Quislan, who glanced at her then said to him: 'But Iroise has asked that you be allowed to join us.' His heart surged, then checked itself when he realised what she was saying. 'I make that offer now – and once. If you stay, you fall beneath our jurisdiction – without question and for all time. If this is not your wish, then leave.' It was said that simply. He tried to gather his thoughts.

'But how can you put it so?' he asked shakily. 'How can I answer, without knowing what such a commitment might entail?'

Quislan lifted back Kynne's arms on to the bed. 'Our code of discipline is simple: we believe that strength comes through obedience; that power is a privilege begotten through strength; and that always, there must be this balance – strength and softness; command and obeisance; the exercise of power, the sublimation of the will.' Her delicate fingers began touching the tight protrusions of Kynne's nipples, examining them, enhancing them, while Kynne murmured with her eyes closed. 'This balance is the key: for each – when each comes to understand her place – there is fulfilment.'

'And what of love in all this?' he asked defiantly.

'Without discipline, Mr Stenner, love is worthless.' She paused. 'The dominator protects the submissive – is that not love . . .? You smile? And yet he looks to her well-being in many different ways.' Then she dealt the death-blow to his pride: 'For instance, there is amongst our men a rule: ejaculation never takes place at depth in the vagina – an elementary discipline. You do not have this in your land?'

Josef was mortified with guilt; he could not look at Iroise.

'Love, then – in the narrow sense I think you mean – such love between two equals is forbidden. For us, love is much wider and more profound – the taking of pleasure from a position of strength; or its giving on demand. And the highest form of love to which these postulants will aspire is that of selfless giving.'

Josef looked at them – Iroise, so gentle, her eyes so forgiving; Kynne stretched on the bed; then the girl with long brown hair. In his heart he knew there was a truth in what the woman said.

'Then why would you want me?' he said feebly.

She almost smiled. 'I do not want you, Mr Stenner, nor do I need you. These women – their direction, their guidance – is my sole concern. I am entrusted with their safe delivery. And it seems your presence amongst us may prove a strength to Iroise. She has admitted what she feels. If you go, she will in time forget you; if she sees you constantly, the temptation is always at hand, and through the passion that denial brings, she will find a greater strength of giving. But, either with you or without you, we leave before first light.'

A silence ensued. Josef did not have the temperament for quick decisions in the face of so many unknowns. He did not believe in sorcery. His head told him that these people were not to be trusted at any level; that what he had witnessed must be trickery; that he should avoid them at all costs. But the head is not the ruler of the will. Iroise looked at him and the surge of emotions came again, as it had done when she had ministered to him after the attack. He had not experienced such feelings for any other woman.

'I wish to stay.'

'You accept the conditions?'

He hesitated. 'Yes.'

Iroise closed her eyes. The Perquisitor watched him without moving. 'You have seen something of the initiations that our Warden has organised? The women on the hill?' Josef threw a malicious glance at Fevrun. Quislan tilted her head. 'Mr Stenner – you should understand that each district has its own ceremonial practices, and they are dear to its people's hearts. Warden Fevrun is held in very high regard in this respect. He is a worthy Commissioner and an able one. We have many converts. Mothers freely give their nubile daughters, masters their maids, and of course, husbands their young brides ...' She hesitated pointedly, glancing at Iroise. The colour drained again from Josef's face. 'Ah – I suspected that you did not know.'

Josef suddenly stared at the woman he loved; her frightened eyes told everything; seeing that despairing expression was more harrowing than any verbal disclosure. 'Alas, her husband is not of our persuasion. That is why Warden Fevrun has had to take her under his wing.'

Shaking, Josef stood up. 'Why, Mr Stenner,' smiled Quislan, 'are you leaving, after all?' He scowled at Fevrun, then walked unsteadily over to Iroise, wavered, then seeing her expression – her eyes – he suddenly collapsed to his knees beside her, taking her in his arms, kissing her face, her neck, her burning, salt-wet lips and tears.

'I shall never leave you – while you want me. Never,' he declared.

'Then there is only one thing more,' said Quislan. 'A test.'

'A test?'

'We need proof of your commitment, Mr Stenner. And since words are all too easy, let us couch it in the terms you seem to understand most clearly: we require your gold.'

'But I have a man – a guide; I owe him.'

'I know this. You may settle your debt – the rest is ours.'

Josef hesitated again. He saw the smile begin to form on Quislan's face. 'My purse is in my room,' he said abruptly. And he could feel Iroise's gaze upon him. When he looked at her, the feeling of delicious warmth swept over him again.

'Kellor . . .' Quislan whispered something to the guard, and the man took Josef's key from him and pocketed it.

'Stand up,' she told Josef. Quislan left Kynne leaning against the bed and dismissed the landlady. The frightened woman bustled out, leaving the third girl standing beside the monk's chair. At a nod from Quislan, the monk got up and fastened something round the girl's neck. Then he urged her forwards and she crept across to be placed facing Josef. The monk then waited by the door.

'Kneel down,' said Quislan. Dutifully, the girl did so, and held her head well back, as if to display the soft, black, jewelled collar round her neck. With each small movement, the blue jewel at its centre lifted. But he was totally unprepared for what came next. 'Sianon – I give you to this man. He is your master. You understand?'

'Yes, Perquisitor,' the girl whispered meekly.

'But –' Joseph began.

'Silence!' said Quislan, and the girl bowed to the floor and kissed Josef's feet. Her shining brown hair unfolded round his ankles. 'She is yours until we reach our destination. You shall look to her needs and her discipline; thus shall you love and protect her. Kynne, you shall not touch. Iroise shall be loved in turn, on your behalf.'

The pronouncement had been cold and militaristic, but when Josef looked at Iroise's face, it was radiant.

'Strip her,' said Quislan to Fevrun and the guard Kellor.
'Take her next door. Only when she is ready – fully,
properly ready – shall you bring her back to me.'

Iroise gasped as they grabbed her; Josef moved forward
but Quislan's eyes met his and the coolness and the weight
once more descended round him like a cloak. 'You are
needed here.' Her small lips made the words so softly that
it seemed he heard them in his mind. He was aware of the
monk's leaving. Then in a daze, he watched Fevrun and
Kellor lift Iroise by the shoulders and carry her through
into the adjoining room. He looked at Kynne, propped
against the bed, her belly thrust out, her nipples still erect.
He looked at the girl – Sianon – kneeling at his feet. Left
in the room were three women and he. And he had never
felt so helpless. He sank limply into the nearest chair.

Quislan had tied Kynne's wrists so high against the bed-
posts that her hips and buttocks swayed above the boards;
her feet and calves stayed on the floor. Her dress had fallen
down again. Quislan lifted it and pushed it over the girl's
head, completely baring the front of her body. Her breasts
shivered and her head fell back, cushioned on the crumpled
dress against the bed.

'Undress her. Make her naked.' The words, spoken to
Josef, caused a freezing numbness down his spine. Sianon's
eyes were already wide with arousal at what she was witnessing. Josef looked upon her youthful face properly for
the first time – at the small nose, the dense brown eyebrows, the clear eyes and soft complexion. The support at
the shoulders of her dress was slender and the dress ill-
fitting. Through its armhole he could see the first promise
of the curve of her breast and above it, the join between
her arm and body, the soft dark line, becoming at its upper
tip a curve, a gently twisted lip, which protruded as the
muscle tightened. Then he heard the sound of smacking
coming from the inner room.

Quislan got up and went to where a pair of full-length
curtains hung from the wall. Josef had assumed they hid a
window; he now realised that they must be hanging against

the inner wall separating the two rooms. She drew back one curtain to reveal an alcove with a wooden grille at the back. The smacking had stopped but now other noises issued from the far side. Quislan stood on tiptoes and glanced through the square slatting. 'Her preparation – she cannot see us – I want you to witness it. Otherwise, you cannot know.' She held the curtain aside and waited.

Josef's eyes remained fixed on the flickering shadows beyond the grille. His throat was dry; he could not swallow. The noises came again, drawing him, just as the sounds on the stairs had done, haunting him these past two days.

Quislan moved back. As Josef passed her, she no longer seemed threatening. Her appearance had shifted: there was a look akin to longing in her eyes, and her small pale face seemed curiously attractive, and there was a slight sweet musky scent, like honey, about her person. Josef heard the curtain drop behind him; he was left alone in the darkness with the scene beyond the grille.

The alcove had been designed for viewing; it projected into the inner room, which had been laid out so that every part was visible. Iroise was kneeling on a folded silk blanket placed on the floor. She was completely nude; even her hair had been tied up to expose her neck. Her arms were folded behind her back, and her knees were open. She was leaning back. It made Josef shiver, that she knelt thus – in provocation and submission combined. He could see no marks upon her body, but then, she was half facing him and the marks might have been elsewhere. Kellor was with her and was crouched on the floor; Fevrun stood a little way behind them. He was naked. While Fevrun looked on, Kellor was examining Iroise, opening her gently with his thumbs, his large hands poised, stretched across her thighs and belly. He whispered to her and her legs splayed wider. Then as he held her sex open, his long large fingers moved, delicately reaching for the top of the place where she was open, gripping it and gently pulling. He was coaxing her clitoris from its hood. It was visible even from this distance; it was larger than Josef had seen it; she was more aroused. Kellor touched it, pulled it, slapped it softly with his fingers and stretched the surrounding skin to keep it out. He whispered to her, then the tip of her tongue appeared through her lips. As he continued masturbating her, her tongue pushed gradually further then, accompanied by a moan, it thrust fully out and remained so, swollen and trembling. Kellor gently released her clitoris and held apart her legs. Then Iroise's shiny, tumescent tongue slowly retreated. And the purpose of the action was clear: to her arouser, her tongue was the visible sign of how near she was to coming; when it was fully out, the stimulation either stopped or changed.

Kellor turned her round, and Josef saw the marks on her bottom. They must have used a belt or strap. He could not understand it – how she could be so aroused when they had done this to her. But she was aroused. He watched the scene continue and worsen, yet could not drag himself away. The longer he remained there, the more the love that he felt for her became tainted by the things he witnessed – the manner of her punishment and pleasure; the cloth that her open sex was placed upon while she was abused; then the intricacies of the stimulation, the licking, the penetration; and the intense arousal she was made to bear continually and without release.

Each man was now naked and had a cord around his sex to keep it unnaturally distended by trapping the flow of blood. Iroise was kept kneeling, their rigid cocks brushing and bobbing against her writhing body as she was stimulated again and again until she seemed to want to sit or crouch. When she swooned, she was supported. Her face was taken in Fevrun's hands. His bulging cock pressed against her pouted tongue as Kellor continued playing with her.

There were already wet lines down her legs – the same wetness that Josef had tasted from her and now being yielded to these others. The cock was directed down into her mouth and slowly pushed until she gagged. But she kept it there; not only that, she took the short remaining exposed length of stem in her hand and began masturbating it slowly into her mouth until her fingers trembled and she gasped and tried to close her legs round Kellor's hand. But Kellor kept her legs open and her buttocks raised. He worked his fingers inside her sex and his thumb inside her bottom. Iroise groaned. The cock in her mouth began pumping. Kellor held her steady, his hand inside her body not moving, until Fevrun's climax was completed. The cock was then withdrawn, still hard, and the hand slipped gently out of her to wet her breasts and belly. She was shuddering, whispering to Fevrun, pleading, her lips still coated with his come. She even licked them in between her whispers. Then a leather cloth was unrolled and stretched across the rounded back of the heavy armchair.

They put her on it, against it, while she was still in the kneeling posture she had retained – as if she were afraid to straighten her legs, or to move in any way. Iroise was moaning, begging them, as they held her sex open and lowered her on to the stretched leather cloth. Then they pushed her knees out and up, so she was frog-legged while they spanked her. When they moved her along the chair-back, the cloth slid with her, and when they eased her shoulders back, it stuck against her. They began to play with her through the cloth. Then suddenly her tongue thrust out again – the sign – and Fevrun bent down and kissed it. His cock curved across her arching belly and poked between her naked breasts. He kept stroking her vulva through the leather. When she gasped, he tilted her forwards. Kellor drew her feet up behind her and put something against her bottom. She began breathing very quickly. Fevrun supported her breasts while the thing that Kellor applied was gradually introduced into her body. Iroise whimpered and pleaded as her nipples were stroked. Her knees suddenly tried to grip the back of the chair. Fevrun prised them apart, then made her sit up and stretch her buttocks open, with the thing still inside her. She began shuddering and her knees started to come together again. But she was not allowed to climax. She was plucked from the chair and lifted to the floor. And the leather cloth came with her. It was part of her and it remained so while they spanked her, taking turns upon her buttocks.

'They will smack until the leather drops to the floor.' Quislan was beside Josef. Unable to move, he watched it happen. Then Iroise collapsed backwards into Fevrun's arms, offering her tongue desirously, pleadingly. 'You think she needs you?' Quislan whispered. 'At this moment – do you think it? When her pleasure is so deep that she is drowning?' A shiver descended Josef's spine. Iroise lay gasping, open-kneed, while Fevrun slowly squeezed her bursting nipples and Kellor drank the sexual liquid oozing from between her legs.

'Come – where you are needed.' Quislan opened the curtains. Josef's subjugated gaze drifted away from the grille. Sianon was still kneeling in the position where he had left her. 'Attend to her. Be strong for her. She shall be guided by your will.'

The drug of illicit desire was dispensed; Quislan had secured the craving. Afterwards would come the guilt; Josef knew it, but the knowledge did not help him.

Sianon's hands were behind her back and her body was slightly turned; he had the urge to slip his hand inside her dress, to gather up her breast, to keep it lifted and to stroke it where it made that pouted lip beneath her arm. He sank into the armchair. 'Undress,' he whispered.

She unbuttoned her dress from the front; it slid from her arms to the floor, leaving her naked, save for the collar round her neck and a thin linen belt around her middle. Attached to this belt was a small gold cross, its arms upraised, its staves circular in section – a perfect replica in miniature of the metal cross above the village. Her breasts were very swollen, appearing concentrated, heavy, much larger than Iroise's – for Josef was already making these comparisons. Her nipples were already firm; his fingers ached to touch them. Then he saw that the lines that he had assumed to be shadows were actually moving with her skin; she had been whipped there, to the sides of her breasts and underneath them.

Quislan had returned to Kynne and the bed but she was watching him. 'Take her on your lap,' she said. It was as if she could see inside his mind. She asked of him only the things that he wanted. He had only to whisper small encouragements and his charge submissively followed. He helped her up. Her skin felt soft and warm, her body kept responding to his touch. He lifted up the small cross and let it fall against her naked belly. Her knees moved open; he felt the drift of rising warmth against his fingers. He could see the swelling ridge of pink skin between her legs; it seemed to move and thicken with a life of its own. He touched it and it opened; he slipped two fingertips just inside; he held the cross lifted and caressed her clitoris gently with his thumb. It was as if the lifting of the small weight from her belly made her more aroused: he touched her only very gently but her labia even now stood out thickly, pouting round his fingers, which were into her only to the tips. And all of this was taking place against a background of renewed spanking from the other room. Sianon responded to those sounds – Josef could sense it in her breathing and he could feel it in the tiny pulses of her labia about his fingers – but she was watching what was happening to the girl tied to the bed. Every time Quislan touched Kynne's breasts, Sianon shivered.

Kynne was hanging by her wrists. She had narrow hips and bright red pubic hair; the backs of her thighs were lifted from the floor. Her body was arched over the end of the bed and her breasts were thrown outwards. Quislan touched them lightly. Then she pushed Kynne's head back to the counterpane and opened her mouth. The girl was looking at the ceiling and could not see the thin wax taper in the woman's hand. Quislan lit the taper from a candle by the bed.

Sianon began to tremble – Josef could feel her pubic lips contract, then swell against his fingers. Then Kynne saw the burning taper and cried out.

'Close your eyes,' Quislan instructed her. 'Stay still. Stay open. Open everything.' Kynne's breathing turned to gasps. 'Wide . . .' Her mouth stayed open; her feet pushed backwards across the floor; her trembling knees moved out and up, laying bare her pubic lips, already distinctly outlined by arousal. 'Push it. Let it open.' Kynne grunted; her

80

sex seemed to swell, than an almond slit appeared in it; only her toes touched the floor as she strained to keep it open. Quislan moved slowly, caressing Kynne's face and kissing her eyelids. The taper trembled; it tilted over Kynne's projecting breasts and the hot wax began to drip upon her nipples. 'Still ...' Quislan whispered. Kynne's body convulsed as the taper was moved back and forth between her nipples, dripping steadily, coating the nipples and their surrounds until the taper was all used up. Then Quislan pinched the flame between her fingers.

Kynne's nipples were imprisoned in shiny yellow pointed coatings and there were pale flat droplets that had fallen stray upon the skin of her breasts. Quislan now removed her leather belt. 'Stay open,' she whispered, unrolling the belt to its full extent. There was a murmur from Sianon. Then Quislan stood back and spanked Kynne's breasts while Kynne was still restrained. She showed no mercy. Kynne tried to arch away but could not save them; the lash, directed horizontally, smacked across them, lifted them up and licked beneath her arms. Her hips gyrated and pushed, her knees began to close, her toes collapsed. Quislan waited until the girl was pushing again, until her belly was distended, and her pubic lips were an open slit. Then the smacks restarted. Kynne's bouncing breasts had turned bright red. Her nipples were still trapped inside their waxen coats. The lashing was delivered precisely and unwaveringly until her legs and sex and mouth stayed open and her breasts stayed pushed out hard.

Then Quislan knelt between her open legs and started to touch. The delicate movements of her fingers seemed a contradiction to the ferocity of the lashing. She held each pubic lip separately: it was as if the girl's sex were a cut that Quislan's fingertips would test and clean, and her clitoris was a bulb, a snag of skin which, through the gentle pressing, she would heal. Kynne remained open-mouthed, but her breathing started coming harshly, and her belly started to move. Quislan asked her to keep still.

There were trickles of sweat running down from under Kynne's arms and across the band of reddened skin

around her breasts. Quislan touched Kynne's clitoris lightly, all the while repeating that she should keep still.

As the harshness of the gasps increased, Josef gently
brushed Sianon's breasts; her nipples were rigid. Her legs
were still splayed; he could feel her bottom start to move
against his lap. He softly squeezed her nipples and she
moaned.

On an impulse, he lifted her down and made her kneel
beside him, turning her so her breasts were pressed against
his thigh. While she watched Kynne, he stroked her shiny
brown hair, then her neck. When he touched the collar, she
gasped. Josef eased her breasts over the top of his thigh, so
the pressure beneath them made them round and hard. Her
breasts were very large. He traced the stripy purple marks.
He circled the wide brown surrounds with a fingertip, then
squeezed the fleshy nipples softly, rubbed them, pushed
them through his fingers, then gently picked them with his
nail. And the picking, the scratching of her nipples quickly
strengthened her arousal, and the whole of the surround
turned hard. He made his fingers wet and pulled her
nipples again, then gently scratched them, wet them,
scratched again, very slowly and lightly, underneath them,
until her breath suddenly caught and her back arched
down and a slight tremble moved through her, then another, a stronger one – was it what he thought? And could
it have happened this way, from playing with her nipples?

Josef turned Sianon's face and looked at it; her lips were
moist where she had licked them; her mouth was open,
breathing quickly, her eyelids half closed. When he slipped
his hand under the hollow of her arm, there was heavy
moisture there. He gathered up her breasts again and made
her straighten up, so he could see below the cross and between her legs – and the pink ridge of her sex glistened
wetly. And he was aroused by this feeling that he had made
her lose control and come, it seemed, by playing with her
nipples. He slid his hand around the back of her neck and
held her, restraining her gently, while he ran his palm up
and down, across the full warm cups of her breasts and the
hard hot lumps of her nipples.

She was still kneeling when Iroise was brought back by the two men. In Fevrun's hand was a broad, buckled belt that was wider than the one used by Quislan. When she was turned, Josef could see the marks of the punishment – the skin of her bottom and the backs of her legs was livid. Fevrun carried the thin leather cloth; it had a shiny wetness in the middle.

Without his realising it, Josef must have released his hold upon Sianon: she was now kneeling a little way from him and watching him apprehensively. He must have instructed her to move away, but he could not clearly recall having spoken. His gaze moved back to Iroise.

A large bowl had been brought and placed on the floor. Iroise stepped meekly into it. And at that precise moment, her eyes met Josef's and sent a shiver of deprivation through his limbs. It made no difference that he himself had only now been caressing Sianon; guilt is not a cure for jealousy. Iroise did not look away, and Josef remained impaled upon the soft, sweet blueness of her gaze until Kellor began to wash her. Then the shiver struck him again: her eyes had closed. Her mouth was open and her lips moved silently.

Fevrun took the wash-cloth from Kellor and squeezed it against the side of her neck. The water ran down her breast and over her belly. The nipple stood out; he touched it and her belly trembled. Then he turned her to face him. There was a hunger as she took his tongue into her mouth. He stroked the stripes across her bottom and she shuddered; he pressed her wet body against himself and lifted her from the bowl, and she clung to him when he tried to put her down. Fevrun made no attempt to dry Iroise but began gathering up her things.

Then Josef heard a gasp: Quislan was holding a lighted taper above Kynne's open legs, holding her labia lifted back and allowing the wax to drip. She held it steadily while Kynne moaned and her belly contracted, pushed and rippled, as her stiffened clitoris and its surround were gradually sealed inside a shiny yellow stump.

Fevrun had taken hold of Iroise from behind; her

thickened nipples slid between his fingers. Josef could still see the drops of water on her skin. Kellor was swinging a short frayed rope in quick, light strokes against the front of her legs. Her arousal had begun again. Her knees were shaking.

When Quislan at last put out the taper, the place between Kynne's legs was standing like a large shiny carbuncle. Quislan fitted a leather cord around Kynne's waist and between her legs; it had a cup that trapped her encased clitoris. Then she untied her and made her get up.

'Kellor,' she said, nodding towards Josef. 'Go back to his room at the inn. There is a purse in his cabinet. There is also a loose floorboard below the window – look there. And move aside the wardrobe – you will find a hole in the panelling behind it. Bring me the traveller's gold.'

Josef was thunderstruck; there was no way she could have known these things. Then she turned to him: 'That was our bargain, was it not?' He simply sat there, open-mouthed. 'Get up!' she shouted. 'See to Sianon – we are leaving.'

At the gates of the manse, he met Cayu, who had fetched his horse.

'They told me you were going with them,' said Cayu, offering his flask. Josef nodded then drank, but when he tried to give it back, Cayu said: 'Keep it.' His manner had changed; gone was all trace of familiarity and ease; and when Josef finally mounted his horse it was almost as if Cayu did not even want to take his hand. When the Perquisitor and her guard appeared, he stepped back from the light of the lamps. And when Josef offered him the payment for his loyal service, he simply stared at it.

'I will not touch their gold.'

Josef told him it was his to give; that Cayu had earned it. The traveller's hand extended anxiously, offering the gold.

As the horses milled about and tapped the cobblestones, Cayu glanced at the carriages being loaded with their innocent cargo, then he looked at Sianon, standing quietly with the traveller's greatcoat about her naked shoulders. The coat was open, the fullness of her breasts barely covered, and her naked, perfect feet were upon the dew-wet stones. Dawn was coming greyly. The traveller's horse gave a start as the manse doors were shut: like lightening, Cayu's solid grip was round its reins, his broad hand softly stroking its nose, his warm breath blowing gently across its flared nostrils until it was soothed. Then without a word, he turned and went.

7

A Peace Offering

With urgent, fluttering, satin-slippered steps, the demesne-lord Rathlen Vengarn – cheeks rouged, skin sallowed by ill-living, but powder-pale hair unruffled and eyebrows stibnite-black – swept down the airy curve of marble staircase, his loose, gold gown flowing out behind him, his ring-cluttered fingers tapping the polished balustrade. Gliding through the liveried retinue flanking the hall, he paused beside the nude slave, Callanis, half reclining in the throne-like chair. And his narrow, pinched nostrils quavered; his pale eyes washed across the warm bronzed body; his thin fingers sidled up to touch the pearl-drop ring dangling from the young man's ear.

There was a cough from behind him. 'My lord – she is here,' announced his major-domo softly. He bore a small, crystal glass perfume dispenser on an onyx tray.

The breath was audibly sucked in through the narrow nostrils. 'Then we must greet her – our Perquisitor.' And the sibilant tones conveyed a hint of pique.

The demesne-lord straightened up, his thin hand extending elegantly, angled like the head of a swan, his fastidious fingers arching, beak-like, to accept the proffered dispenser. Soft fragrant clouds misted his tender pink neck. He took one last, longing look at the young, perfect creature in the chair then, smoothing his gown, proceeded gracefully through the outer doors and to the top of the semicircle of steps, where he balanced, fingertips pushed together, nose lifted, small eyes surveying the carriages and horses throwing billows of dust upon the walls lush with peaches and vines.

The small virago in black dismounted nimbly. The demesne-lord felt a shiver slide through him: he had not forgotten her eyes. So pale and young, she looked, her limbs so delicate, her cheeks so high and narrow, but her eyes . . .

She turned to the horse next to hers, where a red-haired girl, clad only in a shirt, was mounted astride. The horse was bareback. The shiver came again to the demesne-lord. The girl whimpered as the woman dragged her to the ground. Her shirt rode up: he saw her naked belly and the red, chafed skin between her legs; her tight buttocks pushing out; her erect pink nipples peeping. She was displaying herself, open and naked on his steps, oblivious to his presence. The demesne-lord then remembered the rod – very thin and whippy – and he whispered to his major-domo to bring it with the other items. Would that he could use it on her pouty bottom and her legs.

The woman turned to one of the soldiers. 'Valrenn – I do not want her spared. Give her to the men.' The girl began sobbing softly. Taking no heed, the woman beckoned to a monk to follow as she strode determinedly up the steps.

The demesne-lord's heartbeat quickened. He spread his hands in nervous greeting. 'Narven bids you welcome.' She stopped directly in front of him, two steps below him, her hands on her hips, and looked up. His head turned half away, his fingers hovering to shade his eyes.

She laughed abruptly, 'Vengarn –' making him wince at the discourtesy, 'I shall not use the gaze on you again. That was my promise. You have helped us. We require shelter and sustenance for the night.'

'It is our privilege to provide it, Perquisitor. My house is your house for the duration of your stay.' The demesne-lord of Narven bowed, moved his hand down but kept it with the other, close to his chest and still did not look her straight in the face. The memory was too vivid. 'Tormunil is our guidance,' he ventured, glancing at the monk. When neither one replied, he said: 'Dinner is laid on in the kitchens for your party. But I would be honoured if you yourself would grace my own table.'

'I eat with my men.'

'Then yourself and your guard,' he said anxiously,

'whosoever of your choosing.' She seemed to relax a little, so the demesne-lord moved aside, sweeping open his arm. His major-domo had returned with the things he had requested. The Perquisitor marched inside, leaving the others on the steps. She glanced briefly around.

'Your house is very beautiful, my lord,' she said flatly. And Rathlen Vengarn bowed again but his spirits were lifted – because at least she had addressed him by his correct title. Emboldened now, he said:

'I have a gift for the Perquisitor.'

She stared at him. Trembling slightly, but with sparkling eyes, he pointed to the young slave half hidden in the chair, so still he might have been sleeping. The demesne-lord's lips quivered, then pursed the words: 'For you . . .'

He glimpsed a fraction of a frown before the reply came swiftly: 'Servulan takes only women.' But she was watching the slave now, and the demesne-lord knew, if anybody knew, the nature of that look.

'Not for the abbey – for you, Perquisitor,' he said softly. 'My personal gift.' He brought his fingertips together in an arch above his breast, and his polished nails glistened. She walked across – her stride, her limbs were perfect – and stood above the nude figure. The demesne-lord waited. She took her gloves off slowly, took the young man's chin, lifted it and stared into his eyes. The demesne-lord heard the soft, long sigh, as if all the breath was being drawn from that youthful body, a sigh he had often heard, though brought about in other, more delectable circumstances. And the feeling stirred below his gown, where he was naked and shaved. Coming slowly, it was a feeling that was so balanced and so sweet, the weight of warmth between his legs, still hanging, swaying gently as he moved across to watch.

Callanis appeared to be in a dream; his eyes were softer than ever, the pupils wide. He was on his side, his legs open, his perfect balls like heavy velvet eggs, his penis in its jacket, still relaxed, and yet half swollen, wide but slightly curving, the head still nipped inside its skin.

The Perquisitor lifted his leg. 'You have dildos I can use on him?'

'Of course.'

'A range of sizes?'

'Oh yes.'

'Bring me the set.'

She was an expert. She put the first one in smoothly, then began to twist it, slowly, and only every now and then. The penis lifted, half inflated, arching in response, each slight twist detected, the clothed tip of it repeatedly kissing his inside leg. The demesne-lord moved to the head of the chair and watched her with a sweet ache in his belly. On the small table were the carved shapes – narrow ones, thick ones, bulbed or tapered, large and small, some smooth, others grotesquely distorted. With them were the other aids to pleasure that his servant had anticipated might be needed – the ivory spheres, the thin, bone-handled whippy rod, and the small, soft leather teat.

The Perquisitor gradually drew the dildo out of Callanis. It was tapered the wrong way round; the withdrawal was a shedding, the soft folds of the anal ring drawn gently out as if to follow. Then the second one went in.

It was larger, broader, rougher, more tight of access, more precisely shaped, with a cap, and an exaggerated, heavy swelling below the head. When the heavy swelling began to be taken, and the folds of tender skin reversed, Callanis moaned, and the head of his penis squeezed out through its skin as if pushed. His full stiffened penis, no longer touching his body, trembled as, step by staccato step, the dildo was now turned.

The Perquisitor left it in him, then examined his balls gently, squeezing them with her small pointed fingers, then tested the tube along the underside below the glans.

When the second size was taken out, Callanis groaned with pain at the withdrawal, which was more prolonged, accompanied by repeated turning. The Perquisitor now selected the very largest dildo, which thickened to the base and carried on its surface twisted, ropy veins. She made him hold his leg up in the air.

'I want you to say, "Please",' she said to him.

'Please . . .' he whispered, then gasped as the tip pushed a short way in through the rim.

'The full insertion will take time – you are narrow. You have to keep saying it. Each time it goes deeper, say, "Please". Now – again.'

'*Please* . . . Aghh!'

'And each time I turn it, moan.'

At this point, the demesne-lord turned away – not because he did not want to watch that place being so unnaturally stretched, being made progressively to swallow something it was not designed to take – but because at that moment, he wished to savour the sounds, the moans, the sudden gasps she had not asked for, the sweet, interminable, murmured half pleadings, the intermittent scuffing of the ever-stretching limbs against the chair, and the Perquisitor's grunts as she forced the entry. When the demesne-lord turned again, Callanis's knees were balanced in the air, and the knotted stub of the dildo projected thickly from below his heavy balls.

The major-domo looked on, the Perquisitor stood back. The young man's penis looked fit to burst. It was angry red, its blue veins bulging; it was purple at the head, and so stiff it would not even tremble.

The Perquisitor then extracted the dildo so quickly that the lip of the anus was left drawn out, pouting and thickened into red-pink folds. It contracted in a spasm when she touched it, but the folds would not retract. She held his rigid penis gently. It took a long while, but it eventually subsided to a half-inflated state. Then she cradled the young slave's head. His feet slowly sank down over the chair-arms. She waited until the penis actually lolled. Then she took up the thickest dildo again, wiped it and began pushing it very slowly into his mouth, allowing his head to sink back to permit the alignment that would allow him to take it deeply. Before a half of it was in, his belly was arched upwards and his penis was stiffer and more veined than it had been with the dildo in his anus.

Standing above him, she dripped her spittle on his up-turned penis. It began running down the underside. The effect was almost immediate – he started breathing quickly, nostrils dilating, penis throbbing like a heart. The Perquisitor gently rubbed the spittle in.

'My lord, your experience in these matters is greater than mine: you hold it. But make it hurt him when it happens.'

Rathlen Vengarn bowed, stepped forward and gently seized the end of the fleshy shaft. Moaning exquisitely, Callanis twisted on to his side, his penis curving over the edge of the chair. The demesne-lord's fingertips remained with him, maintaining the pressure very gently. Then he deftly fitted the blind leather teat over the cap of the penis, gently but tightly, containing only the end, sealing it off, but leaving the rest of the penis accessible and naked. When he drew the fine cord to its final tightness, the penis gave a harsh, stabbing single pulse and the slave's lips closed tightly round the dildo in his mouth.

The demesne-lord now explored at his leisure the underside of the penis with his thumb, pressing softly, moving gradually upwards until the reaction was again triggered, then stepping swiftly away and watching the slave trying to cope with the approach of his climax.

When the shudderings steadied, he used the thin flexible rod to whip – once only, in order to effect the greater shock – at the base of the stem, where the feeder tube enters the body. Callanis bucked. His penis stabbed and steadied, its head expanding to stretch its leather pouch. The demesne-lord stepped forward – coldly, for such treatments must be cold; therein lies the exquisiteness of the pleasure – held the balls separated so the skin was polished, and whipped down the line of the join, between the balls, striking through to the parts inside, getting to the root of the pleasure.

The slave gasped against the dildo in his throat. The Perquisitor held it steady. The demesne-lord moved forward again, lightly, almost dancing, held the cap of the penis through the leather, waited till the legs were raised so far that the buttocks had left the chair, then he whipped below the scrotum, whipped the muscle joining the root of the penis to that fundamental place.

Then he stood back and watched the young man *in extremis*, the Perquisitor pushing the dildo slowly deeper into his throat, his belly progressively lifting, his penis hard as stone.

It took at most a few seconds, and yet those seconds seemed stretched, because the vision was so delicious. Then it came, the pulsing heavy beat, slowly at first, but building with a sureness that would not stop. It was exquisite to watch him writhing in pleasure, a pleasure that would come now, however much he strived to block it, but a pleasure that, because the naked flesh was not being stimulated directly, would linger on the slow road to fruition, driven only by the balance – the pulsing squeeze against the leather teat, and the pressure from inside him.

Taking pity on himself now, Vengarn took the leather cap of the penis lightly by the tiny strings and slowly drew them tighter. From the slave, the groan was wrenching. Vengarn wanted to put something into him – quickly – but there was not time now. All that he could do was watch, and feel the tremblings through the string.

'My lord – they are not so different, men and women.' The Perquisitor pinched the young nipples, grasping them in her fingers, squeezing them roughly, scratching, as the leather teat about the cap of the penis flooded with come, its pressure forcing opalescent fluid through the material, down the stem and into the groove below his balls. The slave kept groaning, the Perquisitor kept clawing at his breasts and the liquid kept coming until the seat of the chair was wet and the rich smell of semen welled into the air.

The demesne-lord's high thin nostrils dilated as he drank it in.

'I will take him – for training,' the Perquisitor whispered. She took the dildo out of his mouth. 'Your legs,' she commanded the slave. 'Get them up – high up. Feet behind your ears.' She put the tip of the dildo between his buttocks and with the heel of her hand, thrust it quickly in. More liquid squeezed out through the wet leather teat.

'I shall need a plug – at least as wide as this,' she said, 'so he can sit with it in him. I want him properly stretched.'

'It shall be done.'

92

8

Sianon's Story

Sianon knew they called him 'traveller' but his name was really Josef and he was now her master. As she waited uneasily beside him, she watched the Perquisitor and Dom Enken leave Kynne on the steps and march up to the front entrance of the grand house. And she stole glances around her, at the high-walled courtyard, the extensive stable-block below and the gardens stretching into the distance. This place was truly magnificent, larger and more beautiful than any she had seen. Yet it was but a stopping-place on their long journey.

Then she saw her master's eyes, and a darkness in them that frightened her. She had felt it in the bedroom, when he had pushed her aside, and she saw it later, when his servant had refused his gold. He was resentful of the Warden, but the Warden had remained behind. And on the journey, the traveller had not spoken; for the last few miles he had ridden ahead of her, to be closer to the one he really wanted.

Sianon looked up: there was a sudden scurry of servants from a side door. Dom Enken had returned to direct them. The horses were taken to be stabled, and the remainder of the party were led through lush water gardens to the kitchens, where a meal was waiting. She noticed that the monks chose to eat separately, in a side room.

Throughout the meal, Sianon watched her master and tried to judge his mood. Iroise was beside the captain at the far end of the table; she looked desperately unhappy; her eyes were downcast and she never touched any of the food he offered. In the end, he lifted her chin and put the cup of wine to her lips and she began drinking. But then her behaviour towards him seemed to change, because when he later offered the drink again, she steadied his hand. And when the cup was put down, their fingers remained touching. Then after that she started eating.

Sianon's master began drinking steadily as the jugs of wine were freely refilled. Then the Perquisitor came in with the man who must have been master of the house. He was dressed in flowing gold robes. Near the door behind them, a young man who was naked had been placed facing the wall, leaning against it. A servant stood with him. People at the tables turned to watch. When the young man moved, Sianon could see he was sexually excited. It caused a tiny shiver inside her: she had never seen a man used for sexual pleasure; she had not known that such things happened. She glanced at the man in flowing robes.

From a distance, his gaze examined each of the women in turn, pausing at Kynne and one of the others, but finally settling again on Iroise. He spoke in muted tones to the Perquisitor, while nodding towards the young man and then at Iroise. Then he went over to the young man and began to touch him.

The Perquisitor collected Iroise and led her to the door, where she made her watch what was being done to the young man. Something was being put inside him. The Perquisitor seemed to be studying Iroise's reaction to what she saw. She placed Iroise's hand in the hollow of the young man's back, only lightly, yet the young man moaned; his erection bulged. The man in the gold robe began to stroke Iroise's hair. Then he placed something into her other hand, which sank at first beneath the weight. The group then left, taking Iroise, and the object she now carried. Sianon glimpsed it: it was a pure white ball.

She looked at her master beside her; his eyes were glazed and even the cup of wine was pushed away; his fist was clenched and he sat like a statue.

Later, when they were taken to their quarters, Iroise was still missing. Sianon was led from the kitchens, through the gardens, to a room above the stables. She knew that he would want to use her: she would try to please him, she would try so hard to please him, even if he was cruel. But she could hear the others below with Valrenn and Kynne; she knew the sounds they were making.

Her master sat her on the makeshift bed, lifted the coat aside and touched the tender skin inside her thighs. And she was reminded of Kynne, and the way that she had been made to ride bare-legged without a saddle.

He made Sianon lie on her side, facing the wall and told her to remain thus until he came back.

She waited, her inner thighs tingling where he had touched them, her breasts full, hurting, even though he had not. She was thinking of the rash inside Kynne's legs, the mass of bright red spots and raised scratches, and the thick waxed lump that, in the woods, she had watched the Perquisitor gently prise away until it was left hanging. And she was reliving the feelings she had experienced when she had watched Kynne subsequently come to climax during spanking. She could hear the men's voices in the stable below – the traveller whispering and Kynne moaning.

Then he came back, lifted Sianon gently from the bed and led her down the first few steps overlooking the scene. There were no straps used on Kynne, no sounds of spanking. She was kneeling on the straw, her shirt pushed up. There were two men with Valrenn; one was dressed like a servant and they appeared to be deciding what to do with her. Several of the girls were arrayed about the stable, watching. The circle of men closed round Kynne; there were furtive movements. Kynne was lifted back then lowered. Two of the watching girls gasped. Sianon, on the steps, could not see what was happening. Her master lifted the cross from her belly and touched her. She was wet; she could already feel it. Her naked feet were planted on the step. Her naked thighs were open. Her master stood below her, playing with her. It hurt between her legs where he was touching; it ached.

A deep moan came from the centre of the circle of men around Kynne. She was lifted back, gasping, then allowed to squat, still moaning, with her knees held open and Valrenn bent over her, supporting her under the arms, with her shirt lifted and her breasts bulging quickly. The servant held something shiny in his fingers. 'Again,' Valrenn said and the hand holding the shiny thing moved forward, and Kynne's thighs bowed outwards as it was put between her legs. When she was pulled upright, she could hardly stand. Valrenn was murmuring his appreciation and the men were touching her and Kynne was panting.

Putting her to the wall they made her spread. As Valrenn knelt between her legs, it happened a second time: Kynne collapsed; she was held while she was squatting and the thing between her legs was taken out and put back in.

When the deep moan came again, the traveller moved up beside Sianon and held her close, with his hand between her thighs again, coaxing her clitoris, touching her wetness. Then he asked Sianon what she wanted – how she wanted it, suggesting various ways. He asked her if she wanted her bottom spanking. She could not express her needs in words.

He took her naked, but for the cross around her belly, out into the grounds. He carried her choker in his hand; she wanted him to put it on her.

There were others being dealt with. He let Sianon watch from the edge of the orchard. Then he took her a little away from the others and stood her against a tree, while she held her naked breasts and belly pressed against the wood. When he turned her round, her breasts and belly were streaked with green; her sex was aching to be rubbed; she would have done it with her hand if he had asked her. He stripped a twig and held it between his hands and made Sianon climb it. Her labia freely opened round it, so heavy was her wetness. Then he borrowed a short strap from one of the soldiers and took her back inside.

She could still hear Kynne moaning. The traveller stopped Sianon on the steps and let her watch. Kynne was being entered: the two soldiers had used leather thongs strapped round their penises to make them more erect.

But as Sianon's master watched this, his mood suddenly seemed to darken. Picking up the coat, he bustled Sianon coldly up the stairs and threw her to the bed, but left her and went straight to the window that looked towards the house where Iroise had been kept.

Sianon waited. But he stayed at the window, staring. Sianon sat up slowly and quietly and leant against the wall. She pulled the coat around her nakedness. And she picked up the pillow – it was soft and fine and cool, so unlike the harshness of the makeshift bed – and cushioned her cheek against it. Then she put her head in her hands and the pillow dropped to the floor.

She didn't realise what was happening until she heard the sobbing cry – her cry – and felt the hot trickles at the corners of her lips and the taste of salt in her mouth; it was the memory, of something that had happened that afternoon, when her horse had stumbled. The traveller had reached for her – for her – and had taken her in his arms and held her, in a gesture so far-reaching in its warmth, and with a tenderness she had never known. And now all of that meant nothing.

'Sianon . . .' He was there, on the bed with her, pulling her coat back gently from her shoulders, repeating her name – 'Sianon . . .' untying the small cross from round her belly, touching her back, her aching breasts, the place between her legs, laying her naked but for her tears. When he stretched himself behind her on the bed, she could feel that he was naked too. He put the pillow under her cheek, then reached round and gathered her breasts; they were full and heavy in his hand and on his arm. He squeezed her nipples and tiny bumps rose up within the velvety surround. He pinched beneath the teats; Sianon murmured. He stroked and rubbed the places that were marked. Then he asked her gently who had done it: 'Quislan?'

'No – it was my mistress,' Sianon whispered.

'She punished you very well.'

Sianon turned to face the traveller. 'Please – you must understand that it was not that way – not always.'

'Then what way . . .? Tell me.'

She pressed her cheek to the pillow. Then she took hold of the fingers that played upon the marks below her nipples. 'Last night,' she said, 'at the manse, while I was watching Kynne and you touched my nipples, the feeling came. With my mistress, it would come there too. Sometimes it was so strong . . .'

Her breasts moved gently as he touched them with the tips of his fingers. He made the tightness come inside them, the bristling sensitivity, then he kissed them. 'Tell me about her,' he whispered.

Sianon turned to the wall. 'I used to think that she despised me.' She held the traveller's arms around her breasts, above and below them, trapping them, gently squeezing. She closed her eyes. 'She was older than the squire – my master. She was tall and thin, but always stooped with pain. Her coldness towards me made me feel guilty if she caught me smiling. The only time she would speak to me directly was to criticise ... I come from a good family. When my father died, my mother entrusted his affairs to a man who could not cope, and we fell on difficult times. My mother was forced to give me up; my mistress took me in. I was so unhappy.'

'But you said that, with your mistress –'

'Not then – she hated me. However well my work was done, I could not please her.'

'And what about the squire?'

'He was the opposite, in every way – kind to me; always smiling. Except when the mistress was there.' Sianon hesitated. 'But he had a private study, where the mistress never went. One day, he called me in there.' Her voice was a whisper. Her nipples tingled. 'He told me to stand up straight. Then he locked the door.'

Turning, Sianon looked up at the traveller. 'He told me to take my breasts out, to take them out for him. I said I was afraid. "Of me?" he asked. I told him I was afraid of what my mistress might do if she found out. "She would whip your breasts," he answered, watching me. And I cannot explain why, but the words – the threat, the situation, the thought of exposing myself to him – excited me. I was trembling. My nipples hurt with the arousal. And I knew he would see it. It was a sweet, delicious feeling. Even as I did it – opened my blouse and unfastened my vest – I knew it was wrong. I thought of my mistress punishing me.

'He asked me to lift my vest away from my body. Then he walked slowly round me, looking at me. He told me to take the vest off. I watched him put it under a cushion on the couch. Then he explained that I must never wear anything under my blouse again and that, in his presence, when no one else was there, my breasts must be fully naked. He made me sit on the side of the couch with my blouse open while he moved from one part of the room to another and watched me. He said I had the most beautiful breasts he had ever seen. Then I noticed he was holding a short piece of thin bamboo; he kept testing the knots along its length. But he never touched me with it, not then.' Sianon closed her eyes.

'Then one day he appeared in the dairy. I was sitting at the high table. I had kept myself as he had asked; I lifted off my apron and opened my blouse. He came up behind me and drew it down. Then he touched my breasts. And because I had been waiting, thinking about it, every day, expecting this to happen, my body reacted to his touch so strongly, in a way that I did not then understand. He kept touching my nipples. He lifted my breasts and pressed my nipples to the table. He oiled them, placing small pieces of butter on the tips. I felt the tickle as the butter melted. Then he told me he would rub my breasts with something else.

'The first time he did it to me, it felt so hot; the first jet came so strongly that it splashed against my neck. He rubbed it into my skin until its smell displaced the smell of the dairy and my breasts became sticky. It was a warm afternoon. He made me lean forwards into the sunlight of the back window and let my breasts hang down while he stood behind me, fondling them until all the stickiness had dried and tightened on my skin. He made me kneel and play with him again until he splashed against my nipples. Then he rubbed it in until the stickiness had stiffened to another coating. It smelt like milk-nog crusted on the stove. As I knelt there, he made me open my legs and he touched me through my knickers – in all the times he used me in these ways during that first year, he never once took them off me. While he played with me, he peeled the dried layers from my breasts and placed them on my tongue. They turned sticky; I loved the taste. I could feel his fingers turning wet between my legs as my sex started making liquid. It felt so good. I wanted to rub myself against his fingers, wanted to squirt as he had squirted, to splash against his hand. And no sooner had that thought come than my body shook with a feeling so intense – as if I was speared on a stake of pleasure, with the stake pushing deeper, and tiny barbs of pleasure pricking up inside my belly.'

Sianon stopped. She took the traveller's rigid penis in her fingers and toyed with it; she gently pressed the under-surface, then closed her fingers round the head and kissed it while the skin was tight. She left it wet, and she kept hold of it while she took up her story. Each time it dried, she wetted it again. She wanted him to understand what she had felt.

'My master made the pricking sensations come inside me many times after that first day; sometimes they would come twice or more and I would be frightened but he would tell me that it was good – that it was as he wanted for me. One time, he played with me for so long between the legs that when he splashed against my breasts the pleas-ure-pricks came there too; they kept coming while his spendings dripped from my nipples. I felt as if I was spend-ing too – but slowly, all the while that he continued to touch me, not quickly like a man. He always made me keep my knickers on, however wet they became. Then he would not leave me until they were dry. He said that dry, their smell was more arousing.'

Sianon bent her head and put her moist lips softly to the traveller's penis, which pulsed once, then expanded redly and wetly as she slowly pulled away, her hand still around the shaft. She lifted up the ball-sac, pushed her fingers underneath it, and she could feel his hardness even there, and sense it in his breathing. His eyes closed. The saliva she had placed upon him was running slowly down his trembl-ing shaft.

'My master had a long sash that he would sometimes use upon me,' she said softly. 'Upstairs in the house, he would remove my skirt and leave me only in my knickers then wind the sash round and round my middle, twisting it to make it tighter, round and round, up under my breasts, until they felt as though they were bursting. Then he would rub his shaft between them until his fluid came. But first, he used the thin bamboo stick to excite me; it had thickened parts like rings along it, and he would slide it up and down between my legs. And I would open, inside, under my knickers; the stick would be guided in my furrow; my wet would come through the linen, then he would kiss it from the stick. If he was sure we would not be disturbed, he would prolong it and then his liquid would come thinly, like hot water over my skin.

'The sash became marked; its scent used to excite me. When no one was around, I used to take it from the drawer and hold it to my lips and smell it. It was as if the smell – almost sweet, and dusty, like dried milk – made something happen in my nipples. I would touch them with the sash then breathe its scent. He had never made me kiss that part of him, not then, but when I breathed that scent I used to imagine how it might feel, to have it squirting in my mouth.'

Sianon felt the pulse against her fingers, still pressing gently under the traveller's ball-sac. She bent down again, took his penis briefly in her mouth and heard him moan. He was close to spending; she could feel it in the small involuntary movements; and she could taste it in the tiny gulps that yielded salty liquid to her tongue. Again, she left him wet and swollen.

'But one day,' she said, 'the mistress caught me in my dreamings. She saw me trying to hide the sash away. I had never seen her enter the master's room before that day; yet she made me leave and close the door behind me. Then I heard her opening the drawers.

'Soon after that incident, it happened that the squire had to go away for a week. The mistress could not avoid me so much as before, but she still remained aloof. Her coldness started to have a strange effect upon me; it was as if it made the needs of my body more intense.

'I had found a broad belt; I did not even know if it was

101

the master's, but I used to put it round my middle, in bed, or sometimes in the daytime, if I knew it was safe. I had to cut more holes in it so I could draw it tighter. Then late one night, she disturbed me in the dairy. I ought not to have been there but thought no one would be about. I had on the belt and my knickers – nothing else. I was sitting on a milking stool. My breasts were already throbbing and my knickers wet. She came in with a lamp, and just stared at me as if she had known all along that I was there.

' "It is time ..." she whispered in a peculiar tone. Her words confused me. "Sianon – come," she said, taking me into the still-room, where she tied my hands together. I thought I was dreaming. "Sianon," she said, "you will have to help me." '

Sianon paused, shaking. 'She hung me from the ceiling. The effort was almost too much for her, but she did it.'

'You helped her?' the traveller whispered.

Sianon nodded. 'Then she took a rope line and coiled it loosely over her hand. She made the coils into a fan – like this ...' And with her fingers, Sianon showed him. 'Then she whipped my breasts until the skin was livid.'

The traveller shivered; she touched him. Her words came very slowly. 'She ... She whipped me again, then again ... In between the whippings, she collapsed into a chair ... She tried to tighten the belt around me but could not do it ... She did not stop whipping me until she was exhausted.'

'And what of you?' the traveller asked gently.

'There was no part of the skin of my breasts that was not marked. Next day, I was bruised. But that night – while it was happening, while she was whipping my breasts – the wet was running down my legs. She knew it. That was why she did it –'

Suddenly, Sianon broke off. Her new master had touched her. She looked down. Her legs were open. His fingers were against her warmth. Sianon gasped. He held her open gently. 'Deeper, oh master, please touch up inside ...' The pleasure was sublime. He held her still; she felt his fingers, warmly wet, and her moisture trickling into his hand. She wanted it to come then – quickly, the stabbing barbs of pleasure deep inside her. But he made her continue her story while he touched her.

'After the whippings she took me into her bed.'

'That same night?'

Sianon nodded. 'She wore a straight, thin nightdress. She left the belt on me and lay behind me, rubbing my aching shoulders with her bony fingers. And she touched my breasts. While she was playing with my nipples, tugging them and pinching, the feeling of pleasure came through them, as it had done when the master spent against me. She kept touching while it came ... And it happened with you – last night, when I was kneeling.'

'When Kynne was being whipped?'

'It aroused me; it reminded me of what my mistress used to do.' She closed her eyes and shuddered as the traveller's fingers pushed deeper. Then she closed her hand around them, keeping them in place inside her.

'Each morning, she whipped my breasts with the rope and then again at night. She made a short, tight bodice out of knotted, thin rope and fastened it round me. I had to wear it when I slept with her; it was shaped to take my breasts, but it was too small. The ends of my breasts pushed through the holes. Each night she played with them and sucked them. But first, she made me sit on the bed and lean back with my elbows on the pillows while she whipped my breasts. I had to keep my legs apart, but she never touched me between the legs, as the squire had; while my body leaked, she brought about the pleasure only through my nipples. Sometimes, she let me suck her sex when she had whipped me. She knew that it aroused me. She used to fondle my breasts while I was doing it; she used to wet them and try to make me come. Sometimes it would happen to me with her sex still in my mouth. The first time it came that way, she was very gentle with me afterwards, stroking me and whispering, "Now I know ... Now I really know." But if her own pleasure was ever completed, she gave no sign of it. In the daytime, she remained aloof and cold. It made me want her so much. And then at night, she used me, played with me and let me suck her. She never

103

showed true warmth towards me, and yet each night, my pleasure seemed to come on more strongly. Then the squire returned.'

'What happened when he saw the marks?'

'I told him I had done it to myself.'

'And he believed you?'

'I don't know. He became excited when he touched them. When he kissed them, the pleasure came through my nipples again. He told me he was pleased with me.

'The next afternoon I came into the dairy with a pail of milk and found him waiting for me. He locked the door, then told me to undress – shoes, stockings, everything – but again, to leave my knickers on. He touched the marks on my breasts and I became aroused. He sat me on a tall stool with my legs open, then stood in front of me, playing with my breasts. But every so often he would stop and lift me up, then put me down, always with my legs open. Because the stool was tall, my feet did not reach the floor. The lifting and lowering, the repeated pressure of the seat between my legs made me even more excited. He said that he would make the pleasure come that way. The crotch of my knickers turned wet. He rolled them down while I was sitting, turning them inside out around the legs of the stool. Then he put his hands against me, one at the back, and one at the front, as if he would gather me up. It was the first time he had touched my naked sex and bottom. And I was so wet. I could feel his fingers slipping against me.

'I sat on his hands, on the stool, my knickers hanging down, my legs apart, stretched open, my breasts against his arm, and his fingers toying with me – inside, slipping in my sex, slipping in my bottom, until I was gasping, pleading. Then he slid his hands from underneath me and rolled my knickers back in place. Again, he started playing with my nipples, pulling them gently, stripping them down between his fingers, as if he were milking me. His fingers were still wet from between my legs. The pleasure began coming through my breasts, but he stopped me and made me sit further back on the stool. Then he pulled my knickers down again from behind and slid his middle finger up my bottom. He stood behind me, moving it very slowly up and down inside me, taking it out and wetting it between my legs, then sliding it in again. He made me lift while he pulled the crotch of my knickers through to the front, so there was nothing underneath me, then he made me sit so far back that my bottom pushed out behind me and only my belly was on the stool. My knickers were stretched round the front of its legs. He had to support me to stop me overbalancing. Then he played with me in that position.

'The liquid from inside me was running down the leg of the stool. My knob was burning. He never touched it while my knickers were down, but kept slipping a finger into my sex, or into my bottom, or sometimes one into each at the same time. He would leave them in me and touch my breasts. When I was fully aroused, all through my body, he lifted me up, pulled my knickers up and made me sit, but this time forwards. He made me put my hands behind me. Then he took the pail of milk and began to pour it down my breasts and belly. I remember how warm it was, how thick and creamy. He paused to pull my knickers open, then he tilted the pail and just kept pouring, down my breasts, down my belly, through my pubic hair. The warm milk gushed and bulged inside my knickers and I came that way, from the rush of warm liquid against me. Then he pulled my knickers down and crouched between my legs and sucked me clean. I came twice more while he was doing it. The second time, he made me sit forward, on my belly, and he licked my bottom and sucked me from behind.

'After that, he always made me leave my knickers completely off. He came to the dairy many times to put me on the stool. Sometimes he would pour the milk down my back and it would run down the crack of my bottom, across my sex and on to the floor. And he would be playing with my sex all the while the milk was running. He never hurt me. Every time he was away, the mistress would whip me.'

Sianon moved her legs open. The traveller's fingertips, still inside her, probed her gently. Then he whispered:

'While you were with your master and mistress, whose attentions did you prefer?'

Sianon hesitated, then said: 'It was this way: I looked forward to the master going away – because I had the attentions of my mistress. And I looked forward to his return. There was one occasion when my breasts were barely dry from his emissions, and my mistress found me. I told her it was milk. Whether she knew the truth, I do not know. But she whipped them – she kept whipping until the crust broke up like paper and floated in the air. Then she pulled my knickers down and touched me ... And I cannot describe it. She had never done this – never ever touched me there.' Even speaking of it again made Sianon shudder. She turned and stared into the eyes of the man beside her. 'I loved it – every part of it, and all the time it happened – to be shared between them in such a way.'

'Sit up,' the traveller whispered, and she shivered, because the look was in his eye, the look of mastery, and she wanted to be made to do things while she was excited. He made her spread her legs open on the bed. He made her close her eyes and he touched her clitoris while she was still sitting. He took her close to climax, much closer than he knew. Then he asked again if she wanted spanking; he said that he had never done it, but that he wanted to do it to her, that he had never wanted so much to do it, and he showed her the leather. Then he put the collar on her. She was shaking with arousal. 'Kneel up,' he told her.

He turned the pillow over and shook it, then put her breasts on to it, her heavy hot breasts sinking softly through the coolness. He splayed her elbows; her cheek lay on the bed itself, her bottom pushed out behind her. He tucked her knees up to her breasts. 'I want to see your sex while you are spanked,' he said. And when he knelt up, leather in hand, she could see his rigid penis. She wanted it in her mouth. A shiver went through her sex when she heard the swish. The leather descended. *Smack!* Sianon gasped with pleasure; the shivers struck deep inside her. *Smack!* Hot aches kissed her buttocks. *Smack!* The surface of her skin was bathed in delicious tingles. *Smack!* The spanks moved down. Her sex was pouted out behind her. *Smack!* The sweet spanks burned across the backs of her legs, coming quicker, now above her sex, now below it. *Smack!* The burning pleasure in her buttocks softened to a warmth inside the crack, like warm thick fingers probing the mouth. When the leather struck below her sex, her labia throbbed. *Smack!* She was aching to be fondled between the legs, aching to be sucked. She spread her legs wide open. Then the spanking stopped. She could hear his laboured breathing. Then she felt his urgent fingers, peeling her open, prising back her clitoral hood, spreading her anus. 'I want to smack inside the crack – the mouth. I want to open your pubic lips and smack inside you. And I want you to hold your sex and bottom open while I do it.'

Sianon's trembling fingers stretched round her bottom. 'Hold still – hold it open.' Then it happened, as she hunched, breasts against the pillow, bottom in the air. She heard the short swish, then *Smack!* The lick of leather against her sex and bottom made the pleasure burst so deep that everything inside her melted; she could feel her liquid running down into his hand. She collapsed, twisting, taking his bulging penis into her mouth and sucking greedily. She felt him tighten and try to pull back. She pushed her mouth all the way down the stem, then heard him groan in desperation. Her lips kept sucking about the base; his balls began lifting, convulsing. The first jet of hot sharp liquid splashed against the back of her throat. She opened her legs; his fingers searched blindly between them, grasping her wet sex and bottom, clawing them gently, and Sianon came again, his penis still pumping gluts of hot semen down her throat.

And when this second climax came, in her mind, she soared, as in her dreams, up through the air, into the sky, and for a second, she could see everything, everyone, even through the roofs and in the rooms – Iroise and Quislan and the man in the flowing robe, and she could feel the power, her power, it seemed. Then everything was blackness.

* * *

'Sianon – hush. Sianon – please, what is it?' Her eyes flickered open. She was on the bed, staring up into the traveller's eyes. 'You look so pale . . . You fainted.'

'Fainted?' Then her eyes slowly widened and her heartbeat quickened. 'Was it the powder?' she murmured.

'The powder? What powder?'

Sianon closed her eyes and turned her head away. Then she could feel his gentle breath against her ear. 'It seemed to frighten you,' he whispered. 'Was it . . . Was it because of what I did to you? Did that make it happen?'

Sianon looked into his gentle eyes, then pressed her lips against his nipple and whispered: 'I wanted it, so much . . . I wanted you.'

'Your body went . . . I don't know – but I was frightened for you.'

Then Sianon looked at him again and she was sure. She took him in her arms and called him 'Josef' and she held him until she fell asleep.

She woke with a start. He was dressed. It was dark.

'Keep quiet!' he hissed. 'Come on!' He pulled her from the bed. They crept downstairs. The stable was quiet. Her heart was thumping, but she never asked where he was taking her. In the yard were two saddled horses. Iroise was on one. She looked frightened. Her hair was tousled. A richly embroidered, open gown was wrapped about her. Josef lifted Sianon behind Iroise. 'Take the reins,' he told Sianon, then he mounted the other horse. 'Quietly . . .' Once they were through the gates, he shouted: 'Ride!'

They galloped through the night until the horses faltered. At dawn they were still riding, though at a walk. Soon after they stopped, they heard horses in pursuit.

'It cannot be – so quickly?' Josef said. He hurried them off the road just in time; the riders thundered past. The Perquisitor was amongst them. There was terror in Iroise's eyes.

'They will find us!' she cried. 'Oh, Josef – she will kill you!' He tried to calm her, but she broke away from him. At the very moment she ran into the road, a second batch of riders appeared. Josef swept her up and tried to flee, but there was no escaping. Sianon watched him knocked to the ground with Iroise still in his arms. The soldiers began dragging him away. Iroise was distraught. Sianon ran out from the trees to beg the soldiers not to hurt him. He was pinned down on his knees until the Perquisitor arrived. Sianon saw the chilling malice in Quislan's eyes.

'Hold him.' Taking one foot from the stirrup, Quislan kicked him in the face. Then she dismounted. 'Again.' Still dazed and groaning, he was held between the two men. She kicked him again. Blood was pouring from his nose and the deep gash on his cheek. Iroise was screaming, cowering, biting her fist. Quislan calmly looked at her. 'Enough, you think?' she smiled, then turned to Josef's limp, supported frame. 'Perhaps once more.' She stood back, then kicked again, swiftly, hard, as if it were not a human being that she kicked, nor even a dog, but a loathsome, irksome creature, of which she would now be rid. When the soldiers released him, he folded up as if made of cloth. They rolled him into the ditch. Then Iroise and Sianon were dragged by their hair to the horses and taken back to the house.

There, they were tied together naked and whipped, then the large steel rings were fitted inside each of them so they could be given to the servants while Quislan and the master of the house looked on. Kynne was on the master's lap, his penis in her bottom, his fingers toying with her clitoris as if it were a cock. Quislan had the slave; the heavy ivory ball was in her hand, and her hand was deep inside him. His throbbing sex was kept sealed in a leather cap.

When next day the carriages were awaiting departure, this slave was brought out. Quislan had him collared and roped. In exchange, she offered the master of the house any girl of his choosing.

9

Thuline

In his dreams, Josef heard barking hounds, and thought it was the hunt and he was home, planning in his mind his journey. But he opened his eyes to an airy, raftered room with whitewashed walls. Through the open window came the light of woodland green and the sound of running water. Smoke rose lazily from a large iron fireplace in the corner. There was a smell of wheatmeal.

A large figure in a dusty apron loomed over him. A wooden cup was thrust to his lips. 'Drink . . . Drink, lad.' Josef almost choked because the water was so cold and because he was lying down. There was a half-dry cloth across his brow.

'Where is this?' he gasped, pulling off the cloth and trying to raise his head. But it hurt him – how it hurt. 'The women!' he cried suddenly. 'What happened to them?'

The man's eyebrows drew to a white bushy frown then lifted. He blew his cheeks out. 'You mean Thuline?' he said, turning to put the cup on the table. 'She tended you.'

'Thuline?' Josef stared around the empty room. Then looking down, he saw he was naked. But the rest came flooding back. He twisted himself up on to an elbow, then sank down again. His body felt like lead. 'Please – what time is it?'

'Past noon.'

'And they are gone?' asked Josef.

'It happened four days ago.'

'What!'

'You had a fever. No – don't try it . . .'

As soon as Josef attempted to stand, his legs gave way. The man helped him back to the bed then refilled the cup.

'Just drink. You were set upon quite badly – was it thieves?'

'You saw it?'

'No. I found you in the ditch. But I saw the hoofprints: it was plain there had been a struggle.' He gave a wry smile. 'And I doubt you would have done that to yourself.'

Josef stared blankly ahead, then closed his eyes and put his head into his hands. He could feel the contusions round his eyebrows and on his cheekbone. For a long while he didn't speak.

The man said encouragingly: 'You took a stand against them. What more could you do? I counted the prints of at least half a dozen horses.'

Then Josef whispered: 'Thank you – I am in your debt. And I do not even know your name.'

'Nor I yours,' the man laughed expansively. 'But I am Santan.' He threw back his shock of pure white hair. 'This mill is mine. I built it with these hands.'

'Josef Stenner . . .' Josef took one of those sizeable, yet soft hands and shook it gratefully. Then the miller sat heavily on the bed and listened while the traveller recounted his story. Santan's frown re-formed and gradually deepened as the tale progressed; once or twice he pouted his lower lip, or pinched his jowl and grunted, but he said nothing. When Josef had finished, Santan sat there nodding slowly.

Josef said: 'My purse – it must be with my clothes – I would like you to accept it for the kindness you have shown me.'

The miller swayed back, spreading his hands and shaking his head. 'I could not . . . Besides, you have no purse. They took it.'

'Took it? But they have no need of gold – they only made me give up the rest to teach me a lesson.'

'Then I hope your lesson is well learnt,' said Santan drily.

'You don't believe me? She has powers, the Perquisitor. I saw a gold coin melt in her hand.' Santan watched him steadily. 'And I had my gold well hidden in my room yet she knew where it was kept.'

Santan shrugged. 'You never went back there?'

'No – my things were brought to me.'

'Then, for all you know, the room could have been ransacked?'

Josef hadn't considered that. 'The landlord – it's true he was waiting outside . . . But –'

'Thievery can always find a way. And I never yet met an honest landlord.'

'But she knew . . .'

'Aye, once the gold was found – because someone told her.'

'Santan, she was never out of my sight. Except once . . .' He had remembered the display, the curtained alcove into which she had led him. 'Then all of it – everything – was trickery?'

The miller shrugged again.

'But why? If they only meant to rob me?'

'Perhaps the show was not for you.'

'The women?'

Santan got up slowly, then hesitated, looking at him gravely, before sinking his hand deep into his apron pocket. 'I found this beside you on the ground – one bit of gold they didn't take.' He held up Sianon's gold Tormunite cross on its fine linen belt. Josef took it in his fingers.

'I must find them. Will you help me, Santan?'

'You do not know which way they were going. You do not even have a horse.'

Then a soft voice sounded across the room. 'But he will help you. It is not in his nature to refuse. But I shall not let you go anywhere until you are fit and well.'

Josef watched her put the eggs down one by one into a dish until her apron was empty; then she turned to look at him fully. 'You do not know me?' she whispered, and when he frowned at her she smiled. 'Perhaps it is as well he does not remember,' she said to Santan, who suddenly seemed embarrassed. Then she turned to look again at Josef.

'This is Thuline,' Santan mumbled. 'I have corn to grind.' And he left.

Josef covered himself, because she was watching him as she took off her apron. He was thinking of her last words. She had dark flowing hair and rich brown gypsy eyes –

eyes that seemed extraordinarily wide. Her skin was an even shade of palest cinnamon; it was flawless, though her features were pinched as if she had not eaten. Her body seemed slight and delicate. Her breasts were not; and their form was very visibly outlined by her closely fitted bodice. She was much, much younger than the miller. She moved across the room and settled carefully onto the upright chair by Josef's bed, then sat very straight, making him very conscious of her slimness, and of the contrast – the slightness of her body, the proudness of her breasts. But when she glanced away, he found himself waiting for her eyes, which had appeared so large and beautiful.

'The eggs are for you,' she said. 'They will build your strength.'

'Thank you.'

When her eyes drifted back, he did not want to look away from them, but neither did he want her to think he was staring. Her left hand rested on her lap. The fingers were slender, soft, unused to manual work. Around the middle finger was a ring made of leather, in a strip so thick it prevented the adjacent fingers touching. A thin leather twine connected the ring to a band around her wrist; the tension in the twine kept the middle finger slightly lifted. Josef had never seen anything like it. Many unspoken questions moved through his mind, but when she said:

'I overheard part of your story. I am sorry – I was listening,' he felt he had to reassure her.

'It matters not; it is no secret. I hoped your husband might be able to help me.'

'Santan is not my husband.' Her eyes met his and lingered. 'He is a good man. He looks after me.' Suddenly the floor began to shake with a low, continuous rumbling. 'The milling,' she said and her look became wistful. 'Yes, he is a good man. I would not wish to hurt him.' Again, the questions crowded Josef's mind. Then she said abruptly: 'I know the place where they have been taken,' and all other considerations were set aside.

He kept his gaze fixed on her eyes, which did not waver. 'Tell me.'

'It is – it was – an abbey.'

'Servulan?' he said.

'Then you know it?'

'Only by name,' he said. 'Tell me.'

'The Jannites have it. It is a place of training.' She bowed her head. 'Through it, you are groomed anew – to their ways, which are very different.'

'You speak as if . . .'

'I was there,' she whispered.

'You escaped?'

'If escape is what you call it. One of the Tormunite Wardens took me. He –'

'Fevrun?' Josef interjected. Thuline frowned and shook her head, but he persisted. 'Had he sandy hair?'

'No, it was dark. He was a young man . . .' She hesitated. 'He was like you.'

The way she was looking at him caused a sweet unease inside him. He thought again of her having tended him while he was naked, and he thought again of the beautiful slimness of her figure. He could feel the weight of her hand now resting gently on the sheet, and could see her tethered finger moving slightly as she continued:

'He came to the abbey one day. I was singled out. He asked the abbess if he might train me – it is their privilege. Afterwards he told me that I pleased him and that I was to accompany him on a journey. There were others with him. On the road, I was made to please them too; he gave me over to them and they used me as they wished. He told me that all of this was part of my training – the sublimation of my will to the pleasures he had chosen for me. Then I found out it was more: in the places where we stayed, I was used for payment. He had me punished for his amusement. I was made to wear this . . .'

She took it from the bed-rail and Josef then realised this was her bed and it was the only one in the room. Vague recollections came into his mind as she said: 'It is a tether. It gloves one hand completely; the other is left free.'

He wondered – did she know the effect her words were having on him? He was naked under the sheet.

'And now,' she said, 'I cannot achieve full release unless I use it.' She put it over her right hand. With her left, the one with the wristband and the thong ring, she began to unbutton her shirt. Josef glanced nervously at the door. Thuline carried on unbuttoning. It took time, for she had only the one free hand and could not move the middle finger easily. His glance kept darting from the captive finger to the door. 'No – look . . .' she whispered. The task completed, she drew the shirt to one side.

Her left breast showed; it was perfect – large, below delicately-boned shoulders – beautifully full and smooth, the skin soft cinnamon, the nipple very dark. Then she lifted her arm, and he could not believe what he saw there.

Beneath it, in the hollow, was a silver ring, set through her skin, which was nude of underarm hair. He could see no join in the metal and the seal to the skin looked tight: it must have been tight because when she had raised her arm, the ring had lifted. 'He had this put into me,' she said. 'He chained me by it. Then he granted favours with my body to the men he brought.'

Her eyes were yearning. 'Santan would never hurt me,' she whispered. She was shaking. Josef looked upon her lifted, dark-tipped breast, and the ring set through her naked skin.

Then she told him this: 'Last night, when I had washed you, I stayed with you. You were dreaming; you kept saying her name.'

'Iroise?'

'No, it was "Sianon".'

Thuline edged towards him. 'She must be beautiful.' The fingers of the gloved hand touched him through the thin leather; the captive middle finger of her left hand pressed to his lips. 'Do you remember – anything – about last night?' The captive finger moved into his mouth; his lips stayed open; it slid wetly around his tongue and the feeling came inside him, deeply. With her teeth, she drew off the glove. 'You kept saying her name. Tonight you will say mine.'

* * *

Josef was kneeling by the side of the bed, his cheek where Thuline had put it, upon his folded arms. She was beside him on the floor. His back was hollowed. To one side of him on the bed was a large hourglass in a frame, its blue sand hissing slowly through the tight constriction. He heard another egg being cracked. Then Thuline's cool, slippy fingers reached between his legs again and took him where he had never felt so hard, closing round him and squeezing. 'Watch the sand. Seek the timing,' Thuline whispered. Josef groaned. He wanted to pull away from such feelings, but she had him in her hands, between her hands. And the cold glutinous liquid egg was oozing down his rigid length and slipping from his balls. Her right hand never stopped the gently pulsing squeezing, stimulating his fluid flow deep inside.

Recharged, her left hand returned; the captive middle finger pressed between his buttocks; he groaned; it slid inside him to the leather ring. Then the tip of the bedded finger began to move. 'You must tell me where . . . Where is it that I must touch inside?' she whispered. 'Ohh . . .'

He shuddered; his cock felt as if a curved bone had been pushed inside it from behind.

'There . . .? Is that it? Hard inside you, like a ball? Keep still, and let me play ball with you.' The tip of her finger gently pushed and probed and circled. Josef moaned; the leather ring moved against him as her finger twisted; the arousal deep inside him hurt. Thuline pushed in another thickly coated finger, then a third. 'The sand,' she whispered. 'Watch it. Feel it running through the glass.' Josef started gasping; the fingers inside him slowed; the hand dripped yolk upon his cock, then cupped his balls and softly squeezed them at the neck.

'Thuline . . .? he pleaded.

'Again . . .'

'*Thuline?*'

The soft pressure and the nervous touches kept his climax just beyond reach, kept his fluid building.

The sand ran out. Thuline withdrew her fingers. She took the hourglass from its frame. 'Which end?' she whispered. 'The one with the sand is heavier – better.' She coated it with egg.

When the cold glass began to open him, his climax started. 'Stretch,' she whispered. 'Quickly – it comes better with the bulb inside.' Her words finally triggered him, triggered him to pump and triggered him to open. The coldness and smoothness and pressure all at the same time made the aching gland inside him convulse repeatedly, helplessly, harder than he had ever known. His liquid squirted thinly and copiously. Thuline caught it in her hand and drank it.

Then she looped a leather band around the base of his cock. As she was tightening it, the weight of the sand inside him shifted, and he came again, Thuline pumping his cock with the loose tether, her hand cupped round it, but no more fluid being yielded.

She extracted the glass. Then she told him she must leave. He begged her to stay the night with him. 'How can I?' she whispered.

'But what of you – your pleasure?' he asked.

'I am content. Doing it to a man is pleasure.'

'Why? Because of him – the one who took you from the abbey?'

Thuline closed her eyes.

Her shirt was open and her nipples were erect. When he tried to touch them she directed his fingers instead to the ring under her arm. The soft ache of his arousal came back quickly as he toyed with it, because he could feel how excited it made her. But it was as if she meant to keep herself in this state of wanting. 'Tomorrow,' she murmured, drawing away. She told him she would let him play with her then. 'For a long time,' she said, kissing the leather band around his penis. 'Promise? So it hurts me when it comes?' And she asked that he use bondage.

After she had left, he wondered where she had gone: this was her room. And if the room was hers alone, then what was her relationship with the miller?

By morning, Josef had convinced himself that it was platonic. But when he went on to the outside landing, he

117

heard the two of them laughing together below him. Then he saw Thuline kiss Santan – not briefly, but fully on the lips. Santan hugged her gently. They spoke a little more, then Thuline hurried off towards the chicken pens. The look of contentment remained on the old man's face long after she was gone. Josef watched him wind up the sluice, heard the low rush of water, then the heavy creaking. The great wheel seemed to tremble before it began very slowly to turn. There were sounds from within the building, then the familiar rumble through the floor. The miller waved to Josef, then climbed the low flight of far steps and disappeared through a wide doorway.

Josef looked up at the great wheel seemingly rolling towards him through the leafage. He listened to the hissing thread-like streams of water cascading from its frame. And he waited to see if Thuline would reappear. When she did not, he went back into her room. Opposite was a door leading on to the back steps. He followed them down. Finding no sign of her in the yard, he explored a little. He came to a small stable then several outhouses, one with a small mill-wheel. A little downstream, beyond a drop, a footbridge led to an island in the river.

Josef leant on the wooden parapet and watched the water cascading over the weir while he thought over what had happened last night and what he had just seen. Then he felt a hand against the back of his neck – soft, desirous fingers gently tickling. He turned. She was naked on the bridge. The glove hung loosely from her wrist. There were leather cords about her waist and across her breasts.

'Play with me,' Thuline whispered.

Automatically he looked back towards the mill; only the roof was visible. She slid around him, put her hand behind her head and leant against a tree. The silver ring under her arm stood out; the glove hung down; her nipples poked between the biting ligatures. 'Play with me. Suck me. Bind me. Make the pleasure hurt me; make it last.'

Her naked form brushed past him and slipped back across the bridge to the island. Hidden in the foliage on the downstream side was an open-fronted shelter overlooking a still pool in the river.

'My secret place,' she said. 'I swim from here: the water is so deep, so calm.'

Her clothes were on a pallet against one wall. The hourglass was there. And there were other things that bore no relationship to swimming; they made Josef's heartbeat quicken. He looked at Thuline, her nude body so frail, her breasts so full, the twisted double cord biting into them. Then he looked at the objects and the instruments of pleasure.

'Use them on me. Tie me. Make me do things with them in me,' Thuline whispered.

Turning, she wrapped her arms around a low branch of a tree. The glove dangled pendulum-fashion from her wrist. Her back hollowed and she teetered on her toes, almost hanging, her breasts pushed down, straining their bindings, her slim round buttocks invitingly thrust out behind. When he moved towards her, she told him:

'One hour – after that, I go.'

'But why?'

'Because Santan must never get to know.'

Josef nodded.

'Wait!' she said. 'No penetration – with your sex.'

'Agreed.' Josef waited, expecting more conditions.

'Turn the glass,' she whispered.

Josef began her masturbation there, as she hung under the branch of the tree, not using any of the instruments, just his fingers from behind. Thuline's arousal came in waves; he tried to find the rhythm her body sought, that he might control it, slowing the stimulation at the peaks of her unrest. Her sex had been partly depilated: the lower two-thirds were bare, like the insides of her thighs. Its skin was smooth and he could see every detail from behind – every soft bulge, every infold, every edge, and could watch his fingers toying with her, slipping up inside her through her naked inner lips, then coming out silvery wet.

When she continued to move, even when he wasn't touching her, he eased her hands back along the overhanging branch so she was standing upright, on her toes, her legs together, only the tuft of pubic hair visible, her naked pubic mount now trapped between her thighs, the ring quite visible under her arm. The thongs pressed deep into the marrow of her breasts. He had not seen breasts so distinct in proportion to a body quite so slim.

And he had never masturbated a woman while she was on tiptoes. Her legs were obliged to remain together. There was room for only two fingers.

Thuline's eyes had closed; sweet perturbations came between her thighs; her clitoris protruded between Josef's fingers; she began to murmur incoherently. She licked her lips. Her head kept twisting back, her mouth falling open; she let out an indistinct name – 'Rice,' no – 'Reikz,' then began moaning. Josef stepped back and watched her quaking in the slow rapture of her passion, balanced on her toes. He looked at the hourglass; the sand had scarcely moved.

When he took her down, the insides of her legs below the level of her sex were wet with a thick, clear mucus. He took the cord from round her breasts and tongued the thin channels it had made in her skin. Then he carried her under the shelter and put her on the mattress. He unfastened the thong from her waist and kissed her sex, just once, taking its warm entirety into his mouth, experiencing the complete nakedness of the lower lips and mount, smelling the strong aroma of her arousal. Then he looked at the instruments – some metal, some leather. One was like a very small breast-pad; other items were made of wood, and one was of stone – a pair of perfect spheres of polished green marble connected by a chain. He did not know how it might be used. There were also dildos and narrow waxed tubes of wood. And one of the metal instruments was in two parts, one fitting inside the other. The exterior surface was shiny; again, Josef did not know its use.

He turned Thuline on her side to face him, and her breasts moved out across the mattress. He put his hand against her back, at the low place where the back is slimmest and the flexing greatest. She reached across and picked up a dildo. It was heavy, of smoothly waxed leather on wood, the shape and size of a well-distended penis.

There was a thong around it near the base, above the balls. She asked Josef if he were still wearing the leather band she had given him. He shook his head. 'You should,' she whispered. 'I want you to.' She told him she would like to suck him while he wore the leather band. She was holding the replica almost as if it were real, toying with its thong, drawing the tips of her fingers along the smooth surface.

'Your former master – the Warden – was he Reikz?'

Thuline nodded.

'He used this on you?'

'Yes.'

Josef loosened the thong from the dildo. Then he asked Thuline to open her legs. Her naked sex was swollen, her inner thighs bare and smooth. He was burning to take her in the way he had promised not to. 'Where did he use it?'

'In my mouth . . . In my bottom . . . Everywhere.'

'You enjoyed it?'

'I wanted to please him.'

'I did not ask that.'

'I enjoyed it – yes,' she whispered.

'Where did you prefer it?'

'In my mouth,' she said softly. Josef turned away and closed his eyes.

'Show me . . .' he said at last. 'Lie down as you would have lain then – as your master would have put you.' The dildo was in his hand. He told himself he did not need it in her; he just wanted to see her in that pose. Then he would bind her – her breasts again, and her sex. He would put thin cords down into the seam between her inner and outer lips and use them to excite her.

Her body lay diagonally across the bed. One knee was bent, her legs were open, her head was overhanging. 'Don't move,' he said. He began to masturbate her gently, making the waves of pleasure come slowly, making her knee rock softly in the air. 'Your mouth – keep it open; show me.'

She gasped. All four of his fingers were inside her, not probing deeply, but keeping the entrance stretched. He put down the dildo and took up the chained stone spheres. He wanted to put these into her but resisted. She had begun to sweat; her skin was slightly clammy. When she opened her eyes the pupils were dilated, sleepy with desire. Josef picked up the dildo and placed it between her breasts.

'In my mouth . . .' she moaned.

'Shh . . . Give me your hand.' It had no strength. He fitted it inside its leather mitten, sealed it at her wrist and tied it to one of the wooden supports of the shelter. Her left hand was now a stump, its shape completely hidden inside the leather. He put a pillow under her head and lay beside her, kissing her arm as it hung there, brushing his lips along the lifted underside, and licking the place where the ring went through the skin. Then he leant against the wall and drew her hips on to his lap. 'Put your head back,' he whispered.

While he fed the leather-sheathed dildo slowly into Thuline's mouth, he watched the small bulge of her clitoris becoming more prominent within the fork of her bare pubic lips. There was a slight glaze across them on one side, where his fingers had made a trail coming out of her. He began to toy with her – her deep umbilicus, then the tube of skin enclosing the ring under her arm; the nude parts of her sex, and her clitoris. He applied small leather ties to her nipples; he stretched a cord and put it down between her legs, masturbating her clitoris with it as her neck arched slowly back, her nostrils dilated, her lips squeezed round the wet leather dildo, and the muted groans of pleasure issued softly from her throat.

He took the slippery dildo gently from her mouth and turned her on her side. Her arousal was intense; he could tell it by her soft shudder as he lifted her, as though even his moving her body might bring on her climax.

Then suddenly, she froze, staring at the river. The current had slowed.

She tried to sit up. 'The wheel has stopped . . . Santan – he will suspect if he finds me missing.'

'But the sand is still running: have you forgotten our agreement?'

'It would hurt him if he found us out. Do not hurt him, Josef, please? I will come back – I will make it up to you.'

He unfastened her wrist. 'Then make it up to me now. Stand up.' He pulled the ties off her nipples. Then he selected the polished stone spheres.

Her belly was trembling, her legs were trembling as he opened them, but she did not attempt to stop him. And she moaned very, very softly when he put one of the spheres inside her. Her labia closed round it. The other sphere hung like an anchor, rolling gently between her legs. And she moaned again when he put her knickers on her and the dangling weight was captured inside them. 'Keep it in you,' Josef whispered, slipping his fingers under her, touching the bulge through the material, moving it against her. Then he let her complete her dressing and go about her business. There was no visible sign of the instrument's presence but for a slight delicious stilting of her movement as she walked across the bridge.

An hour is a long, long time when you are aroused. Josef waited. After a few minutes, he saw the water level surge again, so he went up to the bridge; the wheel was turning. Thuline was walking down the yard. She crossed to the chicken house and went inside.

Josef followed her, watching her from the door, then creeping up behind her. She gasped and told him: 'No!' But he could see it in her eyes – the fever of arousal. He placed the running hourglass on the straw. It swayed. 'Hold it steady,' he whispered. It became a distraction for her fingers; her sex was his. She was kneeling. He pushed her skirt up. 'Ohhh ...' he murmured, 'Ohhh ...' and Thuline gasped so sweetly, sexually, gently. Everything between her legs was wet inside her knickers. They had turned transparent. He could see the marbling in the dangling ball. He drew them very gently down; her bottom was moist, with a thin wetness; he kissed it. The ball was captured in the gusset; he twisted the hem and the ball descended on its chain and tugged between her legs.

He played with her; she was in turmoil; she aroused him with her sweet unrest. He took his penis out and pressed it to her moistened anus. When she realised what was touching her, she began pleading with him not to do it. But it was as if her anus was turning very soft and was lubricating. He opened her bodice, took her breasts out and held them with her nipples pushing through his fingers. He wanted to put his penis into her and feel the ball inside her rubbing up against him from the front. But again, she begged him, reminding him of his promise not to penetrate her.

Josef sat back on the straw. Then he picked up an egg, still warm. 'Lean over.' He made Thuline lie across his lap face down. He lifted her bodice aside and her bare breasts sank into the straw. 'Open your legs.' He rested the egg where he had tried to put his penis, directly in the cupped, fleshy rim. Then he put a hand between her legs and underneath and masturbated her very gently, very slowly, with the weight of the ball hanging, free to swing. When she was gasping, he lifted the egg away, then placed it firmly and precisely down until it was gripped by the rim. She started to shudder. He waited, then began to masturbate her again. When she shuddered again, he slipped his fingers round the chain and held it still and tight, then released it and she moaned. Again he lifted away the egg. It had clung to the well of her anus. 'Hold it open.' He cracked the egg; some of the white ran down between her legs, but the yolk was captured in the well. 'Open . . .' He slipped his fingers under her from the side and began again the slow masturbation, concentrating on the clitoris and tugging the chain. 'Open . . .' He used his fingers, pressing the yolk gently. She started panting; he could feel her bottom start to open, then the yolk suddenly burst and at that point she came, her clitoris jumping in his hand, the yolk gradually slipping down inside her body with each steady spasm.

Josef pulled Thuline's knickers round her, turned her over, lifted her up and kissed her. When he touched the ball, through her knickers, rubbing it against the slippery pubic lips, her climax came again. He pulled aside the leg of the knicker, let the loose ball drop, then gently pulled out the one that was inside her. But he did not let her close up again. He put his hand inside her sex and continued to kiss her.

124

She had opened out inside; he probed her deeper, then she cried out. His fingertips had touched something hard inside her. A shiver of disquiet moved through him. He touched again – it was metallic – a ring. He gently pulled it and she murmured because it was attached.

'Reikz?' he whispered. Thuline closed her eyes and moaned. She spread her thighs. She held the gusset of her knickers open for him. Then the deep soft contractions came between her legs, provoked by the tip of Josef's middle finger poking through the buried ring.

The mill-wheel had stopped. Thuline became frightened when she heard the miller in the yard. Josef put his hand over her mouth and kept his fingers inside her, still masturbating her. She did not pull away. After a long while of this soft, moist pleasuring, he heard the cart trundling away.

He laid Thuline down upon the straw. The hourglass was almost empty. Thuline pushed it aside. 'He will not be back tonight,' she whispered. Then she took from her bodice a silver chain, long and very thin. At one end was a small clasped hook that would fasten on a ring.

Josef took Thuline naked to the mill, into every room, putting her on the chairs and tables, against the posts, on the floor, on sacks of meal, across beams, arousing her. He used the cords to bind her while he played with her. He wound a leather restraint round her breasts, tight against her ribcage, and made her run across the milling-floor. Then he tied her wrists above her head and masturbated her by rubbing a stretched, wet, leather thong between her legs. He took her to the brink of coming then unfastened her and moved her on. Sometimes he carried her, at other times made her walk. And he kept slipping his fingers into her to touch the metal ring.

At the bottom of some steps, they reached a basement door leading to a long, low room, softly lit from one end, cool and airy, with a bare, rough wooden floor and a ceiling supported by a multitude of beams and posts. Taking Thuline round the waist, Josef picked his way through the sloping bracing timbers and past stalls containing planks of wood and sacks of grain, to reach a more open, yet secluded area at the end. He put down the bag of instruments and let her sink to the floor against a post. Her gaze moved slowly over her surroundings. 'My master used to bring me here,' she said.

'Reikz? He was here at the mill?'

'Did you not know? He used to bring his friends.' She shivered and closed her eyes; her legs sank open. 'Josef – touch me, bind me,' Thuline moaned.

Kneeling beside her, he fastened a cord to the ring under her arm and drew it upwards, so it caught on her nipples. Then he touched her between the legs, where her bare, moist labia rested on the floor. Thuline's eyes stayed closed as Josef drew the cord tighter, so it sank into her breasts. The soft, sweet restlessness that so aroused him was beginning again in her body. His fingers held her labia gently open, nothing more. But suddenly her head fell forward, her belly tightened, her open mouth pressed against his neck and she began murmuring, panting, as his fingers progressively stretched her, found again the ring inside her, and pulled it very gently while her climax came.

Thuline sank back gasping against the post. 'You are like him,' she murmured, touching Josef's face. 'When you do these things to me, you are so much like him.' Her eyes were dark with permissive passion.

'Tell me.'

And as Thuline spoke of the ways she had been used, Josef touched her slender feet, put his hands around her delicate ankles, stroked her open thighs. She told him about the prolonged masturbation that had accompanied the fitting of the rings, about the various ways that had been used to excite her, and the methods of delay – tricks to keep her awake and on the edge of pleasure night after night. And she spoke softly of the whippings and of the use of the glove – how she had come to associate each of them with pleasure.

'And it happened here?' Josef said.

'Sometimes. They brought me here and made me lie on the sacks. My legs were tied up to the posts. It went on for a long time. My master liked to watch me please the others with my mouth and bottom and he liked to watch them playing with me. Sometimes, I would come to pleasure while the chain was still being put inside me.'

Josef lifted Thuline and carried her. He found a low stack of grain-filled sacks between two posts. And there he put her on her back, her head overhanging, and he tied her ankles high against the posts. Then he put the leather-clad dildo into her, all the way in, stroking her inside legs as he inserted it, watching her vulva progressively open to take it. Having done this, he tightened the restraint about her breasts, then let her stretch out on her back, head down, mouth open, while he masturbated her. He took an hour over this one simple gift of pleasure; he timed it with the glass. He had to keep stopping to kiss her ankles, and the insides of her legs, and her nipples poking against the strand of leather pulled across from her underarm. When she came close to coming, he put his arms around her waist and lifted her, her head and shoulders hanging back, but her belly taut while he kissed it. Then he made her sit up fully, with her feet still tied above her head, with her body nearly doubled, and with her belly between her legs, and he masturbated her again in this position until she began gasping, at which time he let her lie down, her head again draped back, her mouth open. When he took the dildo out of her, her sex stayed open. 'Come into me?' she pleaded.

'But you said . . .'

'There is a pad – it is shaped to fit. Put it into me.'

Josef picked it up; he had thought it was a small breast-pad.

'Up inside me . . . Ooo . . . Deep . . . Mmmh . . .' He put it in deeper than the ring; then she moaned again when his penis entered. She was so open, so slippy. Even deep inside, she had opened out, and the surface of his cock kept pressing against her inner skin, lightly sticking to it, pulling free, as if her inside was covered in small, soft, fleshy suckers, each one kissing, cleaving to him, breaking free. The mouth of her sex had closed round him, yet her pubic lips felt soft and wet against his balls. He leant over her, taking slow deep thrusts which made the lips move with him. Each time the end of his cock touched the ring inside her, Thuline moaned in pleasure and Josef felt the hard knob of her clitoris against the base of his shaft.

She tried to sit up against him, but he held her down. Her nipples were enlarged, but soft and rubbery to the tongue. She tried to move her legs, and the movement – her wriggling under him – caused the rubbing, sticky touch of her insides against him and made the tightness come inside him. So he withdrew, pulling her upright, masturbating her again. Then he simply held her. The sweat was running down from under her arms. He pulled the cords from her breasts and let her lean back on her elbows, then fed the dildo he had used inside her, slowly into her mouth. She started whimpering with pleasure, her legs shuddering as his fingers slipped up into her and began straightening the ring. Then he clipped the slim silver chain inside her. Again, he had to wait until her contractions eased before he could remove the dildo from her mouth and unfasten her and take her outside. He wanted to carry her, while she was in this delicious fever of arousal.

The chain hung down between her legs; at times, it touched the ground. He took her down a path leading a short way into the woods. She directed him to the tree where Reikz used to put her. Josef sat her on its low, dished branch, then opened her legs and wrapped the chain around it. He tied the cord of her armpit-ring to the branch above her and fitted the glove over her hand. And he made love to her in that position, her wrists draped over the upper branch, her legs wide open, the slim chain trembling as he entered her alongside it, very gently, but very deeply. Then he held her belly lifted while her sex pulsed softly round him, tugging at the chain that ran below his balls and wrapped around the branch.

Josef withdrew, went round behind Thuline, and slipped inside her again, collecting her teat ends in one hand and toying with her clitoris. When she started moaning again, he began to unwrap the chain, meaning to lift her on his cock and steady her feet against the branch; but the movements – his fingers between her legs, the slippy chain against her thighs – triggered her climax; her soft delicious writhings brought him on. His cock was moving in a soft, wet sea of semen squirting round inside her. She was in bondage; but he was her prisoner, he was spent but hard and she was still aroused.

He carried her back to the mill with the chain still hanging, his semen running down it, and he took her to bed, where he entered her from the front, then from behind, then on his back with Thuline riding. And after he had come again, she tied his wrists to the bed-rail while she straddled his face, feeding the chain into his mouth and kissing him with the bare part of her vulva. When she came to climax, he felt his hot semen slipping out of her and running down his throat.

It was late into the night, as Thuline was asleep beside him, with the restraints around her breasts again, his left hand under her arm, against the silver ring, and his right hand between her legs, softly searching up the silver chain, that Josef looked up and saw the miller standing quietly at the open door.

10

The Talisur

By morning, Santan had made ready a horse and some provisions.

'I cannot repay you,' Josef mumbled guiltily.

'It is my horse,' Thuline declared. She took the reins from Santan, who moved away then stood, hands clasped across the belly of his apron, and watched her. 'He will need Reikz's things,' she added.

Josef stared in bewilderment at her. 'Go with him,' she told him.

With mounting foreboding he followed the miller to a small hay loft in the field behind the mill. Santan moved aside the sheaves of hay to disclose a trunk, which he untied and opened. And there, wrapped in a waxed linen cloth, was a black cloak with a gold Tormunite cross at the shoulder. In a small wooden box were a belt and several trinkets including a black ring, again bearing the cross.

'How?' Josef asked uneasily.

Santan, his jaw set solidly, stared fixedly at the things. Then he picked up the ring. 'I do not blame you for what has come about,' he blurted out. 'I blame him.' There was a fire in Santan's eye. His breathing was short. Suddenly he turned and stared at Josef, his voice now a whisper, but the anger scarcely controlled:

'When he had had his use of her, he left her. That was two years ago. But he made the mistake of coming back. I told him I would kill him with my bare hands if he tried to take her.'

'You mean you . . .?' The unshrinking stare in Santan's eyes stopped Josef speaking.

'He seemed to think this ring would protect him.' Santan gave a short laugh. 'It didn't. He backed off – like a coward, he did.' Sighing heavily, Santan shook his head. 'He was struck by the wheel – killed instantly.'

The miller did not speak again. In the yard, Thuline said to him: 'I will go with him as far as the abbey. He does not know the way.' She was watching Santan steadily. Some unspoken conversation was unfolding between them. Josef tried to read the expression in the miller's eyes. After a long while, Santan nodded slowly, then strode forward and took her in his arms. He held her head to his breast, and Josef watched her lips press gently to the leather of his apron and his fingers spread searchingly through her hair. When Santan moved away, there were tears in his eyes.

Thuline was looking at Josef and offering him the reins. He climbed clumsily on to the horse and again murmured his thanks to Santan, who again said nothing. Thuline mounted in front of Josef, yanked the reins and they left. She never once looked back.

Their journey took the most part of three days, during which time Josef made no advance of any kind towards her. She seemed as preoccupied with her own thoughts as he was with his guilt. Each night, she told him a little more about Commissioner Reikz – his mannerisms, and the things he did with her, in order that the traveller might more convincingly assume Reikz's identity. For this was Thuline's plan to get him into the abbey. Josef had grave doubts about it: anyone who knew the man would hardly be fooled. 'But they did not know him, not as I did,' Thuline said wistfully.

He asked her about Reikz's presence at the mill. It seemed he had requisitioned it as a billet for his men. She said: 'He used to leave me with them when he went away. That happened often. Sometimes he took me along. One day, while he was still gone, the men went too.'

'But Reikz came back for you?'

'After two years – yes. Santan told you . . .? But he should never have come alone.'

'You mean you would have gone with him?'

'Josef . . . Oh, Josef,' she whispered, shaking her head. 'You do not know – how could you?' She stared at him yearningly. 'Would that he were still alive.'

131

And having made the admission, Thuline closed her eyes, then slowly twisted on to her belly and spread herself. 'The chain,' she pleaded, 'put it into me – like he did. Fasten it up inside me, please.' And she shuddered and shivered while Josef's fingers trembled and the hot moist skin inside her gently yielded. Then while she slept with it in place, he remained awake and aroused, toying with it, haunted by the intimate visions she had described. In his mind's eye he saw her, spread-legged, open-haunched, sitting on a pillow. Two men were taking turns with her mouth. Reikz was crouched beside her, watching. Her small spread bottom was writhing on the pillow, her labia opening ever wider as Reikz's fingers milked her slim, wet, silver chain. Thuline's hand was gloved and fastened above her head; her head was held; her mouth was being guided. Her ringed middle finger was provoking the anus of the one awaiting his turn, keeping the erection firm. And her bulging breasts were gently shaking below the buttocks straining to insert the penis deep into her throat.

Late on the third day they reached the traveller's destination. It was a warm, still evening. Thuline dismounted and walked to the crown of a grassy bank at the edge of the woods. She stood in silence. As Josef crept up behind her, the view suddenly opened out: below him was a broad valley with a lake so wide that the mountains of its far shore were shrouded in the heat haze. 'Servulan ...' Thuline whispered.

The abbey lay in a crook of the river feeding into the lake. Its towers and walls of red-brown stone glowed warmly in the sun. Its high glasswork reflected and splintered the light like jewels. Dominating the scene was the magnificent vaulted roof of the cathedral. To one side was a quadrangle of green; beyond were lower roofs and circular structures capped with slated cones of green. In the distance stood a very tall, round tower surrounded by trees. There were two bridges over the river, one leading across to the abbey and the other away from it to a short slipway into the lake.

As they were watching, a carriage appeared, moving quickly along the valley road. Josef recognised the type. It was accompanied by riders. He watched it cross the bridge and roll down the low-walled driveway before entering the open gates and disappearing. He looked at Thuline: she hadn't moved. Then her left hand lifted and pointed. A small craft was moving out into the lake and turning up the valley. 'Over there – on the other side. Can you see it?' Josef squinted but could make out nothing but a few distant islands and terraces of rock at the head of the lake. Judging by its heading, he guessed the boat might be making for one of the larger craggy promontories. Then he realised that there was a regularity in the terracing and that what he had assumed to be crags were in reality ramparts. But they were massive, too large for anything man-made: the structures must have been over two hundred feet high, enclosing an area of several hundred acres – an entire bowl in the lower hillside.

'Tormunil?' he said.

Thuline shivered. Her left hand came to rest upon a branch above her head. The action at first seemed almost casual – until she let her weight be taken by the arm. She swayed; the ring below her arm protruded under her shirt. Josef could smell her scent. He looked again at the abbey and the boat – a fear crossed his mind, that Iroise and Sianon might already have been and gone, but he put it aside – then he crept away to the horse and began unpacking Reikz's things. Thuline remained staring out across the lake.

Coming back and standing behind her, he said: 'Wish me luck, Thuline.'

When she turned there was already a strange look in her eye. Then she saw him in the Tormunite cloak.

'Wish me luck,' he said again softly. She nodded slowly, but the look was still there, and when he came towards her again, she moved away and said abruptly:

'You must take me with you.'

'But –'

'Stay there!' She began undressing. The road was only a

few yards away. He was at a loss to know what to do. 'Do you not see?' she said. 'You have to take me back, otherwise they will not believe you are Reikz.'

'But – Santan?'

Thuline was shaking – her body was trembling; she was shaking her head fiercely – refusing to listen. She continued undressing until she was naked. 'There must be marks on my bottom – fresh marks,' she urged.

'But –'

'Do it!'

Josef stared at Thuline, quaking, naked. All the sexual things she had told him Reikz did to her came flooding into his mind. The turmoil of emotions took him, sweeping him away. He ran to her and took her shaking body in his arms and began squeezing her so tightly that she could not breathe. He would not put her down, but lifted her higher, so his face was in her breasts. The smell of her – her nakedness, her warmth, her sexual passion – overpowered him. He kissed her belly, sucked her nipples, sucked the ring under her arm, put his fingers to her naked sex.

'The Talisur . . .' she moaned. When he let her down, she ran to the horse, pulled out the box, extracted the black Tormunite ring reverently and began to push it on to his finger. 'Put it on. Keep it on – while you punish me,' she begged him.

And something happened to Josef then, as the cold black metal bedded at the base of his finger and he felt Thuline's lips against it, bestowing sweet, submissive kisses. He looked at the beautiful, vulnerable girl crouched naked in front of him. And he tasted the power that this ring conveyed – the power it seemed to have over Thuline. It thrilled and frightened him.

'Whip me. Whip my bottom. Please – there must be marks.'

She bit him through his trousers, then took his penis out and sucked it, slipping a thong around its base. She pulled his balls out too, then kissed the ring again, frenziedly. The feeling came to him as he put her to the tree. When he unfastened his belt – Reikz's belt – she started moaning in anticipation. He let the leather slide up between her legs.

Then with each smack, his penis swung, her bottom jutted; and her hands slid further down the tree. The bare part of her sex lips pouted out behind her, plucking and dabbing at points in the air. He put the silver chain inside her, chained her up against a waist-high branch and leathered her again, the thin chain stretching up over her clitoris, slipping across it from side to side with every jerk her belly made. When her bottom was well marked, he bundled her onto his lap with her legs straight in the air and fucked her until her wetness started running down his balls. When she tried to touch herself, he stopped her, pulled out and made her kneel with her legs apart and her breasts on the grass. Then he fed the chain completely inside her and spanked her again until it had slipped out and dangled to its full extent down her legs. She was on the point of climax when he made her lie flat on her belly with her legs wide apart.

He knelt astride her, facing backwards, his balls resting in the hollow of her spine, and began to masturbate her slowly, barely touching her, concentrating on the wet, nude part of her labia, with only the moistest, lightest brushes of the chain against the clitoris itself. When she began squirming with pleasure, he laid into her inner thighs with the belt, leaving the skin bright red. But immediately after, very gently, he stretched open the cheeks of her buttocks. And as Thuline's anus went into its first dilation around the pushing bulb of Josef's penis, her climax came. He could feel it through her body. He did not otherwise need to touch her, but held just the bulb of flesh pressed into her. Her back hollowed deeply; her pushed-up bottom took suck upon his penis; and her sex pouted open, its nude lips gulping fish-like round its shiny silver chain. It caused a curious pleasure inside him, that her climax had come thus, through the stretching of her anus by the wet bulb of his cock.

11

The Abbess of Servulan

As he rode through the gates, Josef glimpsed female figures in pale blue habits moving round the cloister overlooking the quadrangle, and he heard gentle voices singing. A youth ran out to meet his horse, then a monk-like figure in grey came hurrying from the other direction. 'The guest-master,' Thuline whispered. The monk eyed the half-clad figure of Thuline suspiciously, then squinted up at Josef.

'Your business, sir?' he asked warily.

Removing his glove, Josef displayed the Talisur ring. 'I wish to see the abbess – now.'

The monk bowed away. 'My apologies, my lord,' he muttered anxiously.

'Commissioner Reikz,' Josef corrected.

'At once, Commissioner.' Then the man scurried off.

Josef dismounted, his heart pounding in his ears. He felt that he was sure to be unmasked. But he forced himself to leave Thuline with the horse in the courtyard while he pretended to look around casually. The carriage they had seen entering the place stood empty on the cobblestones. The singing seemed to be coming from the upstairs rooms in the building opposite. Josef walked over to it and began ascending some steps at the side, then glanced back. Two monks moving slowly across the courtyard passed Thuline without looking up.

Ahead of Josef at the top of the steps was an arched walkway between two buildings. It became a terrace overlooking the quadrangle where the blue-hooded women moved in twos and threes. He scanned these small groups, looking in vain for some feature he might recognise. Then one of the women looked up and his heart leapt into his throat: he caught a glimpse of blonde hair. Could it be?

She whispered to her companion then, head bowed, continued walking.

The mind is a strange creature: in that split second, and with one tiny clue, she became Iroise, and the girl beside her, Sianon. Reikz was forgotten and Josef's eyes darted wildly about, already looking for Quislan, ready to conjure her evil spectre from the shadows.

When he looked again, the two were disappearing quickly.

A door in the wall behind him looked as if it led down to the quadrangle. Josef took hold of the heavy-ringed handle and twisted it. Before the latch had even lifted, the voice of the guest-master resounded dissuasively behind him: 'Commissioner – the lady Abbess will see you ... Now.'

Josef followed him with guarded grace, which turned to foreboding when he realised that Thuline was now nowhere to be seen. In the courtyard, he was handed over to an old monk and the guest-master hurried away. Josef was taken through a door at the far end of the yard and down a long stone corridor with tall windows on each side. At the end, they came to an octagonal area with rooms leading off it and a staircase spiralling up through several levels towards a pale aquamarine domed-glass ceiling. Josef could smell incense. With great difficulty and with frequent stops, the old monk escorted him up the first flight to where a short corridor with magnificently frescoed walls and ceiling terminated in a pair of black-lacquered Gothic doors. Josef hesitated, attempting to give the impression he was at his ease by looking through one of the windows. The sight greeting him put an end to that.

The girl was naked. She was in a corner of a neatly laid-out formal garden. Two monks were with her. She was fastened into one of three curved devices resembling open cradles. Her ankles were bound to an overhead spar crowned with the Tormunite cross. Her head and shoulders draped back; her arms dangled. Her breasts, sex and bottom were exposed. She was sexually aroused. The monks were alternately working and spanking the exposed parts.

'Commissioner ...?' the usher wheezed. One of the

137

heavy doors now stood open. Josef took off his gloves and walked briskly in.

At the far end of the room was a large, black, altar-like desk with a solid, carved chair behind it. But the Abbess of Servulan was not sitting there. She was standing to the right of the desk. Lit from above, her cassock glowed crimson. It pinched her narrow waist, expanded roundly at the hip, then dropped straight to the floor, concealing her feet completely. The impression conveyed was of a cylindrical, solid-based, red statue in a vertical shaft of light. Her sleeves tapered to the wrist. Her neck was bare: the collarless cassock lay close against her skin, reinforcing the impression of a statue with the clothing painted on it. Her hair was cropped short and looked washed of its colour – but she was quick-eyed and when she finally moved, quick-limbed.

A thick velvet cloth covered the desk and overhung each end. Thuline was sitting naked on it. Then the door opened again behind Josef and someone was ushered in by the guest-master, who hurried to the Abbess and delivered a whispered message before retreating.

There was now a young nun in pale blue standing quietly to the side of the desk in shadow. Josef found himself peering at her, trying to see beneath the dark of the cowl.

'Are you looking for another?' The Abbess's clear voice echoed across the room. He was taken off-guard.

'I . . . I am sorry?'

'An apology from a commissioner is strange meat indeed.' Her quick eyes glinted. 'But I ask again: why else have you brought back Thuline?'

He wondered what answer to give. 'She wanted it,' he said truthfully.

'What an extraordinary reason . . . Let me look at you.' She glided towards him. 'I do not seem to recall you . . . Commissioner Reikz?'

From the outset, she was forcing him to make excuses. He tried to put some backbone into his delivery: 'Lady Abbess – I stopped here only briefly, and that, some long time ago.'

She moved closer, apparently staring at his face, yet throwing frequent oblique glances at the hand bearing the ring. 'No, I do not recall you. But have you been brawling?' She was staring at the marks on his face.

'As happens sometimes on the road – but none of it of my doing.'

'But this is your doing?' She turned to Thuline and lifted her arm, exposing the silver ring.

'It excites her.' He folded his arms.

'You seem to be evading my questions – is this a trait?'

'On the contrary, I have returned a girl without preconditions and have answered the more pertinent of your queries. So, if you would be so good as to –'

'Commissioner please . . .' Her tone had changed. 'It was not my intention to hinder nor to cause offence.' But her proud eyes told him otherwise. She turned and beckoned. 'Vernel . . .' The figure in blue gave a start, then moved forward nervously. 'You may lower your hood, Vernel. The Commissioner may wish to look upon your beauty.' The slender fingers lifted back the cowl. And she was beautiful – slim-necked, graceful, full-lipped, blue-eyed, with dense blonde eyebrows and softly freckled cheeks. 'Vernel is yet a novice. Lift your arm, Thuline. Take it Vernel, take hold of the ring. Put your fingers through it.'

Josef watched the slim fingers sliding smoothly though nervously through the ring. He watched Thuline's eyes close and her nipples gathering. The Abbess asked her to lie down across the desk and made Vernel kneel on it beside her. Then she opened Thuline's legs and touched the twisted, naked pubic lips. There was already moisture seeping out, and the lips looked slightly inflamed and swollen. Opening them, the Abbess put her fingers in. 'And you have ringed her here . . . More space,' she whispered. Thuline's knees splayed open. All the finger-ends and the thumb had disappeared. Thuline's bottom was moving the cloth. 'More space, Thuline.' The hand probed deeper, the fingers now unseen and the wrist turning gently, 'Legs out . . . Legs out . . . There.' There were soft sucking sounds from Thuline's belly, which lifted as the fingers tugged the buried ring; the stump of the Abbess's hand was wet; the naked pubic lips clung to it. At their junction, Thuline's erect clitoris formed a brightly swollen ball.

'Your tongue, Vernel, across her nipples.' And Thuline shuddered. 'Now the ring, wet it. Put your tongue through it. Vernel has a good tongue, does she not, Commissioner? Up girl . . . Legs up.' Thuline's knees went into the air, with the Abbess's hand still inside her, until Thuline was doubled over with her knees around her ears and almost touching the desktop. The Abbess examined every smooth projecting knob of Thuline's spine, then gently spread the bottom cheeks. 'Vernel – come taste. Search out her earthiness. Fill her soft brown cup with honey.' The shiny, soft-pointed tongue pressed and probed the dark velvet skin. The slim young fingers stretched it. Josef saw it open to a narrow roundness, saw the wet tongue sliding in and out, saw the contractions of Thuline's pubic lips about the Abbess's hand. 'Your tongue, Thuline . . .' The Abbess gently lifted Thuline's head so she could lick her own clitoris. Thuline shuddered quickly as she came, then her head fell back and she came again as Vernel's tongue continued moistly to open out her pulsing anal rim.

Withdrawing her hand, the Abbess pushed Thuline on to her side, leaving her panting. A monk had appeared from the shadows; he carried an ebony platter bearing a small broad plunger, which he placed on the table.

'Vernel – lift your habit.' The girl seemed to be naked underneath it. Sliding his hands up, the monk grasped her by her slender waist and the Abbess picked up the instrument. 'Wait – perhaps the Commissioner would care to . . .?'

Josef's tongue adhered to the roof of his mouth, preventing him speaking. He shook his head, feigning indifference, though that was the last thing he was feeling. 'At least then – would the Commissioner hold Vernel for me?'

She was testing him; Josef knew this well. The Abbess looked at the monk, then tilted her head; he moved aside.

Josef's trembling fingers took Vernel round the bare waist as she was kneeling, head down on the desk. 'Hold her under her thighs, Commissioner. Now lift her buttocks.' She was small. Her sex and anus had been completely depilated. The skin was smooth, perfect, the narrow beige funnel velvety, deep but tight. The Abbess ran her index finger gently around it. 'Hold her.' Vernel's breathing was already coming rapidly. The Abbess clutched the small broad plunger like a knife. A viscid liquid oozed from the end. She put her thumb to the shaped end. Vernel's bottom trembled in anticipation; her body sagged. Josef put a hand below to steady her and he could feel the delicious down-bulge of her belly, punctured by the soft slot of her navel.

'We do not touch her sex,' the Abbess warned him. 'Instead, she gets it here . . .' The barrel of the plunger tapered to a wide smooth nozzle which the Abbess adeptly fitted to the fleshy funnel. Vernel moaned gently as the nozzle probed the centre of her velvety surround. 'Take hold of her round the legs. Stretch her anus open with your fingers . . . There . . .' The Abbess rotated the plunger; the fleshy rim opened round it and the nozzle slid inside. The rim tried to tighten like a closing flowerbud. Vernel gasped. The Abbess was slowly depressing the applicator. 'Take her belly in both hands.' He could feel it gently writhing, expanding downwards. 'And touch her breasts.' The nipples made hard points at the dangling ends. And the applicator kept moving steadily. Vernel's face was to the cloth; her tongue protruded, licking the thick plush strands.

'Bring Thuline closer,' the Abbess instructed the monk. He lifted her leg and held her haunches. Vernel's slippy tongue now licked slow lascivious circles round Thuline's still-moist rim.

'Do you unto others . . .' the Abbess whispered. 'For you see, Vernel herself is not permitted to receive the tongue there. And therein lies the sweet irony: before her therapy was begun, she never knew she craved that particular pleasure . . . Self-awareness – the key that lies within us all. Servulan tries to free it.'

The plunger was now withdrawn empty, but Vernel did

not stop moving. She moaned with deprivation as Thuline's open buttocks were eased away. 'Leave her,' said the Abbess. But Josef could not resist first pulling the pale blue habit gently up Vernel's back, exposing her swaying breasts, so he could see the hard tips moving. The Abbess spread Vernel's legs and showed him the rigidly projecting clitoris.

'We must not permit her to bring her legs together in this state,' she explained. 'We want the feelings to come the other way, through her bottom. With some, it can be made to happen through training. But I should warn you now – not to go inside her once she has been treated. It is necessary to wait two hours at least.' The Abbess rubbed Vernel's naked back, making the skin move up and down across her hips, making it pull the anus. Vernel moaned. 'There . . . Is it good, Vernel?' she whispered, but the novice did not answer. She seemed far away. Josef watched her silvery tongue protrude cravingly through her open mouth and across the cloth. 'Keep your head down, and your knees up. Let it sink inside you . . . We have many treatments, many clysters, Commissioner. One must take care not to confuse them. The function of this one is to enhance the sensitivity of the skin inside and thereby to enhance the anal pleasure. It is a good part of the training in her case.'

She clicked her fingers at the monk. 'Stay with her while she finishes. Have someone see to Thuline. Get her a cell.' Then she turned and looked at Josef. 'Commissioner – perhaps you would care to tell me the reason why you asked to see me?'

From the way the Abbess was so attentive to him, it seemed to Josef that she had some purpose far deeper than that of politeness to a visitor. Perhaps it was because he wore the Talisur. The ring certainly had an influence: everyone who recognised it treated him with great respect. And he found the burden of pretence being gradually leavened by the privileges that the deception seemed to bring.

'So – you wish to understand our methods, Commissioner?' They had left the octagonal tower and passed along a covered walkway some yards above the level of the gardens. There was now no sign of the naked girl. The Abbess stopped at a large recessed door protected by an iron grille. 'We welcome scrutiny – but there are rules to be adhered to, where outsiders are concerned, and procedures of our own which are sacrosanct. I must have your word that you will respect them.'

'You have my undertaking.'

'And there are places that by rights should be closed even to you.' She tugged a bell-cord. A panel snapped open in the heavy door behind the grille, a female face peered out then after a delay the door opened. 'Sister Sutrice – unlock the iron.' The nun eyed Josef with suspicion. 'He is permitted,' said the Abbess. 'Sutrice . . .'

The grille was opened. The Abbess stepped over the threshold and Josef followed. 'Sutrice – Commissioner Reikz shall require to be robed as a tutor.' Then she turned to Josef. 'Sister Sutrice oversees the Training Cloister. She will escort you.' Then she hesitated. 'I am sorry – but your attire must be correct: you cannot wear that ring, not here, beyond the iron. Sutrice will keep it safe for you until you leave.'

He looked at the Abbess, wondering what she might be planning. 'I cannot part with the Talisur,' he said firmly.

'A good start, this, after you have given your word.'

'I gave no undertaking on the Talisur. Take all else, but I will keep it.'

'Then slip it into a pocket, out of sight,' she said, glancing at the nun.

'I keep it on – where I know it is.'

'As you wish.' Stepping back, the Abbess said abruptly: 'Shall you leave now?'

'Madam . . . Lady Abbess, I have agreed to be robed in the manner you require. Now I request that you show me your procedures – as was promised.' He took a gamble: 'For I know it to be my right.' And he held up the ring.

The nun's eyes glittered. The Abbess stared at him coldly. 'Very well.'

12

In the Training Cloister

Sister Sutrice led Josef into the robing-room. 'Your things will be kept safe,' she said, taking his cloak. She had narrow bony fingers. Her eyes were close against the thin bridge of her nose. They were sharp, scrutinising. Her appearance fitted her post as overseer.

It soon became clear that she wanted him naked. How Reikz would have reacted, he did not know. But for Josef this was another test. A young nun was sitting in the corner. She watched him complete his undressing. At a word from Sister Sutrice she got up, walked round Josef, studying him, then began to search the array of large mahogany wardrobes. He leant nude against the table. Returning with a grey habit and sandals she stood in front of him, staring at his crotch. 'She must make an estimate of your size,' Sutrice said, 'for the sheath.'

'What sheath?'

'It must be worn. According to the Rule of Janna, at the first stage of the noviciate the initiants are forbidden to look upon a man's naked flesh. But again according to the Rule, they must be mindful of the response which their actions might elicit. This is the solution.' The young nun picked a thin silk one from a large flat drawer. 'The sisters make them,' said Sutrice. It had cords that fastened round the waist and between the buttocks.

Josef had great difficulty controlling his arousal as the young nun's soft fingers unrolled the thin sheath around his penis and his balls. When she fastened the ties, she noticed the ring; then her fingers deliberately took hold of him again, slowly and gently shaping the sheath around him. It was obvious that she was expert at administering pleasure to a man; moreover she enjoyed it.

'Jacelyn!' Sister Sutrice, frozen-faced, glowered at the young nun, then moderated her tone for Josef. 'Should you need replacements today, Jacelyn will fit them.' He stared in surprise. 'Commissioner – because the novices must not look upon a man's naked flesh is not to say that it cannot be used.' But her gaze again struck pointedly and coldly at the young nun who, casting frequent nervous glances at Sutrice, began helping Josef into his habit and sandals.

'And now, the cachet.' Sutrice held it up. 'Use it sparingly.' It was a soft pouch, such as might contain a watch on a chain. She carefully removed from it a pendant of frosted deep yellow grains resembling crushed wax or amber compressed to the shape of a heavy lens. As the cachet swung, its textured surface shimmered. Impressed into one side was the Tormunite cross.

'Use it – how?' Josef asked.

Sutrice smiled thinly. Her hand closed around the cachet, her pale eyelids sank shut and for a second she seemed to shiver. 'Sparingly,' she whispered, staring at the kneeling Jacelyn. Then she pushed the cachet back into its pouch and fastened the chain around Josef's neck.

'Shall we . . . ?' She indicated a door at the opposite end of the room. 'One moment . . .' She had noticed the young nun's eyes still lingering on Josef. Standing over her, Sutrice took her by the chin and stared at her. Jacelyn began to tremble then to cry. Sutrice continued to stare. The whimpering girl removed her veil and released her long hair, which hung in a column down her back. Her face was looking straight at the ceiling. Sutrice moved round behind her, took her by the hair and drew her, crawling backwards, on her knees across the floor. Then she tied her hair to a cord hanging from the wall. Finally she wrenched her habit open from the shoulders. Round Jacelyn's neck was a closely fitting chain, fastened by thinner chains to rings through her nipples. Sutrice played with the piercings, pinching them, lightly smacking them. Josef felt arousal as he watched. Sutrice smiled at him; she wetted Jacelyn's erect ringed nipples then left her restrained and exposed and ushered Josef through the door.

Beyond it, they came into a low hall. 'Your arrival is well-timed, Commissioner. We have some postulants, new today.' His heartbeat quickened.

He scanned the frightened faces – there were about a dozen, but he recognised none. Yet his heart never slowed: they were being examined by the 'tutors' – monks dressed as he was. The young women were in a line. All had been made to shed their clothing. All were shapely. Sutrice led Josef on to a low balcony overlooking the line. He was close enough to hear the soft trembling in their breathing. 'Their bodies – so charged with unleashed excitement,' Sutrice whispered eagerly. 'These first few hours, they will remember always. It sets the scene; it has to be right. Watch . . .'

Suspended from the ceiling was a long horizontal bar. The nude initiants had been made to grip it while two of the grey-garbed tutors moved along the line, looking at them. The girls were already very uneasy. A third tutor did nothing but watch their expressions. When the two had completed their traverse, the third one consulted with them, then the girls were rearranged, but with no obvious pattern to the regrouping. A freckled girl from the middle had been taken to the far end. She now seemed much more nervous than the rest as the tutors, one at the front, the other behind, moved slowly down the line towards her. Each girl, still gripping the bar, was meticulously examined between the legs. One of the tutors sniffed his fingers. As the victim burned with embarrassment, Sutrice whispered: 'She will pay close attention to her toilet in future.'

The men were becoming aroused by the touching; since their habits fastened only to the waist, the initiants could not fail to notice. 'Look again at the last one in line,' said Sutrice. She was shaking long before they reached her.

Then one of the other girls was singled out and put in front of the line. She was short, blonde and small-breasted. Again there was no clear reason for her having been selected. But in her case, the explorations went deeper: she was masturbated standing. It was done very slowly, one tutor in front of her, squeezing her between the legs, rubbing with his fingers, probing, the other behind, touching her only intermittently but opening out her buttocks whenever she made a murmur. Suddenly her breath caught. The one still playing with her whispered to her then lifted aside the shoulder of his habit and bent down. Chained around his neck was a cachet in a pouch. Her cheek came to rest against his naked skin. He kept toying with her sex. Her legs splayed open and she buckled. Her nipples brushed his rigid silk-sheathed penis. He pulled her up and put her face to his shoulder again and continued masturbating her. Then he took the chain from his neck and drew the cachet from its pouch. It glinted golden yellow.

He put it between her legs, gently put it into her, slipped it in as if into its soft-lipped pouch. The chain hung down between her legs; but she was already on her toes, gasping. It took only a few seconds. He touched her clitoris to help her; the one behind her spread her bottom cheeks and stroked a finger in the crack. Her mouth opened wider – she started to shudder and moan – then her teeth sank into the shoulder as she came. The tutor caught hold of the trembling chain, gently pulled the glistening cachet out of her and returned it to its case.

The line of young women was shaking as the third tutor now moved along, peering into each face – hesitating here and there, but not saying anything or touching anyone – until he reached the end. The last one in line was shuddering more visibly than the one who had been brought to climax. Yet nobody had touched her. He told her to take her hands down from the bar and keep them clasped behind her neck. Then he moved her slowly backwards so she could not see where she was being pushed. She reached a tall stool. He lifted her on to it, warning her to keep her hands behind her neck. Then he stood back. Her freckled breasts were shaking gently, her deep pink nipples were hard. He came back and opened her legs, perching her heels on the cross-staves of the stool. Then the other initiants, exchanging apprehensive sidelong glances at her, were led out of the room.

Sister Sutrice stepped down from the platform and

beckoned Josef to follow. She went over to the girl. 'Your name?'

'Toinile.'

'Toinile – you have been chosen. Keep your legs spread, your tutors have placed you thus for a purpose. Now, will you do for them precisely as they ask? Deny them nothing?'

'Yes . . .' the girl murmured.

'The cachet . . .' Sutrice held out her hand. Josef took it from round his neck. Sutrice held it up and the girl started breathing very fast. 'You know what this is for?'

'Y-yes,' the girl stammered.

'Good. Whenever it is offered, you shall spread your legs in readiness. Is that understood? That is all your tutors shall ever ask of you, Toinile – obedience. Now close your eyes. Lean back. Keep open.' But the sister did not use the cachet. She took Josef out of earshot and explained:

'She does not know it yet, but she will be kept aroused by watching the others and not being allowed to touch herself or come. But she will sleep beside them while they are pleasured. She will watch the cachet being used and the clysters being given. And oh, she will be swollen. She will have to be tied with her legs apart or she will try to use her sweet, soft, freckled thighs to squeeze herself to pleasure. During the daytime she will be fitted with a cup.'

'And what of the –?' Josef began, but his words were cut short by Toinile's moan. Two of the tutors were with her. One was standing between her legs, the other was behind her, holding her upright. Her out-thrust belly trembled.

'We have to mark them, you see, the chosen ones – so when they are being passed around, everyone is aware of the restrictions.' She led him back. Toinile's legs were still wide open. Fastened through her inner labium was a ruby stud. 'And of course, the piercing and the constriction of the lip can but enhance the sexual feelings. None of these pleasures can they fully understand until we teach them. But you were saying . . . ?'

'The others . . . ?' he asked weakly. But he was watching Toinile on her stool, the tutor behind her, her head held back, her nipples hard, belly distended, inner lips already distinct and separate from the outer, their arousal very clear.

'Each novice is given under the supervision of two tutors. They stay with her night and day. She may be totally innocent of the exigencies of pleasure so we take nothing for granted. We go back to basics, Commissioner, and begin afresh. And the first thing she must learn is that nothing – no function of her body – is to be kept secret. With some, this takes time. You wish to see it in operation?' She turned to the tutors. 'Bring her.'

They moved into a series of interconnected rooms. 'The day rooms,' said Sutrice. Only a few were occupied. 'The novices here have been with us a short time; their capabilities are still being explored.'

On a bed, a young woman wearing only a bodice was being masturbated continuously by two monks. Her supple body was draped across one man's lap; she seemed aware only of the oily fingers drawing circles in her open wetness. Sutrice quietly questioned the monks. Then she whispered to Josef: 'When they come to us, they have scant realisation of their true potential. Her tutors have been with her since last night. They have lost count of the number of times she has come to pleasure; yet her climaxes are getting stronger; and her case is not that unusual. It often happens that the devout ones are the most lubricious.'

The girl was ruddy-cheeked, straining. They adjusted her position on the bed. Even as she was being moved she started to moan. The hands between her legs were slowing. The other hands caressed her hair, drew it out in long strands. Then she was drawn up the bed to where a carved wooden phallus jutted from the headboard. Her mouth was fed around it while her open sex was gently oiled and rubbed. It was as her bodice was still being unlaced that she came, her legs convulsing open, her naked belly thrust against the oiling hand, the gap in the bodice drawn aside, one swollen nipple and its bulging areola pushing through the lacing. 'The undressing at the point of climax helps them, as a rule,' said Sutrice. 'And look at this one ...'

Beside the bed, Toinile was trembling. 'Shall we leave her here to watch?'

In the next room, a naked novice was kneeling, head down, on the bed. Josef saw a row of sheaths laid out in readiness beside her. Sutrice made enquiry of the monks, and the girl was temporarily turned on her side. She was short-jointed. Her breasts were small, her belly bulged softly. A fine jewelled chain had been fastened between her labia. 'She is a virgin,' said Sutrice, 'new this week, chosen by the Abbess specifically to be taught anal coitus.' She watched Josef, as if judging the effect her words were having. 'With the soldiers who visit us, it is much in demand.' Again she hesitated. 'The chain is worn only as an indication that the usual access is not to be developed; it could never prevent insistent entry.' Sutrice moved closer to Josef. 'There are two shifts, each of two tutors; the sheaths are dry hessian; no salve or lubrication is ever used.' As she spoke, the treatment was recommencing. 'The tissues will fill out, soften and extend. And the novice is always masturbated during penetration; the pain – an exquisite hotness, a burning in her bottom – serves but to augment her pleasure.' Then she said to the monk who had turned the girl over again and was beginning to mount her: 'Touch her here, between the legs; keep her knob moist. Do not stint – let the pleasure take her freely when the sheath is inside her.' At the first true gasp, the sister turned again to Josef: 'How long would you think, Commissioner? How long to train a novice to a predilection for such ways?' She was studying his eyes; he had great difficulty withstanding her gaze. Then it suddenly softened. 'Come with me,' she whispered.

She had led him into a room with a solid, velvet-covered table in the middle. On the wall were glass-fronted sloping cupboards, filled with dildos of every imaginable shape and size, every surface texture, every type of material. She placed three in turn on the table – a bone one, curved, polished, long as a forearm; a thick one carved from soapstone; and a lead one coated with gold leaf. Then she locked the door. 'Choose one,' she whispered. Her eyes sparkled. 'I shall put it into you.'

'What is it?' she asked when he didn't move. 'A woman cannot penetrate a man? I want to. Lean across the table. Each of these is very smooth. We have lubricants. I shall masturbate you with your anus stretched. Just a little, I shall do it. Then we can return and see how she progresses.'

Josef did not answer Sutrice. She waited awhile, watching him, watching his arousal as she stroked the dildos. Then she opened another cabinet and chose several for the girl. He stared at the rough, notched surfaces.

She took him back to see the girl, now in a sitting position. Her legs were thrust out to the sides, she was being lifted up and down the coarse-sheathed penis, and her clitoris was being gently sucked. Sutrice gave the monks a studded dildo. The girl was drawn back off the penis, back across the monk's belly. The dildo was put into her anus while she lay on her back. Her small breasts shook, the chain between her labia trembled; her clitoris was masturbated wet.

Sutrice stared calmly at Josef while the girl was in climax. He thought again of what she had wanted to do in the room; Thuline had said Reikz made her do things like that to him to keep him aroused. And later, throughout the evening, those thoughts would come nudging back into Josef's mind, when he least wanted them – the thought of the girl in climax with her anus stretched and the thought of the velvet table, of Sutrice, and the dildos of soapstone, lead and bone.

Sutrice led Josef onwards, to a place where a girl on a bed was nude above the waist. Her breasts were being sucked. They looked not only large, but also quite swollen; the surrounds were brown and bulging, as if her breasts were capped and the nipples distended from pressure into the teats. 'She is being trained to lactate. And she is a virgin. You seem surprised. Already she has some secretions. There are preparations that can help. With some girls, it comes quickly. What matters is the constant stimulation. We have one with us now who began lactating freely after only a week.' Looking sidelong at Josef, Sutrice then whispered: 'Should you wish to train her breasts, it can be arranged.'

On the next bed, a young woman was tied by the feet to a bar below the ceiling. Two monks were with her. One was watching the other oil her between the legs with a brush.

'She is going to the soldiers. They do not have the self-control possessed by tutors. She needs protection.'

'With oil?'

Shaking her head, Sutrice took a small casket from the watching monk and opened it. 'These . . .' They were tiny gold trinkets on fine cords. 'They go inside the womb. They represent the spirit that protects her. They increase the flow of monthly blood – a signal she is safe, whatever the means of love, however many suitors.' She showed him some of the individual designs: a snake – 'Desire,' a minute penis – 'the spirit of her sponsor, protecting her when she is put to other men,' and a miniature Tormunite cross – 'the purest protection of all.' Sutrice kissed it. 'When any of these is inside, she cannot feel it. But there are larger ones. Of these, should we choose them, she would be quite aware. As would the lover . . .' She showed him one shaped like a conical stem with a lip in the middle and a ball at the narrow end. 'When she thrusts, it slides down the penis; the male climax is taken with the metal ball inside.'

The girl was now moaning from the prolonged masturbation with the oil-charged brush. 'The moment is near. It is inserted at the point of climax. Which one has been chosen?' It was the tiny gold penis. 'Will he put you with other men?' Sutrice whispered, loading the charm into the guiding tool. The girl climaxed as her sex was being opened. Insertion followed swiftly. Her sex contracted, the labia folding softly together.

Sutrice left her and the journey continued. They emerged into a large brightly lit arcuate room. The inner wall had a series of partitioned cubicles; some were occupied. At the far end of each cubicle was a darkened doorway sealed by an iron grille; it was impossible to see into the passageway beyond. When Josef attempted to venture towards one of the grilles, Sutrice drew him back. 'Beyond the iron, there may be visitors, like yourself, though not so privileged,' she whispered. 'They are sometimes permitted to inspect but only from a secluded distance. A few are sponsors – who may of course dictate the training. We are often asked to train a novice to a specific end. Only when the training is successfully completed will she be returned. Take this one: she is being taught to climax orally – when the penis discharges into her mouth.'

The monks with the girl were nude except for their sheaths. She was draped between them. Josef had not seen erections quite so hard. The ends of the sheaths were saturated, where she had been sucking. One monk was milking himself for her. 'The liquid seeps through; if they do it gently, it can run almost continuously, very slowly. Her sucking helps to draw the liquid; she drinks it; she acquires a taste for it.' The girl's lips closed round the sheathed cap of the penis. The other monk took a feather to her clitoris. 'As with the teaching of anal coitus, the association is made. In this case, the pleasure between her legs; and in her mouth, the taste. In time, she shall be put as concubine to a guest who is not her sponsor. By then, she will have learnt how to make the pleasure build inside a man. She will have her first naked one to milk with her mouth, and it will be a stranger's. And oh how richly that first flood will come; how strongly she will climax.' Sutrice closed her eyes. 'With others, it is only the cane that is allowed to precipitate the pleasure. Witness . . .'

She directed him to a cubicle where a girl was lying face down on a narrow, high, altar-like divan that was capped by a soft white mattress. The structure was just wide enough for her to lie with her hands resting to either side of her head. A pillow positioned under her belly had the effect of raising her buttocks. She was sobbing gently. The monk beside her held a long, thin cane. There were straight, pink marks across her buttock cheeks. Sister Sutrice took the cane from the monk. The girl tensed visibly. Sutrice waited for the buttocks to relax, but the sobbing did not stop completely.

Without realising what he was doing, Josef positioned himself by the girl's head. He had been driven by the desire to watch her face. It was half-buried in the softness of the mattress. From the corner of his eye, he was aware of someone moving in the shadows beyond the grille.

The rod fell swiftly three times; the sound of the blows went through him. When the fourth one came, no longer able to contain herself, the girl squealed. Her legs were trembling. 'Relax.' Sutrice whispered. Three cruel thwacks came again in swift succession, the girl emitting hard tense grunts, then crying quietly, open-mouthed. 'Enough for now,' Sutrice whispered. She glanced towards the grille, then touched the girl's hair. The victim's thumb had slipped into her mouth. Her tears ran down her cheek and wetted the thumb. The seven thin bars the sister had scored across her bottom stood out firmer and darker than the rest.

'Turn her over.' Josef saw her fully for the first time – her nipples, rose pink, her breasts soft and large. 'Flagellation – for some girls, it reigns supreme. No man, no unassisted tongue can fully match it. Look here. Her clitoris is quite erect. And it is the caning that brings it on, the pain, this special sharp-sweet pleasure in the soft flesh of her buttocks. She does not understand it. You do not need to understand. Enjoy . . .' The girl moaned with pleasure as Sutrice began to play with her clitoris. It was oily moist. She slid the tips of her fingers in between the lips. 'The secret is to masturbate freely, but to stop at the brink and let the caning work her to completion. With some, you can cane till the syrup is running down their thighs. To cane against a wall is good, or with her simply standing, or with someone holding her between the legs. Then there are the refinements – the inner thighs, the mouth of the anus, the insides of the labia. Each of these discrete pleasures, she will be taught to enjoy.' Then Sutrice showed Josef the clamps and weights for holding the labia open during this precisely focused caning, and she asked him if he wished to watch. But when she attempted to show how the clamps were fastened, the girl climaxed wetly against her hand.

Sutrice did not scold her. Rather, she shook her head, cast a glance towards the hidden watcher, then asked the monks to bring her to the brink again, attach the clamps and cane inside her.

Throughout these excesses, Josef was still attempting to retain the calm aloofness he assumed to have characterised the man he was impersonating, neither complimenting nor criticising Sutrice, but secretly fighting the deep arousal he experienced every time he allowed his gaze to linger on such scenes. But the test was only just beginning. 'And now to basics,' said Sutrice.

She took him downstairs to a bathroom area, which proved to be empty. But beyond it, he could hear voices. The next room was only dimly lit; the air was cool; the scent was faint but distinctive. There were three monks and two nude novices, one of whom was kneeling on a plain wooden bench. She was awaiting her turn, and facing away from the monk sitting next to her on the bench. His erect, sheathed penis was poking through his habit as he massaged her between the buttock cheeks. The second girl was being suspended over a hole in the floor by the other two monks, who supported her in a sitting position. Sutrice went over and spoke to the monks; then she spoke to the girl, touching her briefly. 'It is hard,' she said equivocally when she came back. She sighed. 'They find it difficult; so private a matter after all. Notice her face – how rosy. You have observed how cool it is in here? But she is warm. Her sex is burning. It has been four days. The longer she leaves it, the firmer the yield and the more difficult the delivery. But it will come; it must. And she is kept excited till it does. She will come to associate this necessary function with pleasure.'

The girl moaned. The monks lifted her aside. One of them held her to his chest, his hands under her knees, her breasts upon his shoulders, while the other examined her. He took some cream from a small wooden dish and put it into her, then he wiped his fingers on a cloth and she was again suspended.

From the other side of the room came a moan of

resignation accompanied by words of encouragement. The kneeling girl had begun to deliver. Josef's gaze was drawn; the feelings churned inside him. No basin had been brought. The monk began playing with her sex as he pressed his hand into the perfect bowl of her back. She moaned again; he toyed with her. Sutrice took Josef round in front of the crouching girl. Her hands were pressed to the bench, her head was bowed; her nipples were erect. He wanted to take her hot, flushed face and kiss it. The monk turned her over and made her lie along the wooden seat. He squeezed a thin line of cream between her labia and began gently to work it in.

The other girl had been lifted into a kneeling position above the hole. Her legs were gradually eased apart and she was masturbated slowly. Her yield began descending then stopped; her belly was supported, her head lolled back. When she groaned, her cry was echoed by the one on her back on the bench, whose knees had now been lifted while the yield was gently pressed back in. 'A long, sweet process,' said Sutrice as she led Josef away. 'And afterwards, this . . .'

Josef stood stock-still at the entrance to the next room. A beautiful novice was kneeling naked on the floor. She was being given an enema. The monks had deployed themselves around her; the tube snaked up from between her buttocks to a container hanging from the ceiling. It was being refilled. As the pressure built, the young woman began moaning. 'This is not the first time, truth to tell,' Sutrice said. 'She has come to want it. Each time, she likes it better than the last. They are most careful with the insertion; in her case, we do not want the tender inner tissues sore.'

The girl was holding her sex open and her legs were trembling as the monk was touching her. The tube swayed gently under the weight of the flow.

'Sit down, Commissioner. You may have her on your knee.' Before Josef could stop her, Sutrice went over to the girl. She watched the leather container sag as the last of the liquid emptied. The girl murmured as the tube was taken out of her bottom. She was helped up. She walked unstead-

156

ily. A strange shivery feeling came inside Josef as he watched her moving – like Thuline had moved with the ball inside her. The feeling intensified as he sank into the waxed leather chair and took the naked girl on his lap and felt her when her belly was so swollen and her sex was so aroused. She was indeed beautiful. She trembled as she held her sex open for him to touch. He lifted the Talisur ring and let her kiss it and she shuddered so strongly that he thought she might come against his browsing fingers.

'She needs more; she can take more,' said Sutrice. He was reluctant to release her. But he watched her kneel again, and saw the bag refilled, the flow tested, the tube inserted, the sweet distension of her belly down between her legs and he listened to her gentle moans and murmurs. 'On the master's knee,' said Sutrice when the bag was empty.

Josef had never felt a belly so sweetly sexual in its distension. The silk sheath was tight around him; he had the aching urge to pull it off and push his naked cock into her soft wet crotch and rub her clitoris slowly while he held her bulging belly.

'Again,' said Sutrice, and while the girl was being done, she whispered: 'Look – she cannot bear the pleasure.' The girl was then turned on to her side and played with, then lifted in a harness while she was emptied. 'They are not finished yet.' She was still aroused. The soft tissues that the tube had stretched were gently anointed; a clyster of cream was made ready for her sex. Sutrice and Josef took their leave.

'There is one last room that you might like to see,' she said. It was larger than the others, and the young women – four or five – moved freely around it. They were nude save for short, tight, seamless pale-blue cotton jerkins enclosing their breasts. On one table were some small gold cups. Sutrice indicated them and asked Josef would he like to sample? He saw the cups were empty. Sutrice then asked the girls to display themselves for their visitor. Even their walking excited him: they seemed to have been chosen for the perfection of their buttocks and the large size of their

157

breasts, which provoked him. 'You may pick one if you care to,' Sutrice said. When he didn't, she selected one with long yellow hair and bade her lie upon a narrow marble table that was covered with a closely fitting white sheet. The girl lay face down. Her full breasts bulged under the compression and the jerkin tightened across her back. Her legs opened and her thighs dropped over the table edge. 'Put your hand here.' Sutrice directed his palm to the naked part of the girl's back, into the hollow and against the warmth. He could see the girl's pulse in her neck. Sutrice put her hand between the girl's legs, which moved more open as the hand moved deeper, until the girl's eyes closed and she gasped softly and then emitted a long slow sigh. Sutrice expressed approval as the sigh deepened. 'Slowly . . .' she whispered.

Then Josef could smell it, faintly, warmly. Automatically his hand lifted and his fingertip trailed up the groove of her spine. Her sigh became a moan. A wave of strong scent drifted up and the cloth began to darken in a growing circle of moistness centred between her legs. As the circle expanded, the darkness turned visibly liquid as the wetness welled from below her belly. 'Slowly . . .' The girl's mouth was open; her vest was wet and the dark area on the sheet was still growing. He could see her breast through the wet cloth; the nipple was firm. When the edge of the patch reached where her hair lay on the cloth, the flow stopped. Sutrice removed her saturated fingers from between the girl's legs and turned her over. 'Camomile,' she whispered, inhaling deeply. Driven by the heat of the girl's body, the rising smell was hot and strong. Her wet vest was sticking to her breasts; the hair between her legs was glistening. Josef's cock was throbbing in its silk sheath.

'Expose yourself,' Sutrice instructed the girl. 'Pull your vest up.' The heavy wet breasts slipped out. 'Commissioner – kiss them,' she said. His head was buzzing. 'Kiss them like that, even once,' she smiled, 'and you are lost. Are you afraid?'

Josef kissed them one by one – the nipples – and the girl murmured, and the wetness was on his lips when he was taken from the room. He did not attempt to wipe it away. Neither did he lick it. 'You are lost, Commissioner,' whispered Sutrice as she stared into his eyes. 'And I wager you will never leave us.'

He was given a cell for the night. It had a bed, a chair, a writing-table and a view overlooking the lake. And there was a locked door opposite the bed. A tray of food and water had been left. The bed was not uncomfortable but still he found it impossible to settle. Propped up on it, he prepared to sit through the encroaching darkness. Then a nun bearing a lighted candle appeared at his door.

'The Lady Abbess wishes the Commissioner to join her,' she said shyly.

As Josef crossed the threshold of the Abbess's private quarters, he stepped into a harem. The air was perfumed. Erotic murals adorned the inner sanctum; nubile bodies draped the cushioned floor. Opulence and sexuality surrounded him. A girl, flushed with pleasure, was being shaved between the legs; another was being tongued. There were devices strewn about the room. The Abbess, in a grey, tent-like nightrobe, was ensconced serenely on a soft divan. On her lap lay a nude girl with her legs in the air and her smoothly depilated sex exposed. The Abbess was stroking it. Its lips were very prominent. The girl's breasts were rising and falling with her gently laboured breathing; a timeless, soft laziness pervaded this scene.

'Commissioner, tonight you are my guest,' the Abbess said cordially. 'Take your time; examine them; select one of your pleasing.'

Looking round the room, he recognised the girl who had been put to have her anus stretched. Then his gaze was drawn to a young woman standing nude against the wall. And he could not move – he had never seen a pose more voluptuously erotic – it was Vernel, whose belly he had held that very evening while her bottom was stimulated with the plunger. And now she was here, facing the wall, leaning against it with one hand. She was half turned, so one breast was exposed. But her stance was stilted; for her other hand held one buttock lifted open as a young nun filled the brass clyster from a bucket on the floor.

Josef turned again to the Abbess. The girl on her lap was swollen, not from any punishment, but simply from this prolonged pleasuring. The Abbess's fingers plied gently upon her bloated, pinkened labia. As the movements turned more searching, her belly lifted and her tucked-up legs jerked wantonly open.

'Samarkin has been with us five days. When she came here, she knew nothing of her body. We have had to teach her. She is kept bare down here so she understands her wetness – what it feels like, what it means.' The fingers gently pushed inside and lifted. The broad ridge that had already formed about the hood of skin now raised and widened; Samarkin murmured and her vulva opened. It was filled with wetness which was about to spill. 'Each night, I masturbate her until she falls asleep. Sometimes, this does not happen till the early morning ... But I see you are attracted by Vernel.'

He had heard her catch of breath. She was being clystered. Josef watched her – her eyes closed by pleasure, her open lips pressed to her forearm, her throat moving gently as she sucked the skin; her anus stretched around the shiny nozzle; the nun on the floor gently forcing the plunger in.

He moved round. Samarkin's head was fully back and her long silken hair was spread across the floor. There was a bulging leather dildo next to her; cream was oozing from its tip; her hand had fallen beside it, but she was oblivious of it. Her mouth was open; she was breathing rapidly. The Abbess had changed the movements of her hand. 'Look at her breasts,' she said, for she was watching Josef. It seemed her attention could be divided in this way; she did not need to concentrate entirely on what she was doing to the girl and yet what she was doing was so effective. 'Her breasts,' she repeated, cupping the vulva in her hand. And it was true that they had changed in shape, had become more gathered as though there was a straining, rising creature in each one. The nipples stood up on cones. Samarkin's knees jerked gently and she gasped. The fingers rubbed her rapidly one last time then the Abbess quickly lifted the swooning girl to her feet. She made her stand, legs apart, and hold her vulva open. 'She did not know how swollen she could become until I showed her. Few men ever take the time to know it.' The liquid from inside Samarkin started running down her legs. The Abbess took an oval hand-mirror. 'Hold your pinkle open.' Samarkin's labia projected, but they were soft and malleable, showing no resistance as her fingers held them open. The Abbess brought the mirror closer and they touched the glass, making the girl shudder. 'Take away your fingers.' The mirror was pressed upwards; the labia slid fully open; an elliptical patch was left on the glass. 'You are so wet, so wet.' Her fingers moved up Samarkin's shaking body. 'My robe will be dripping before we are done. And tonight is to be your vigil. Lift your chin. I want this gentleman to see your face – so beautiful, you are. Now hold your pinkle open; let your belly bulge – oh yes, so sweetly – let your tears of love drip out of you.' Josef still wore the cachet around his neck. He ached to take it off, to put it into Samarkin, to make her pleasure come. 'Commissioner – my novices are learning for you.' The Abbess looked proudly round the room. 'Now let us see how my girls prepare themselves for the soldiers' way of love.'

One of the girls promptly lay on her back then tucked-up her legs until her mouth and sex and anus were in line above one another. Then two others used cream-filled dildos on her.

'And what of Leah? How has she progressed?' The Abbess began to examine the novice who had had her anus stretched. It was swollen, reddened. The touching made her murmur. While she lay face down on the soft sheets, the Abbess gently pulled the thickened fold of tissue and asked about the sensation. Leah referred to it as 'burning'. The Abbess asked her to describe how the tutors played with her during penetration, how it had felt the first time she climaxed, and how many times it had happened. Even as she whispered her replies, Leah was lubricating on to the little chain that held her pubic lips together. Then the Abbess explained: 'While you are with us, you will take your pleasure only during anal penetration. Is that understood? And you must keep yourself always at the ready – the functions of the body must not be allowed to interfere; the access must at all times be kept free.' She caressed Leah's hair, then turning her on her side whispered: 'I understand that when they began with you, there was a problem.'

'Yes, Lady Abbess.'

'And how was it overcome?'

'With a clyster, Lady Abbess.'

'Then you know what must be done in future?'

'I must ask the gentleman if he wishes to give it.'

'And if he does not?'

'Then one of my sisters, or myself . . .'

'You have learned well. And I trust there is no impediment now to access?' The Abbess took Leah's moist clitoris gently in her fingers. She took a rough wooden dildo in her hand. 'I would prefer not to wet it, because I want you to feel it. I want it to hurt you – just a little. Shall I wet it?'

'No,' the girl murmured, 'I . . . I want to feel it,' then she shivered and turned away her face.

Her climax came before it could be fully inserted. The Abbess turned to Josef. 'Take Leah with you, for tonight. Or perhaps you would wish to take Vernel?'

Soon after that, when Josef took his leave and the Abbess drew open her door, two monks were blocking the corridor. Sianon was between them – Sianon whom he had all but forgotten. Her eyes threw Josef a frightened warning. She brushed against him as she was dragged away. The incident was over as quickly as that. He stood, pole-axed by the shock.

'Commissioner, you look pale – are you unwell?' the Abbess asked.

'A little,' Josef whispered. 'That girl . . .'

'You know her?'

'No.' He shook his head, for there was a strange, eager expression in the Abbess's eyes.

* * *

162

That night, he took no one to his cell. He sat on his bed, listening, awaiting his chance to steal out secretly through the darkened corridors and go looking for Sianon. As he waited he relived the meeting over and over in his mind. Surely it was not a chance encounter? But there was something else buried in those recollections – a memory of the extraordinary hardness and fullness of her breasts, their heavy weight, but of something yet more. Then it came to him what it was: dark oily patches on her vest, darkness only round the nipples. And some of it had touched his hand, a milky wetness on his fingers that had brushed against her through the cloth.

When the midnight bell sounded, he was back in the corridor. He could hear no sound from the Abbess's room, so he crept cautiously on. There were several ways Sianon could have been taken – stairways both up and down. Josef tried the doors along the main passageway. The third one opened quietly and he heard a gasp.

There was a man – not a monk – on a chair. A nearly nude girl was on his lap. His hand was down her knickers. They were pure soft white. He was kissing her slowly. But she was gasping into his mouth, climaxing. Another man was watching. The knickers bulged as the hand moved about inside them; they were turning yellow and wet; the saffron stain spread out as she was climaxing; the urine started running down her leg.

The man pulled the wet yellow knickers down. The watcher dropped to his knees in front of her. The other one's wetted hand closed round her breast; her belly bulged forwards. Josef saw the moist thickened lips of her sex being opened, saw the droplets of wet clinging to the pubic hairs, saw the brass nose of the clyster start to enter. Then he backed away, turned and Sister Sutrice was staring at him. At her waist was a ring heavy with keys. There was no hint of surprise at his presence and she was carrying a bottle of wine. She closed the door quietly.

'Commissioner,' her tone carried mild contempt, 'at this hour, curfew prevails. I thought to find you in your cell.' Then her voice softened. 'I came to offer you a nightcap.'

163

She pressed the bottle gently into his hand. Then seeing him glance towards the broad door at the end of the corridor, she deliberately moved across to bar the way. 'The chapel is out of bounds. There is a vigil. May I escort you back to your cell?'

He had a choice – to risk a disturbance or to follow meekly. Too late, when she had gone, he heard the key being turned to lock his door.

13

Milk and Honey

The tiered candelabrum that Dom Gregor set in place
threw softly wavering light upon the chair in the choir-stall
where Sianon was displayed. Far below, in the dark body
of the chapel, a river of clustered points of light kept vigil
for a young, punished novice fastened to the altar. The
novice-mistress crept in quietly and stood behind Sianon's
chair.

'What news, Sutrice?' the Abbess asked her.

'He will not be going anywhere, my lady. I saw him
drink the doctored wine.'

'And he does not seem to understand about the ring?'

The novice-mistress shook her head.

'Then we shall continue to amuse him until the Perquisitor's return.' Wiping her hands, the Abbess said gently:
'Sutrice – attend to her. She is crying.' Then she drew her
cloak about her nightgown and departed.

Sister Sutrice, now half in shadow, leaning on the balcony, faced Sianon. On the wall beside her were the proud
instruments of pain and truth. Dom Gregor and the young
monk, having placed Sianon as Sutrice had redirected,
moved back.

'Leave us for a little while. I shall recall you.' There was
a controlled, frightening softness in her voice.

The special chair was of polished solid wood, with
patches of cushioning restricted to the centres of the panels
the seat, the broad armrests, the curved, short back, and
the distinctive ledge-like headrest that projected behind.
The cushioning was worn and discoloured from use.

Sianon was alone with Sutrice.

'Put your head back.'

She stared up through tear-filled eyes at Sutrice, framed

against the arched stone ceiling and haloed by the glow from the candles.

'You like her – Anaisa?' Sutrice asked gently. 'The Abbess?'

'Yes.'

'Is that why you denounced him?'

'*No!* It was not I –'

'And what of me – do you like me too?' Her smile was ironic.

'I . . . I . . .'

'You do not know me, do you?' Sutrice sighed. 'Oh, but you will, Sianon. Lift your vest. And put your hands back on the armrests . . . Your tutors have almost plucked you bare already. How long is it now – a week?'

The novice-mistress drew back to collect something from the wall. 'You know what this is?'

Sianon shook her head.

'It goes between your legs – a sling. It's made of horse-hair. I can make you wear it. And these,' she held up a collection of small, barbed metal balls, 'I might have them put inside you.' Sutrice crouched down and stared at Sianon. 'Why did Anaisa keep you for two days? What happened with her?'

'She . . . She made me share her bed with a girl she was pleasuring. She hardly touched me. She put a smooth stick inside me –'

'Where?'

'In my bottom, just inside the rim. It had something on it, something that made the desire come strongly. And each time the other girl was brought on to pleasure, my breasts were played with and the stick was turned.'

'What else did she do?'

'She talked to me. She told me what was happening to my breasts and what else would be done.'

Sutrice pushed Sianon's vest tightly under her distended breasts and held it there. It was the first time Sutrice had actually touched her; Sianon was beginning to cream between the legs as well as through her breasts. Her labia bare of pubic hair now, quickly turned wet. Sutrice spread open Sianon's sex and the feeling intensified, the feeling of creaming. She lifted back Sianon's vest, exposing the heavy waxy secretions on her bulbous nipples.

'She let you suck her?'

Sianon was dizzy with excitement at the recollection – the strong, musky smell, the barely audible moans, the lady Abbess coming in her mouth, the warm loving fingers in Sianon's hair.

'She was like my mistress,' Sianon whispered. Sutrice asked about her; Sianon told.

'But I am much younger and more demanding,' Sutrice then said. She stretched back the skin of Sianon's breasts, and the milk squirted and ran like teardrops down her side.

Then Sutrice moved away again to look down at the novice in the chapel.

In her breasts, Sianon was experiencing the sensations that came upon her each morning when her tutors began the day's ritual, and she would wake already aroused. Dom Gregor had explained that it would be so. He was the older master. He had white wispy hair and a craggy, fissured face. His skin was thick and freckled, and hard against Sianon's tender lips when Sianon kissed him. For she was allowed to kiss him sometimes on the lips when her arousal came on strongly. Gregor permitted it, without his responding, but even the warmth of his breath, like new bread from the oven, made Sianon glow from the happiness she felt inside. First she would be given the bitter drink that helped to make her breast-milk come. Then when Gregor touched her with her legs apart, the pleasure would swell inside as if to drown her, pushing in her throat until it overwhelmed her and Sianon would be crying, on the bed, crying tears of pleasure, weeping her arousal from between her legs, wetting his fingers. And he would anoint her body with it, the sign of the tau, upon her engorged nipples and her lips, and gently murmur, *'furor uterinus.'*

The young monk would be watching, learning. While Dom Gregor slept, he would keep vigil over Sianon and maintain the stimulation of her breasts. She would sometimes wake in the night, the ache of pleasure between her legs, and his soft young fingers would be inside her. She would be yearning for release. His penis would be hard; she would feel its hotness through the silk. She would want his bare flesh in her mouth, but he would pull away and tie her hands and rope her by the ankles, then gently work her nipples till the pressure from inside her made them leak. Every pleasure that she underwent, these two men controlled.

By the morning of the fifth day, she had been depilated by gradual plucking, to the extent that most of her labia were bare. The hairs were removed from her bottom upwards. She was constantly masturbated during plucking. When she was near to climax, her clitoris would be held by Gregor. Her secretions would by then be thick, and his fingers would keep her on the point of slippage. The tiny pricks of pain as the hairs were taken out would stab like needles in her pubic lips; her prepuce would be held back; her clitoris would be bursting. While she was in this state, Gregor would ask her to recount to him stories of the spankings in the chapel, of the novice-mistress, and of the girls Sianon most desired. She would be encouraged through pleasure to divulge her innermost sexual thoughts. The names would trip from Sianon's tongue – Vernel, Roslin and Castyrian – and the memories of their lewdness would seduce her. The sweet prickling pains would bathe her pubic lips, and her clitoris would want to burst between his softly squeezing fingers. Then the deep ache would come to Sianon, as if a wet soft hand were probing her womb, and she would feel her sex begin to contract and her wetness running down her bottom.

After each session of depilation, the remaining pubic hairs would be laved back with a wetted brush to make the bare place feel to her more extensive. Then she would be smacked there, on her pubic lips and on her anus. The younger monk would use his fingers. The older would support Sianon's head and let her kiss him. His craggy face would stay immobile and Sianon would be burning with arousal once again.

Gregor would compliment her on the sounds her naked

sex made during smacking. Then he would at some point make her kneel up, and the collection vessel, a fine, shaped open-lipped glass, would be put between her legs. Her labia could fit inside the rim. By this time, she would be lubricating freely, and her clear sexual liquid would slide into the glass. She would have to offer the glass for them to drink from. Gregor used to say she left an aftertaste like honey. When he had drunk of it she would be dressed. They might wash her first or leave her wet as a preparation for the trials and pleasures of the day.

It was memories such as these that kept Sianon sexually excited as she lay open on the chair, her breasts and belly leaking, awaiting Sutrice.

Sutrice came back. She opened a small trinket box that was inlaid with mother-of-pearl. Inside it was a collection of thorns. She said that she would later use these on Sianon when she was more aroused; that she would push them through the skin of Sianon's labia and nipples, then masturbate her with the thorns in place. 'Your tutors have been too gentle with you; I fear they do not understand.' She stretched the skin of Sianon's nipple, and the feeling came inside Sianon's breast, like a soft sexual sneeze, and again her nipple squirted. 'Get up,' Sutrice said.

All Sianon wore was the stained cotton vest and the soft white cotton boot-socks. Sutrice took her down the wooden staircase from the choir-stall to the floor of the chapel.

It was dark except for the double row of candles down the aisle and the larger clusters round the altar. A group of novices were keeping vigil; two of them were at the altar, standing in front of the girl. Sianon was led up the steps of a side altar which was in darkness. 'We must not distract her,' Sutrice whispered, looking through the bars.

Sianon recognised this novice; she had seen her often at the spankings. The Abbess herself used to bring her and afterwards take her away. But now it seemed she had been given to Sutrice. And tonight the punishment was different.

The girl's lips were cracked and dry. A coil of leather lay between her legs and glistened across her belly. She had been plucked completely bare. Her legs were in the air; they had been fastened to a vee-shaped frame that had been placed against the altar. The insides of her thighs were shaking. There were no marks on or even near her vulva yet her vulva was more swollen than any Sianon had seen; it was small, but despite this, intensely swollen. It was as though it had erupted like an overblown pink flower, all the petals bloated and pushed out, standing separately, soaked with the liquid being slowly given up from inside her. The innermost surface of the flesh was on the outside. The entrance was constricted by the swelling. She almost appeared as if she had three sets of labia, a tiny extra pair forming wings about the clitoris. Her clitoris remained hooded, but oh, how thin and stretched was its covering; it was like a thick red pellet trapped in a tube of translucent skin.

Sianon knew the cause; the instrument lay beside the girl on a pedestal. Her labia had been treated with an unguent to make them swell. Sianon had once seen it being done to a novice. It had made Sianon feel very funny in her belly, to watch this happen. The novice had come to climax without the need for touching. She had stood there, trying to keep still, trying to keep her hands at her sides, trying to keep her thighs apart. But all the time, she was climaxing, and everyone watching her knew it. They wouldn't let her sit until long after it had happened.

But this girl was being kept in arousal. Perhaps this was the purpose of the vigil.

Sianon's gaze turned to the novice-mistress. Not much older than Sianon, yet she filled her with a dreadful excitement; there was something evil about her eyes. Sianon could not look at her without thinking of the ritual spankings that took place in the hall adjoining the chapel each afternoon. Sutrice directed them. The novices were assembled naked or in their vests. Then Sutrice would walk slowly among them; it was as if she could read every transgression in their frightened eyes. She would select one, look at her from back and front, have her lift her arms. Then she would ask her intimate questions. Sometimes the girl would be taken aside for more private questioning. There would be no pattern or reason in the original selection; everyone was vulnerable, everyone felt guilty, and frightened of betrayal. When this happened, Sutrice would treat the implicated girl with great severity, casting her in front of the others like a wrongdoer, flinging her to the floor. Then she would be punished at length by the monks while the others watched with bated breath. And Sutrice's eyes would be circling the room – perhaps selecting for tomorrow.

A thick belt would be buckled round the girl's back, under her arms and above her breasts. It would be drawn tight. Then she would be suspended by the belt against the wall; it had a heavy brass link that fastened over a hook. Her buttocks would then be spanked by two monks standing one on each side, using leather belts and delivering blows alternately. The procedure would continue for a long time, but there were interludes when her feet were allowed to rest on stools set wide apart while she was masturbated. Then the spanking would resume.

Sometimes she would be supported sitting the wrong way round on a plain wooden chair, her breasts and sex pushed through the open back. The exposed parts would then be spanked. Or she might be bent across a stool, her knees tucked up, her sex projecting. The punishment would progress from her buttocks to her sex as her arousal mounted.

While this was going on, other monks with small light straps would circulate among the novices, snapping at their naked legs, sometimes making them crouch or kneel with sex lips open, and playing with them from behind.

The young novice now on the altar was being treated again. Sianon shuddered; but she felt pleasure as she watched. The feeling frightened her.

Sutrice put her hand round Sianon's neck, at the front, just holding her, while the treatment was completed. Sianon's nipples were up, her clitoris was out between her legs. The tip of the plunger was taken out; the girl was already moaning.

171

Sianon was taken back into the gloom at the side of the chapel. She heard the gasps, saw the legs kick against their bindings, glimpsed the fire in Sutrice's eyes, then felt her shaking body taken by the shoulders, turned, and her throbbing nipples being pressed and squeezed, then pushed against the freezing marble stonework. She felt her anus being played with, her knees being opened, and her hot wet sex contracting round a bulge in the ice-cold, sculpted stone. She felt the lips moving down her naked back, the tongue-tip slowly licking her running sweat then, so precisely, probing her anus, rimming the flesh, which opened as her labia sucked and slipped against the polished stone.

Sutrice stood up. She pushed something cold and metallic into Sianon's bottom. At first, Sianon thought it was a clyster, and she tensed, waiting for the cool, deep pleasure. But it was to keep her anus stretched while she was walking. Sutrice took her back onto the main altar and to the tethered girl, whose sex had become even larger. The clitoris had extruded through its tube. A slender hand was between her legs, attempting to push the coil of leather inside her.

'Her name is Samarkin,' said Sutrice. 'You may have her tomorrow night – but you must treat her rightly.'

In the corridor outside, Sutrice stopped. There was an intense look in her eye – desire and domination intermixed. It put a sweet terror into Sianon. She wondered why she had been chosen. Sutrice put her hands – both hands – between Sianon's legs while she kissed her. The kiss aroused Sianon; the pressure came in her breasts. She felt her cotton-booted feet sliding open across the smooth tiles and she felt Sutrice's fingers pulling at the metal stretcher in her bottom.

Sutrice told Sianon she would make her climax during urination. She took her down a spiral staircase, but kept stopping on the way to play with her. There was a thick rope down the central column that she made Sianon hold while Sutrice stood below and behind her, looking up between her legs. She said she liked Sianon open. She put her fingers inside her; they slipped without restriction because

Sianon was lubricating freely; they pressed up against Sianon's bladder, making the first feelings happen, setting the seeds of the prolonged pleasures to come.

The soft whispers of the monks echoed through the low arches of the basement vaults. A young, clothed novice was sitting on a wooden table; she had not seen Sutrice and Sianon enter; she was watching the nude girl on the marble slab. Nearby was a plain wooden bar on supports above the floor. Across the room a heavier beam stretched across an alcove. This part of the vaults was warmed by the heat of a large fire against one wall. Sutrice took Sianon to it. The fireplace was of intricately sculpted stone. There were tongs and pokers and pots beside it. On a table next to it was a row of moulded yellow candles shaped like cocks. The area was lit by candelabra and row upon row of these candles, some having burnt longer, others shorter.

Sianon looked at the patterns of wax running down them. She looked at the bottles and jugs on the table where the novice sat. Then she looked at the girl on the slab. The monks had turned her round and sat her up to drink, but had kept her legs open. Sianon could see she had been played with. It looked as if her sex had been oiled. When she had finished the mugful, one of the monks refilled it by pouring in a small quantity of wine then topping it to the brim with water. Then they administered this heavily watered wine by mouth.

Sutrice brought a little of it for Sianon. It was very sour and astringent. She waited until Sianon had finished. 'There is no hurry with her,' she said of the girl. 'She need drink only as deeply as she wishes. But the thirst remains, however much she swallows, and then the need comes quickly. Even so, some we have to help.' She pointed. Hanging from the fireplace was a very thin brass tube with a nozzle at the tip.

The girl on the slab had been opened and made to sit forward, with her spread, oiled sex against the polished stone. One of the monks dipped his fingers into a pot of honey-coloured paste which began to melt as he put it into her. Sutrice stood close by Sianon. 'She takes a long time,

173

this one. That is why I like her.' Sianon trembled. 'She will smell like myrrh when she pisses.' Sutrice looked at Sianon. 'Oh . . .' Then she turned her round, her back to the warm stones by the fireplace. 'Are you jealous – now, so soon – that I like her?' She went over to the girl. The monks moved away. The girl swooned back in Sutrice's arms, and Sutrice kissed her, more deeply than she had kissed Sianon, pulling at her nipples with a gentle milking action. But no milk came out of her. The monks went over to the novice at the table and began rubbing their hands softly sideways over her clothed belly and breasts as she sat there. One began to remove her knickers; the other selected a fresh candle and warmed it by the fire, but when he went back with it to the novice, Sutrice said: 'Not yet.' She was feeding the other girl more drink. 'Attend to this one. Put her to the bar.'

Then she came back to Sianon. The girl's belly looked slightly swollen. She was lifted gently and helped to bend over the bar. Then her wrists were fastened to her ankles. One monk played with her; the other smacked her with his bare hand. They took turns. It took many minutes, during which Sutrice alternately watched the proceedings and paid attention to Sianon, plying her with watered wine and kisses. She showed her the beam across the alcove where she would be made to sit, and the hook above it where her wrists would be fastened, then she brought her back to the table where the novice was sitting and began to play with her.

She was about to take the metal stretcher out of Sianon when the girl who was bent over the bar began to pee. Sianon was leaning against the table. Her anus immediately tightened against the lip of the stretcher and Sutrice had to wait. The girl squirted – it started during the smacking, which was immediately stopped. Both monks began to play with her at the same time. She was still head-down, her wrists tied to her ankles.

Her urine trickled down her inner thighs, slowly, then it flooded. She cried out in pleasure. 'It is the spurting,' Sutrice whispered, 'the sweet, hot spurting against the clitoris that makes it happen. And then urine flowing where it shouldn't keeps it on.'

Sianon moaned; Sutrice's wine-soaked fingertip was dabbing at her clitoris; her anus was in spasm round the stretcher. She was on the brink of coming, her cheek against the table, where she had collapsed. The girl was still urinating, her sex held open, pulsing, the liquid now running onto the floor.

'Come round,' said Sutrice quickly to the novice beside Sianon. 'Open your legs . . .' She lifted her and drew her knickers quickly down. To Sianon, she said, 'Kiss it.' The knickers were round one ankle and the lubrication was already trickling. Sutrice held Sianon's hair back while she drank it. 'Do not suck, just let it run into your mouth,' warned Sutrice. 'She must not come to climax yet. And nor must you.' She pulled her off the novice and took her to the tethered girl. 'See what I do with the ones I like. Kneel down,' she said to Sianon. 'Now lick it.' The girl immediately came to a second climax. Sutrice then instructed the monks to take her away. They carried her with her legs still open.

Sutrice stripped Sianon of her vest, stood her against the beam and masturbated her. But she did not remove her cotton boots. She put the novice in a chair, leaving her clothed but bare of knickers. One of the monks had returned. He stayed with the novice but did not touch her. Sutrice turned Sianon round. Sianon was ashamed to pee: the swollen feeling was there inside her but she was ashamed to do it in front of the girl and the monk. Had Sutrice been the only one, Sianon could have done it. She liked being played with by Sutrice.

The beam was higher than the bar; it pressed under her breasts as she stood there. There was a dense cloth padding on it that was heavily stained. Sutrice removed the stretcher from Sianon's bottom then ducked under the beam and appreared on the other side. She began to touch Sianon's breasts – the waxy coating of seeped milk that had congealed around her nipples. 'No – keep your legs open,' Sutrice whispered. She gave her more to drink. Sianon's head tilted back to take it, but her breasts stayed on the beam. 'Let your belly out,' said Sutrice. She reached underneath and held it, gently squeezed it. Sianon moaned. When she had finished the cupful, Sutrice tied her wrists together with a silk band. She had the monk assist Sianon onto the beam, but it was Sutrice who hung Sianon's wrists on the hook on the ceiling. Then she told Sianon this:

'I want you to control it. You may beg to be allowed to piss. But do not let it come until I give permission. Then when I say so – you stop. I shall play with you and keep you drinking.'

Sianon was suspended with her booted feet a short way above the floor. Sutrice had climbed a step-stool and sat sideways in front of her on the beam. The novice was watching – her habit had been lifted to allow her naked legs and bottom to touch the seat.

Sianon was near to climax. 'Lean back,' Sutrice said. She kept playing with her clitoris. Sianon gasped. 'Do it,' Sutrice said, 'just a little – wet the beam.' Sianon spurted. 'Again . . . Oh, shhh . . . Too much.' Sutrice offered her the cup. While she drank, Sutrice milked her clitoris. Sianon moaned.

'Oh – please?' she whispered.

'Finish it.'

The tip of Sutrice's finger pushed against her tiny hole. Sianon shuddered. Hot urine splashed briefly on Sutrice's fingers, made them slippy when they played with Sianon. Sianon moaned and pleaded. Sutrice spread her legs; another little spurt came quickly. The monk moved over to watch. The flow had already stopped. The small puddle of pale yellow soaked into the padding, which was warm on Sianon's bare labia. Sutrice climbed down. She dabbed Sianon dry. Then she put a folded fresh cloth between her legs. 'Hold it in,' she said to Sianon, then turned to the monk. 'Give her some more to drink.'

She went to the novice and began touching her between the legs until the novice began to swoon. Then she selected a cock-shaped candle, cut off the burning end to leave a moderate stump and put this into the novice. She made her sit up with her habit lifted and the balls of the candle balanced on the edge of the chair.

After giving her another drink, the monk had moved Sianon back along the beam, so she hung by her wrists, with her breasts thrown forwards and the weight of her body pressing against her bladder.

Sutrice returned with a crop, which she hung on the hook where Sianon's wrists were tied. She lifted open Sianon's leg. A small mark was on the surface of the cloth; its underside was yellow from urine pressed out of the padding. She had the monk hold Sianon's leg open and bent up. 'Now again, when I tell you – just a spurt.' Sutrice began the slow masturbation, one hand on Sianon's belly, lifting it, the other between her legs, rubbing the labia and the clitoris with the fingers flat. The feeling came between Sianon's legs, as if a thick cold needle was being inserted into her bladder. 'Not yet – when I tell you,' Sutrice whispered. Sianon felt the rubbing fingers suddenly turn slippy, but they did not stop their slow rotation and their gentle stimulation of her bladder. Her climax was building. She bit her lip. 'Not yet, my beauty . . . Get the ice.'

While it was being put into Sianon's sex, Sutrice's enquiring hands explored her, smoothed upwards under her aching swollen breasts and under her arms, then down again between her legs, against the sensitive depilated places. Then as the pressure mounted, she held Sianon between the legs, cupping her vulva, rubbing her clitoris with her thumb, pulling her nipples gently – not enough to make the let-down come about, just enough to make her ache. When Sianon shivered and spurted in her hand, Sutrice made her lean back. Then she took the crop and whipped the facing surfaces of her thighs, three strokes to each thigh, before she opened her and played with her very gently until all the ice had melted and flowed out. Sianon began to shudder and move. 'Sit up.' Sutrice held a thumb against the tiny hole. 'Let it come,' she whispered. 'Let it flood.' Sianon moaned and hung back on her arms; the thumb kept pressing. The first squirt sprayed against her leg; the second against her clitoris. Sutrice pressed harder and milked it with the other hand; the spray went everywhere; Sianon was coming. Sutrice took her thumb away, but kept masturbating Sianon with hands now bathed in the stream of warm pee broken only by the stabs of Sianon's climax and the wiping of the liquid over Sianon's legs and belly. 'Sit up,' Sutrice said again. One of Sianon's cotton boots had filled with pee. Sutrice left her sitting in the warm wetness soaked into the pad and went to suck the girl.

Sianon watched, breasts aching to be milked, legs burning, open, sex still aroused. The girl started to climax when the candle was being taken out; she came to completion in Sutrice's mouth. The monk was holding her under the arms. Sutrice pulled back. 'Keep her open,' Sutrice told him. 'Tie her knees back. Leave her in this chair. Use a stream of liquid on it. Do not let her climax again if you can avoid it.'

She returned to Sianon and kissed her shuddering belly, still moist with urine. She opened her with her thumbs, then rubbed her finger up inside her, bringing down the last trickles of her pee. 'I shall be your dominatrix. You will be my slave.' The slick wet fingers pumped at Sianon's plump teats; Sianon looked at Sutrice in acquiescence; the letdown happened; the climax started in her breasts; coalescing beads of blue-white milk appeared on Sianon's nipples.

Sutrice did not drink it. She let it run down Sianon's body. But when Sianon had been lifted down, she opened her labia and fitted the hair sling between them.

She took her outside in the dark beyond the cloister walls, making her walk, then run, then pushing her against the wall of the round tower and masturbating her with the wet hair sling. Sutrice held Sianon upright. Her climax came harshly; again the let-down happened, and her climax came again. And again Sutrice did not drink from Sianon's breasts; she let the milk well and trickle. She told her she would take her to bed. Then she put her hand down inside the hair sling between Sianon's legs.

While they stood there, Sutrice's hand inside Sianon,

Sianon's bulging naked breasts shedding slow warm milk from her nipples, three men emerged from the foot of the tower and took the path towards the ferry landing. One was hefty, head and shoulders above the others. A stumbling, naked girl was in their midst. She had collars round her wrists and ankles. The girl was Iroise.

14

Vernel

Josef opened his eyes. He was sprawled across the bed. The cup of wine lay spilled beside him. He must have fallen asleep with it in his hand. But it was morning and the door to the corridor stood ajar.

Then he heard a splash of water: someone was beyond the inner door opposite the bed. He got up quietly, opened it and peered round it.

The room – a bathroom – was empty, but the bath had been filled, and towels made ready. The surface of the water was still moving. Another door on the far side led from the bathroom. Josef tried it; it opened to a far more comfortable room than his cell. Again there was no one there. But this second room had three exits: whoever had filled the bath must have left through one of them. He glanced around. The place resembled a study; there were extensive bookshelves, a heavy writing-desk, chairs, a *prie-dieu* and a large oak table. But there was also a bed, ancient, wooden-posted, its headboard covered with ornately curlicued carvings. The centrepiece was a projecting polished phallus.

Moving closer, Josef stared at the device. The varnish had paled along its length; in places it was completely worn away. He recalled all too vividly its use in the Training Cloister – the way the novice had been encouraged to take it in her mouth while she was being played with. But he imagined other things too, other juxtapositions of naked girl and phallus, legs being opened, toes clinging to the knobs in the carvings. There were grooves around the posts – marks where securing ropes had been anchored. Again he looked at the phallus; the paleness darkened rapidly near the base, where the last of its length had never been fully taken.

He opened a drawer in one of the several cabinets by the bed, revealing instruments of penetration and sexual pleasure. There were clyster syringes, creams, gold trinkets. As he looked down, the black Talisur ring glistened on his finger; he thought of Reikz, perhaps here in this very snuggery with Thuline, beginning her training. Images of power and perverse sexuality inveigled Josef's mind.

After a while, he retraced his steps and stared at the bath. He wondered about the meaning of these preparations: why had the door to this room been opened for him, if not for a meeting, perhaps unauthorised and secret? Would it be Sianon? The only way to find out would be to co-operate.

As soon as the warm, scented bath-water came into contact with his skin, he turned unaccountably tired; he might have dozed. Then, hearing a sudden sound, he jumped, making the water overflow onto the tiles.

A chair with a robe draped over it had mysteriously appeared beside the bath. The water was now tepid. The door to the study stood fully open. Sounds drifted through, shuffling, flicking sounds of pages being turned, and occasional sighs and murmurs.

Josef stepped soundlessly from the bath, ignored the robe, covered himself with a towel and tiptoed to the open doorway. And there he held his breath.

He had never watched a woman do it on her own. But this was no ordinary woman: it was Vernel – mistress of erotic poses; Vernel whom he had watched perform anilingus on Thuline; Vernel who had leant nude against the wall, awaiting the clyster; Vernel of the tight, deep-cleft buttocks; Vernel of the pure blue eyes, of the freckled face, of the straight, blonde, silky hair; Vernel whom, so light, he could surely lift without effort and place upon his lap. Josef recalled the Abbess's words: *She is being trained to anal pleasure*. And he recalled every soft insertion, every sweet gasp of arousal.

She was kneeling on the chair, nude but for her knickers, and nude in essence for they had been pulled down to her knees. Her soft, blue-grey vest had been taken off and lay on the table. Even from behind he could see her hand between her legs, her fingers moving, her bare sex lifting. Delicious irregularities crept into her breathing.

Her breasts were on the table, in front of the angled heavy book whose pages Josef could not see but Vernel's available fingers turned at intervals while her eyes darted like frightened butterflies over the pictures: he could tell they were pictures from the immediacy of their effect upon the movements of her fingers, and by the sudden interruption of her breathing. A moment later, she moaned and pulled her hand away and sank forwards on the table, her knees thrust open, but her eyes still on the picture and her body slowly heaving. Josef did not know whether her climax had actually come or been deliberately prevented. Then he realised that her gaze had left the page and was on him – so innocently, it seemed. She didn't move; she was still kneeling, legs open, her knickers round her knees. Her gaze was melting his insides.

Then she spoke. Addressing him as 'Commissioner' she asked how she might please him.

A soft shiver went through him as he moved into the room. He thought of Iroise – on that first night, she had asked this same thing. And he thought of Vernel exciting herself in readiness for a man she had scarcely met, because that man had power and influence.

'Who sent you to me?' he asked her gently.

'The Lady Abbess.'

'Vernel,' he said cautiously, 'do you know a novice called Sianon?'

Vernel nodded eagerly, then her expression changed. 'She is very pretty.' She knelt straighter, making her breasts more prominent.

'And if I wanted to see her?' It was the wrong thing for him to have said. Vernel's face dropped. 'Just to –'

'My lord must ask the Abbess . . . Do I not please him?' Her beautiful blue gaze met his. And again they were the very words Iroise had used. But Vernel was unafraid, unashamed. Hauling herself up to a sitting position on the table, she made no attempt to bring her legs together to hide the clear evidence of what she had been doing.

Josef looked at the open book on the lectern. It was tall and leather-bound, the pages heavy. The left-hand page was covered in a perfect illuminated angular script which he could not decipher. The right-hand page was a painting so detailed that it looked like a real scene clipped by a Gothic frame. There was a man's jewelled hand resting on a girl's inner thigh, encouraging it open. Every hair upon her pubes was picked out individually as a fine black line. A woman's hand was on her other thigh. The skin was drawn back from her clitoris. Her labia were stretched and swollen around the head of a thick-bodied snake.

The geometric mosaic of brightly coloured scales was cut off precisely by the line of contact with the swallowing pubic lips. The woman supported the snake with one hand; the other helped stretch the girl; the unconsumed coils writhed off the picture.

Leaning on the table, Josef turned the page, expecting in the next picture to see just the tip of a tail dangling between the girl's half-closed pubic lips.

But instead he saw an oblique view of the girl stretched on a divan on her side, turned away, one knee bent, the head of the snake still inside her, its body stretched up between her legs, across her belly and between her breasts, her arms around it, clasping it in an embrace. The woman – a fine lady – was sitting behind her on the divan with a second snake in readiness.

'Please, Commissioner – you must tell me what you want,' Vernel whispered.

'Turn the page,' Josef said. Vernel twisted on to her side, adopting the attitude of the girl in the picture, exposing the eye of her bottom. Josef sat behind Vernel on the table. He could not see her face – her eyes – as she stared at the new picture.

The head of the second snake was sliding up the girl's anus, which, itself like a snake's disarticulated jaw, had expanded to permit it. Josef now felt sure that the subject of the image could not be real. But this did not make it any less arousing. He thought of what he had seen being done to Vernel with the plunger. The Abbess had said that it would sensitise the inside of her bottom. What was she feeling as she watched the girl's anus being stretched by a snake?

She was trembling, breathing quickly. Josef drew her knickers from her ankles and turned her onto her back. He cast aside his towel. She licked her lips at him; her legs sank open. Her depilation was complete, her pubes completely smooth, perfectly naked, slightly red. Her sex looked tight, the outer lips closed, the inner lips squeezed out to a round-edged rim, like an extruded tube of liquid. Josef knelt on the chair and split the tube. He let the two halves touch his naked belly. Their moisture made them cling. She asked distractedly about the pleasing.

'The plunger,' he said slowly, softly, fighting back his excitement. 'I saw it being used.' He felt her clitoris pulse against his belly.

'We have them here, my lord,' she whispered.

'Show me.'

She got up. 'Wait – put your vest on.' He wanted her the way he had seen the novices in the Training Cloister. And he wanted to take his time. The soft woollen cloth was lifted by the strong push of her breasts. The vest draped short, its thick hem suspended high above her belly. Below it was a space. Josef put his fingers up through it and found her nipples. They made hard shapes through the cloth. The naked hollow of her navel faced upwards, inviting the tip of a finger to fill the cup. He lifted her vest above her breasts and asked her to hold it there. Her breasts protruded, pale of skin, dark and thick of nipple.

'Go over to the mirror,' he said. 'Face it.' It was a full-length mirror with a leather-clad level bar in front of it near the middle. He brought across a chair and sat behind her. Then he made her move her knees apart. 'Keep your vest up,' he whispered. There was something about her arms thus occupied, that aroused him. 'When the monks play with you – do you like it?'

'Yes, Commissioner.'

'Move closer to the mirror . . . What do they make you do?'

'Anything,' she whispered thickly. 'Everything.'

'They have sex with you?'

She whispered: 'They are not supposed to. They are only supposed to train me and to play –'

'But they do?' he said urgently.

She nodded, lips trembling.

'How?' he asked. 'How do they do it with you.'

'In my bottom . . .' Vernel whispered. He moved her forwards till her knees touched the glass.

'And you like it there?'

'Yes.'

'Because the Abbess has trained you that way?'

'Yes.' Her eyes were upon him through the glass.

He had to know about this pleasure. He made her straighten up. Then he gently prised open the cheeks of her bottom. There was no visible sign there of the way she had been used, no swelling. They must have taken care with her. The wrinkled skin was warm pink. She murmured when he touched it. 'Keep your vest up,' he reminded her. He could see every bone in her spine. He moved to one side so he could see her breasts reflected in the mirror. She was leaning on the bar. While he touched her anus, he watched her belly trembling as the pleasure deepened. Her inner lips had swollen. Their reflection was visible below the bar. They appeared so vulnerable, so sexual, because they were so completely naked. He knew now why the novices were always depilated: everything was visible, everything was made sensitive, there was nothing to obstruct the administering of pleasure or punishment to that perfect sexual part. He made her bend until her breasts and elbows rested on the glass while he examined her in detail.

There were no hairs below her anus, none, not even fine ones. It formed a deep, smooth, slippy warm pink well. When he touched it again, she moaned, her hips angled suggestively to one side, her breasts slid down the glass and the urge to go inside her was nearly overwhelming.

He let one hand move round the front, retrieving her nipples, warming them after the glass's chill, then moving down to stroke her inner lips. When he stroked her anus

185

with his thumb, she immediately became excited again. He could feel her flesh responding, wanting to open.

Her breathing changed when he asked about smacking – had they smacked her, did they do it routinely? Her anus pouted to a dimpled nose; she was pushing, wanting to be entered there; the skin around the tight crater was hard and raised. He tickled this skin; her anus stayed pouted; he wanted to wet it. He could smell it on his fingers, a slight, definite animal smell and it aroused him. He turned Vernel around. Her nipples had engorged. He sucked them and left them wet. She looked as if the jelly of her breasts had been drawn by the stimulation up into the teats, which had fattened and sat upon her breasts like rounded, pointed-tipped dollops of hot flesh.

Her belly jerked; a spasm had come through her and her knees were giving way. Josef continued petting her anus from underneath. The skin sheathing her clitoris was bulging; her hands were tightly gripped about the raised hem of her vest. 'The monks do this with you?' he asked.

Again Vernel answered, 'Yes.'

'And they clyster you?'

She shivered. 'Each morning and each night.'

There was a soft buzzing in his ears. 'Go on . . .'

'They make me kneel up on a table. My arms are fastened to straps suspended from the ceiling. It is in case I pass out.'

'They hurt you?'

She shook her head.

'Then what?'

'One stands in front of me and plays with me. The other feeds in the clyster from behind. Each time it is empty, he refills it. The first one plays with me and puts things into me at the front. I am forbidden to bring my knees together. Ohh . . .' She closed her eyes. 'It is so strong a feeling. You cannot stop it; they oil the muscle to keep it slippy; you cannot stop the clyster going up inside. And when it pumps me . . . Ohhh!'

The shudder travelled up her thighs. Her labia were wet as she spoke of these things. Josef slid his fingers up her sex. Her legs stiffened. He continued to rub her anus softly. His cock bulged at the thought of putting the nose of a clyster syringe inside her and squeezing the plunger while she was so aroused.

'The Abbess mentioned soldiers,' he said.

'Sometimes, when the ferry comes, the crew and soldiers knob me.'

'Show me what you mean.' He let go of her. She walked unsteadily to the *prie-dieu*, but did not kneel. She bent from the waist, put her breasts over the velvet edge, closed her eyes and twisted the tip of her stiffly held middle finger against her bottom. Her legs splayed, her bottom opened and her finger began smoothly masturbating it. Josef went to her and rubbed her hot protrusive nipples as she quaked. He put his hand over hers, sealing her finger up inside her bottom. And he cupped then smacked her belly as it bulged down. The smacking made the juice start to trickle from inside her. Her umbilicus turned slippery with sweat.

Josef stood her up and asked her to show him where the instruments were kept – of course, he knew, but he wanted her to help him choose.

She opened the drawers one by one. His eyes swept over the contents – plungers of various sizes, hollow dildos, and jars of creams, all neatly arranged on white linen. He picked up a very slim syringe with a long straw-like flexible spout. 'What is this one?'

'For the man – it goes down the stem.'

Taking her freckled face very gently in his hands, Josef whispered: 'And can it be used in the same place on a woman?'

Vernel began trembling.

'Fill it.'

She used a colourless gel.

'Now do it to yourself,' he said.

Her hands were shaking.

'Wait – it will not hurt you?'

She shook her head, but her hands were still shaking.

He watched her fingertips searching out the minute hole.

At the insertion, Josef shivered. Then he watched the squeezing. She was standing up, standing there doing it. His shiver kept coming. But he was unprepared for what happened next. He heard her sudden catch of breath, looked up at her pallid face, then the instrument clattered to the floor. Her legs buckled but he managed to catch her in time. She climaxed in his arms.

Her clitoris was rigid; her labia were pouted like a tube of glossy pink icing; she was still moaning as he helped her upright. She said that, inside her belly, where she peed from, it felt cold and sweet and tingling all over; that from within, she could taste the liquid she had put there. Josef's hard-on came as never before.

'Go to the table,' he told her. 'Look through the book. Choose a picture.'

She could hardly walk. He picked up the syringe and wiped it.

Vernel was leaning across the table. The buzzing in his ears strengthened steadily as her shaky fingers leafed through the pages, slowed then stopped.

Josef moved around the table, watching – her expression, her open-mouthed breathing, the way her poise adjusted and her body moved, her slender fingers on the page; he noted that now, one hand kept her vest always lifted – because he had earlier asked it of her and had not countermanded the instruction.

Other images of sexuality flashed through his mind – the gold trinkets used to protect from conception – he wondered if she had one inside her; he imagined it being put in. He relived the moment of her recent climax – the powerful arousal it had induced in him. The aftertaste was sweet, prolonged, thirst-making as a drug.

Already, she had become engrossed in the paintings on the heavy vellum pages. Her vest kept falling down as she leant forward; she rolled it up; she lifted one foot from the floor; her naked belly touched the edge of the table; a shudder ran through her and she closed her eyes.

Josef peered over her shoulder: the picture was of a bare-sexed girl sitting on a man. She was sitting on his

188

penis; she was lifted back so the point of entry could be seen. The cock looked thick and squat, triangular in section, and the distension of her anus looked unreal.

There was a long-tressed girl beside her, opening her with one hand, the fingers of the other poised to enter her vagina, as if to reach inside to touch the cock lodged in her bottom. Another man was making ready. A leather thong was wrapped around his cock and her head was being turned to take it. In the background was a standing girl being rubbed between the legs. Her feet had been tied apart. Because the picture was so large, every detail could be seen. The girl's sex was red and full and weeping.

Josef moved behind Vernel. He eased her small belly on to the edge of the table. Then he opened her legs. Her body sagged gently; the pressure was brought to bear and her sealed-together labia stood out behind her in a ridge, warm to the fingers, stiff as a captive cock beneath her skin. He played with them until she gasped and her breasts touched the page. The tiny trickle had restarted. 'Lift up,' he told her. She was supported on her hands. He moved round to the front and turned the page. She stared wide-eyed. It showed a girl draped backwards across an overturned barrel, her head and shoulders to the floor. She wore a vest like Vernel's and it had been pulled back to expose her breasts; a naked man was holding it. His cock stood up as he crouched. Her feet were being held apart while her naked thighs were smacked.

Vernel was absorbed in the picture. Her belly had lifted. Her nude red labia brushed the edge of the table. Unlike the girl's, there were no marks on Vernel's thighs. Josef pinched inside them and she moaned in pleasure.

Then he crept across the room. He opened the top drawer. It contained a set of egg-sized glass balls, some partly filled with quicksilver, others with weights. There was a small, flat strap and a double dildo. And there were strips of soft cloth for binding. In the drawer below were the smaller plungers and the hollow dildos, one of which bulged with cream. He took it out. The stem was rigid, though coated in soft leather; it was designed to ejaculate

189

when the balls were squeezed. He placed it carefully on top of the cabinet. In a third drawer, deeper than the others, was a thick brass clyster syringe and a large flask of bluish-white cream. The flask was very heavy. He looked across at Vernel. Her legs were gaping and she was leaning on one elbow, touching herself, murmuring. He could see her fingers teasing at her labia, which stood out starkly, thickly, itchily between her legs. He picked up the bulging dildo.

She did not take her hand away; she kept touching herself while the dildo entered her and her sex gradually accommodated it. But her breasts shook as her labia spread. On the page before her was a rigid cock that a girl was holding firmly at the root while a large dense globule of white ran down beneath it from the tip. 'Kiss it,' Josef said. Vernel shuddered as her pouted lips touched the globule on the page, and the soft shaft of the dildo slid deeper inside her.

In one swift movement from behind, Josef gathered her up with the dildo now a part of her and carried her to the bed.

Projecting horizontally from the headboard was the carved wooden phallus. He made her suck it, on her back, with her shoulders on a high round pillow and her wrists fastened to the headboard and the dildo still between her legs. Her head hung back, her breasts pushed out, her legs were free to move. He watched them lift and open while he touched her. He scooped her breasts up to cones, then let them fall again and shake. He teased her clitoris with his fingers. When she was writhing, he kissed the soft skin inside her thighs. Then he filled the brass clyster. It took a long while for the oily cream to slide from the flask. He stood where she could watch him. She had ceased to suck; the worn, polished phallus glistened beside her cheek. He secured the lid of the clyster and sat on the bed. Her rolled-up vest made a band under her arms. Her nipples stood stiff as stones. He tested the spout of the clyster: it was flexible, about three inches long, half an inch wide, slim enough for any bottom. 'Is this how they do you? Raise your legs.'

First he eased the dildo out of her, but kept it nearby, kept it handy, putting it on her belly, where the leaked, thinned cream that had been inside her made a smear. There was a sweet musky scent coming from the leather. The stem of the dildo was warm, and rigid as a cock on the point of coming. He slid it up her belly till it lay between her breasts. Vernel murmured; her pubic lips had collapsed and a clear full wetness ran from inside her to her bottom. Her anus pulsed and pouted when the running wetness touched it. Josef started to feed the tip of the clyster into it. Her legs jerked open, though the pressure he applied was slight.

'Push . . .' he whispered to her. Her anus opened. He watched the full three inches of the nose of the clyster slowly slipping into her bottom before the widening at the barrel made her tighten. He depressed the plunger very slowly. Vernel gasped as the cold fluid oozed inside her. He kept pressing; she was breathing rapidly; he left the clyster in position and lifted up her head, which was rolling gently, eyes closed, sweet lips wide and searching till they found the phallus and took it greedily. And as the squeezing of the plunger began again, Vernel's lips pushed up the phallus, and little grunts of pleasure shuddered through her nose. When the plunger would depress no more, Josef slipped the clyster out of her to refill it. Her bottom tightened in a spasm as the tip was withdrawn.

She was moaning as he spread her legs apart again. But they balanced, open, while the nose of the clyster unsealed the muscle and the heavy wad of coldness issued slowly up inside. When the charge had been delivered and the tip came out, the muscle clenched; she leaked a glistening drop of creamy fluid. He put this to her clitoris, gently masturbated her with it then refilled the clyster. When it slid in for the third time and the plunger was depressed, Vernel almost climaxed. The phallus had been shed from her lips and she was wriggling. Her belly had tightened to a ball.

He eased the clyster gently free then very softly pushed the dildo up into her sex and sat beside her. Then began the deliciously slow process of toying with her clitoris, stroking her distended belly, kissing her dewy underarms. When she was again on the lip of pleasure, he held her legs apart and waited for the danger to seep away. It was doubtful she would be able to take any more cream in this position, so Josef unfastened her and retrieved the dildo. Then he filled the clyster again, picked Vernel up and took her to the mirror, where he kept her knees tucked up and her toes against the bar, then let her body sink until her vulva hung below it. When he pressed her down, her belly touched the bar. His hand, dangling at the front, recommenced her slow masturbation. He was able to continue this for only a few minutes.

As he eased her body back to relieve the pressure that might lead to climax, he could see her anus in the mirror. Holding it gently but firmly with one hand, and balancing her against his chest, he slipped the nose of the clyster in. The soft skin bulged pinkly as it entered and a blue-white dollop escaped to the floor. Vernel emitted a long, continuous sexual moan as the new cream squeezed inside her. Then Josef lifted her down and carried her back to the bed. He put the open book beside her. He asked her to play with herself, but not to come. Each time she gasped and took her hand away, he asked her to continue. And he turned the page for her. The periods of masturbation became shorter, the gasps of pleasure sweeter; the hand was each time cast further away. She never looked at him; she could not take her eyes from the images on the page.

While Vernel continued to touch herself, Josef filled the clyster. She had to kneel on the bed, head down, elbows to the floor, in order to be able to take it. Then when he turned her on her side and introduced the dildo into her sex, a tube of creamy goo was expressed between her buttocks. He rubbed it gently round her sex lips. Then he pushed the rigid head of his cock against her and he was in.

It was as if the hot skin of her bottom burst. Deep inside her was oily coldness. She started to squirm across the bed. He could feel the cream inside her, squishing around him. 'Ahh!' she gasped. Each time she tightened up, the underside of his cock stroked the dildo through the inner wall of

192

skin, and the cream squeezed out against his balls. 'Oh! Ooo. Knob me!' Vernel cried. He tapped light tiny love-strokes upon her clitoris. As she writhed, he pulled back until just the bulb of his shaft kept her bottom open, rimming it in short quick slippy strokes. Then he withdrew. Vernel pleaded: 'Put it in me – let me come with it inside.'

Josef went over to the table and picked up the small plunger. Vernel started to shudder when he filled it with the clear gel. Putting her on her side, next to the book, he asked her to continue looking through the pictures. Her body, her belly, were shaking. 'Knob me,' she moaned.

He knelt astride her, lifted her leg, and slid his shaft up her bottom. The pressure of penetration pushed the balls of the dildo to one side. Heavy with liquid, they rolled against her belly and hung against her leg. The cream inside her was now hot and fluid. It began spilling out – running; she could not control it; her sex and buttocks and legs were oily wet. He made her keep touching herself as he turned the pages.

The images in the book ran out, leaving only empty Gothic frames. Vernel was delirious with pleasure. She began whimpering as he lubricated the spout of the small plunger with the oil she had extruded. Very gently, he pulled the balls of the dildo down, drew back her clitoris and tentatively touched the tiny hole. 'Oh, yes. Ohh! Oooo . . .' she pleaded. 'Do it!' When the spout pushed into her, little stabs of pleasure moved her. As the gel was fed inside her, 'Ughh! Unnnh!' she gasped – gutturally, open-mouthed. Josef waited. It took only seconds, but it seemed a soft sweet age. He watched her face. He gathered the balls of the dildo against her. When her first cry of unstoppable pleasure came, he squeezed them. She tried to curl forwards; her forehead touched the page; he slipped his other arm under her and round; she drew it up between her breasts – just like the girl in the picture with the snake. Her mouth sealed round the finger bearing the Talisur ring and sucked it deeply. She had a blinding climax with it in her mouth. Then he squeezed again, squeezed every last drop of fluid from the dildo, and Vernel kept crying with the pleasure; kept sucking the Talisur; kept coming, her anus tightening round his cock in pulses, bringing him on. He felt as if his gland would never stop pumping come. Then the muscle of her anus seemed to burst and all the hot cream from inside her gushed against his balls. He collapsed against her, and with the pressure of his body on her, Vernel climaxed again. The tightness in her bottom hurt him. He was still hard after he had withdrawn.

Josef looked at the Talisur, wet with her kisses. He looked at Vernel in her abandon, and he thought then of Iroise – the contrast, the way this one seemed unafraid to take her pleasure to fruition. Iroise had always run away from it. She had run away from him. He could not see it otherwise. But he could not forget her. And at that point the remorse swept over Josef like a dark tide: Iroise – where was she? He stared again at the ring; then he picked up the book. A chill came over him.

The picture had changed; the Gothic frame was no longer empty – but Vernel had not turned the page. He blinked; then the page was blank again. He closed his eyes and tried to remember what he had fleetingly seen: water and a boat. Then he looked again; the picture was there, faintly, as if through a veil. The boat was moving! He turned the page; his eyes widened in disbelief. The place figured was a chamber in a castle. A naked girl was being held upright by a large lordly figure; a shadowy figure was on the stairs; another person was on the balcony. The girl's eyes were blue; soft blonde ringlets framed her cheeks – she was Iroise.

From the bed, Vernel saw it happen: the Commissioner closed his eyes, seemed to waver, tried to hold on to the book. Then he fainted. The book tumbled open on the floor. She stared in frightened disbelief as a door beside the mirror opened. The Abbess stood there. Vernel looked at her, then at the blank page of the book. 'The ring . . . ?' Vernel whispered.

The Abbess smiled. 'Our wait was long for him to try to use it.' She stepped into the room. From the opposite door appeared the two monks who had been waiting patiently. One crouched over the impostor's crumpled body.

'Shall I retrieve the Talisur now?' he asked.

The Abbess shook her head. 'We await the Perquisitor – we would not wish to break the thrall.' She looked down at the book and the blank page. 'Would that we could see where he is taken.'

Then she stood above Vernel. 'You did well, my child, though you do not know it – well to take the ring that way. And it gave you pleasure, I can see.' Vernel was lain on her back. 'Knees up,' said the Abbess, 'knees up tight below your chin . . . There now, you can surely take it?'

Her hand moved into Vernel, fingers in the front, thumb in the back, stretching her to gasping point. Her knees jerked partly open. 'No – knees up, I said, tightly to the chin. It keeps the cunt constricted. Ohh . . .' Vernel's head twisted to one side. The sweet sexual faintness came upon her. The fingernail inside her kept plucking at the gold knob protruding from her womb.

'Take her into the garden. Leave her like this – tie one leg up against her body, so she cannot close properly. Smack her sex and anus on the hour; I shall come to see how she progresses.'

15

The Pleasure-Garden

Only when morning came did Sutrice take temporary pity and unfasten the hair sling, pulling it from the groove of Sianon's buttocks and the slit between her legs. The inner skin, hot and damp, was covered in tiny red scratches. Sutrice examined them zealously. Then she fitted the stretcher into Sianon's anus, with Sianon gasping on her back, her legs held open in submission. After three turns of the stretcher, Sianon came. Nothing touched her sex or clitoris – it happened because of the prolonged arousal, followed by the invasive opening of that super-sensitive place, and because she knew that Sutrice would just keep twisting the instrument and stretching her open until her climax came.

Sutrice then kept Sianon fully dilated and played with her nipples until they yielded milk. But again, she did not drink it, though Sianon wanted her to. The milk was at first bluish-white, then it turned creamy. Sutrice made Sianon's nipples squirt and let it run down Sianon's body. The feelings – the squirting, the trickling and the constant pumping of her breasts – made Sianon's untouched clitoris ache with pleasure.

In these few hours, Sutrice had obliterated all thoughts but sexual ones from Sianon's mind. She had dominated her through the night, using her as her plaything, keeping her naked but for the hair sling, but never letting Sianon touch her properly. Sianon felt intense sexual desire for her. She could express it only through submission and through the liquids that her breasts and vulva yielded. Sutrice had hardly whipped her, yet still, not since being with her mistress had Sianon experienced pleasures so profound.

'Anaisa will wish to see you before we go into the gar

den,' said Sutrice. When Sister Sutrice spoke of the Abbess, it seemed always to be with disdain. Last night, Sutrice had made Sianon tell again precisely what the Abbess had done with her. And it was after that, that the whipping had come.

'I want her to be pleased with you – you understand me?' A shiver went through Sianon. Sutrice wiped away the milk and removed the stretcher. She gave Sianon a fresh vest and cotton boots, then took her to the orangery, where Dom Gregor and the other monks and novices were gathered. The sun was shining. The day would be warm. The light came diffusely through the frosted glass roof. The smell of flowers drifted in from the gardens to mix with the scent of bergamot. A monk was extracting oil from the rind and measuring it into tiny bottles.

Sianon was placed on a couch amongst potted vines. She felt excited, deep inside. Her breasts felt good, warm all over, throbbing with gentle fullness to the tips. They swung out as her hands slid back across the seat. The drink that she was made to take each morning was being mixed for her. There were other novices distributed amongst the foliage, each being prepared in some way, each being gently stimulated, two tutors to each young woman, two rigid penises sheathed in silk.

After a time, the Lady Abbess arrived and began to move around the orangery, her sleek red robe stark against the glaucous green. She came over and spoke in secretive tones to Sutrice, whose eyes narrowed. Then Sutrice hurriedly disappeared. The Lady Abbess approached Sianon and watched the silver cup being lifted to her lips. Sianon took the bitter cloudy liquid in greedy gulps; her brown eyes watched the Lady Abbess from the sheltering silver rim. Sianon's legs sank open; the Lady Abbess smiled. Sianon felt hot between her legs, inside, though the hair sling had long been taken away. The Lady Abbess moved closer. Sianon's legs trembled wide. Sutrice had warned her that the Abbess must gain no clue as to the bond that Sutrice had forged between herself and Sianon, and that Sianon must offer herself freely to the Abbess. But even as she did so, Sianon was lubricating at the thought of what Sutrice might do to her afterwards. She could not believe that Sutrice would leave her unpunished.

But the Lady Abbess was distracted by sounds of smacking – a body stretched, a vest uplifted, naked, slim, round buttocks smacked bare-handed; then feet on tiptoes edging open, a moistened hand between the legs, a gentle urgent gasping.

Sianon moaned. Her nipple was between the Abbess's firmly squeezing fingers, which took her through the cloth. The Abbess lifted up the vest on one side to expose the other breast. She touched the oily, hot, fleshy protruberance. Then she bunched the vest above both breasts and Sianon was naked to her pure white cotton-booted feet. 'Look – her breasts.'

All of their substance had gathered to a standing roundness. Her nipples poked out as pear-shaped droplets oozing a waxy yellow liquid.

'Lady Abbess, she was played with through the night,' Dom Gregor said. 'The more they are played with, the more they leak, the more she seems to want it.'

'That is as it should be.'

'But we have never known it come so quickly.'

'It depends upon the girl. Be grateful she is bountiful.' She lowered the vest.

The wet had formed a runnel in the cloth below the nipple. Sianon's legs and sex were open and her clitoris was red. Nobody had touched it, though she had offered it.

The Abbess had the monks lift Sianon to her feet and lead her round the orangery. The girl who had just been smacked had been tied head-down while she was given a clyster. Sianon was made to stand, legs open, and watch. The monk behind Sianon eased her bottom cheeks apart. She felt the head of his silk-sheathed penis probe her. As she watched the plunger of the clyster sliding smoothly down into the inverted girl, the mouth of Sianon's bottom softened and pushed. She felt the Abbess lift her vest again and bunch it on her nipples, then she felt the Abbess's gentle fingers moving down between her legs, brushing past her open sex and reaching underneath to displace the push-ing cock and gently rub her anus. 'Has this one been clystered?' the Abbess asked.

'The instruction was no – that she was only to watch, and that we devote our efforts to her breasts.'

'The instruction from whom?'

'Sister Sutrice.'

A look of annoyance threw a shadow over the Lady Abbess's face. She took Sianon by the arm and drew her behind the foliage. Then she put a finger, then two, into Sianon's anus, examining its size and shape.

'Who stretched you?' said the Abbess. The Abbess made her tell. Then she played with Sianon's anus until Sianon did not want to stand: she wanted to kneel, for the Abbess, so the Abbess might go deeper into her.

A little later, as Sianon, still shuddering, looked up, she saw Sutrice's face glaring at her through the fronds. All of the touching, the deep examination, the offering of herself, must have taken place with the novice-mistress watching.

'Come . . .' The Abbess helped Sianon up and led her away from Sutrice. One by one, the girls had begun to disappear into the gardens with their tutors. But the orangery was extensive. There was a glint in the Abbess's eye as she took Sianon through into a hot-house. A group of monks, stripped to their sheaths, surrounded a com-pletely naked novice who was being pleasured during urination. 'Does this excite you?' the Lady Abbess whis-pered. But she could tell that it did. 'And what of this?'

It was a girl whose hair had been shorn and whose legs were stretched round a smooth bar. Her pubic lips were wide open and her clitoris was touching the wood.

'Her knob is being lengthened. There are potions that can help distend it.' Sianon remembered the treatment be-ing applied to the novice in the chapel. 'When it is large enough to make a head, this will be fitted behind it . . .' The Abbess showed Sianon a tiny ring, then she put it to the end of the girl's knob and the girl moaned softly. The ring was pushed. She gasped. 'Get a ball,' said the Abbess to the monks. 'Put it inside her.'

199

The instrument was made of lead which was sheathed in gold. The girl was lifted back. When it was inside her, her labia projected open as a consequence of the weight. It excited Sianon to see this. A potion was brought and her labia were treated. They continued to swell after the treatment was over. She was made to sit on her sex. Then her knees were brought up. Her body rolled forward; her arms were pulled back and held, so the front of her torso made a curve and all the pressure was between her legs. She moaned on the verge of climax, her knees shaking, her feet supported in the monks' hands.

The monks' breathing was strained; their penises looked as though they would burst their sheaths. Only the Abbess was calm, as she held ready the clitoral ring. Sianon was aching with desire; she wanted her nipples fondled. At last, the gasping girl was lifted back.

Even without direct stimulation, her clitoris had engorged. The tiny ring was brought to bear; she moaned; the potion was brought again. 'When fitted properly, the ring will need to be cut, then clamped into place.' Sianon shuddered; the Abbess made her crouch, so she could no longer see the girl except for her head and shoulders, and her feet captive in the stirrup-like hands. When the potion was rubbed between her legs, the girl's toes curled up, her head fell back, her torso lifted and Sianon briefly glimpsed her nipples before the Abbess lifted Sianon's vest above her breasts and moved Sianon's legs apart while Sianon was still crouched. Then she tugged and twisted Sianon's weeping nipples until her knees splayed wide open and her labia touched the warm stone flags upon the floor.

The Abbess called for assistance. Her eyes had narrowed as she looked at Sianon. 'She shall have her clyster now. But put it into her sex; I feel that this is where she needs it.'

Sianon was drawn backwards to the floor. She was panting. Her knees were trembling. The heavy syringe of polished brass was poised between them.

'I am not looking,' said the Abbess, half turning away. 'If you do what you should not, I shall not see.' Sianon's heart was thumping as the silk-sheathed penis was unsheathed and the monk crouched behind her facing her feet. Her head fell back between his knees; her body arched. She gagged. Her lips pushed wetly down his penis. The thick brass barrel of the clyster stretched her puffy pubic lips till her thighs ached from yawning open to create the space. And when the plunger was depressed, her breasts jerked quickly, her belly bulged, the monk's anus up above her opened and shut in sturdy pulses as his semen began pumping.

When he withdrew from Sianon's mouth, the plunger was still moving; her mouth was open and her tongue was slick with viscous liquid. It arched up gently as the heavy white cream extruded round the cylinder enclasped by her pubic lips. The warm, stretched burning sensation came inside her and her welling yellow milk trickled down her breasts and soaked into the vest wrapped under her arms.

'Sutrice . . .?'

'My Lady?'

The Abbess sighed. 'You are never far away, it seems. You saw the traveller?'

'He is still unconscious.'

The Abbess studied Sutrice's face. Then she said: 'Take charge of her – for the present. Do as you think fit.'

When the Abbess had departed, Sutrice wiped the excess cream from Sianon's sex, cupped the flesh in her hand and held it while the burning reached its zenith then began to ebb. She dripped cool water onto Sianon's clitoris, then placed the wet cloth on Sianon's breasts. The water running down Sianon was cloudy with the milk she had extruded when the clyster was inside her. Sutrice dried her then helped her up and took her out into the open air.

A grassy slope led down below the cross and the chastisement chairs to a pool and fountain. A nun and nude novice lay together on the grass. Nearby, a novice was being spanked by two monks. Another was in harness. At the edge of the fountain, a girl was being held with her legs open while a fine jet of water played between them. Sutrice took Sianon closer and instructed the monks to move away.

'Take her head. Support it in your lap,' she told Sianon. Already the girl was moaning. The jet of water, swaying slightly in the breeze, moved erratically back and forth between her legs. 'Give her your breast,' said Sutrice. 'Feed her.' The girl sucked lustfully. The pleasure swelled in Sianon's nipple. 'Hold her. Guide her,' Sutrice whispered. Sianon's fingers slid down between the girl's legs, opened the labia, drew back the hood. The stream of water sprayed across the clitoris. The girl's lips clamped to Sianon's nipple. She felt the suction deep inside her belly. Her other nipple stood out hard. Sutrice milked it. The spray of water drummed the girl's knob; she stiffened and groaned, her hot, moist lips enveloping Sianon's teat. The one that Sutrice milked dripped upon the girl's face. Sutrice kissed the droplets away, then tried to lick the very nipple that was suckling. As her tongue pursued it deeper inside the girl's mouth, the girl climaxed. Sianon held her hood back and she felt the clitoris jabbing up between her fingers, hard against the spray.

Sutrice detached the girl from Sianon's breast and turned her over. She directed the monks to keep her with her buttocks stretched, so the stream of water drummed upon her anus. 'Leave her thus until it learns to open.'

Sutrice laid Sianon upon the grass. Her sex was weeping warm, thinned cream from the clystering. Sutrice wiped it. She removed Sianon's vest and wrapped a strip of bandage tightly round her breasts, sealing the nipples. Then she played with them through the bandage until the girl undergoing anal stimulation by the fountain had climaxed again.

Many of the novices had been taken amongst the trees. Sutrice made Sianon voyeuse to several of these scenes of protracted masturbation. It was as if Sutrice was attempting to discover those practices that most aroused Sianon. Sianon knew there were many novices more beautiful and desirable than she, yet Sutrice never left her side. Sianon suspected it was because her breasts were giving milk. But then, Sutrice had never sucked her breasts directly: she would only stimulate the flow then let it run, leaving it to dry or sometimes wiping it away. But Sianon liked the feel of Sutrice's fingers on her nipples, making the ache intensify, the skin of her breasts and neck flush red, then the ache turn cool as the fullness overflowed.

In a glade they found the Abbess with Vernel, lying on her side. Vernel's leg was tied up against her body and the Abbess was smacking her anus with a wet knotted rope.

Close by was a girl secured to a tree. It was the same girl, Samarkin, who had been the subject of the vigil in the chapel. At Sutrice's command, the monks stood back. Her ankles had been fastened as far apart as they would go; her nude sex lips protruded achingly as a result of the continual treatments. 'They were already prominent – some girls' are,' said Sutrice. 'But now they are larger and more beautiful.' Sutrice watched Samarkin for a little while. Then she took a bundle of thin, soft hazel twigs and whipped her, first her breasts and then her belly above her swollen vulva. Then she began to kiss the marks.

It was when Sutrice's lips and tongue were caressing the girl's marked breasts, and nipples distended by the whipping, that Sianon started to tremble. A feeling of sweet faintness came to her, like the timelessness before a climax. Her own sex was swelling up; she could feel it, like a heavy weight pushing out of her. The scene – the fastened, aroused girl, the swollen vulva, the breasts, the marks, the cold administration of the whipping – reminded her so closely of the pleasures she had suffered with her mistress. Every soft, clipped moan that Samarkin made aroused Sianon even more, because she understood so well all the burning, stinging feelings, the aftershocks, the end-pleasure of the whipping as the sensations flooded back into the skin.

Seeing Sianon's state, Sutrice asked the monks to take her aside, saying: 'Keep her within earshot. Slap her gently, between the legs. Put things into her. Stimulate her breasts.'

While it was being done Samarkin was whipped again. Then Sianon was brought back. Sutrice unfastened the girl and made her kneel. Then Sutrice pulled open the skirt of her own habit. She glanced at Sianon, who was staring at her legs, clad to the tops in pale silk, clinging stockings. Sianon glimpsed the shiny black bush of pubic hair before Sutrice moved astride the girl's face. 'Come here,' she whispered to Sianon. 'Kneel beside her. Watch and listen.' Then she caressed Samarkin's long locks, pushed them back to bare her neck, then drew her face closer. The girl's mouth spread wide enough to take Sutrice's black-fringed vulva. Sutrice angled, bent her legs, held her skirts lifted and positioned herself so she was sitting in Samarkin's mouth.

Then Sutrice shivered and Sianon suddenly understood what was happening. The girl coughed as the first spray struck her throat. Sutrice gently pulled away, staring at her. She held her face again and stroked her throat. 'Swallow,' she instructed her. 'As it comes, keep swallowing, keep pace and you will not choke.' The frightened, aroused girl tried to lick the moisture from her lips. Sutrice eased her head back. 'Open as wide as you can. Put your tongue to the roof of your mouth. Keep it there. Now again ...' She placed her sex inside the open cup of Samarkin's lips then closed her eyes. The girl emitted a muffled sound, raised her hands – as if to touch Sutrice's belly and somehow control the flow. Sutrice murmured gently as it came. Samarkin's hands collapsed limply, her head falling further back, and Sianon could hear the hollow squirting, and could see the girl struggling to swallow steadily.

Sutrice eased away; the last few drops fell inside the open mouth. Then Sutrice gently dried herself on the girl's locks. She turned to Sianon. 'A perfect submissive – she refuses nothing. Kiss her.'

Samarkin remained with lips wide open. Sianon kissed them, licked them, put her tongue inside to sip upon the last of the essence gathered in the well. It excited her, the strong taste, the thought that it was from inside Sutrice. And she was aroused too by the depth of the girl's submission; it put a curious feeling inside Sianon – a jealousy, but a loving jealousy. She wanted to show Sutrice how much she desired her. Even as she was kissing the girl and seeking every remaining drop of Sutrice's liquid, Sutrice was already touching Sianon from behind, between the legs. Sianon was thinking of Sutrice's silk-clad, slim, cool thighs.

'I shall show you how to whip her,' Sutrice whispered into Sianon's ear. She left Samarkin kneeling while she chose a single thin flexible hazel cane. Then she instructed her to bend forward until her shoulders touched the ground. Her head was twisted, her cheek on the grass. Her back was deeply hollowed. Sutrice made her shuffle her knees forward until her sex pushed out behind her. She showed Sianon the profile from the side. There was a smooth, short bulge at the place where the sex adjoined the anus. When she laid the cane horizontally against it, it touched only this single spot, below the cheeks of the buttocks but above the labia. 'Whip it. She will cream.'

Sianon whipped it numb. She had never felt so powerful an excitement. Samarkin was moaning with submissive pleasure. A thick drop of her lubricant was dangling between her legs. 'Leave it,' Sutrice whispered. 'Come here. Give me your tongue.' Sianon climaxed when Sutrice kissed her. It happened with no hand between her legs, no squeezing. Her tongue sought Sutrice's. 'You forget your training,' Sutrice whispered hoarsely. But Sianon could see that her dominatrix was pleased. Sianon wanted her to put her thigh between Sianon's legs and peel her stocking down and let Sianon's naked vulva kiss Sutrice's skin. Sutrice was stroking Sianon's hair and searching her eyes. 'We must take her back and share her.' Then she touched Sianon's sex very gently and Sianon came again.

Sutrice took them to a bedroom in a part of the abbey where Sianon had not been. There was watered wine ready. Samarkin was laid on the bed. Then she was stimulated slowly. Sianon was allowed to give her the watered wine to drink. Some of it spilled about Samarkin's neck because she was on her back. Sianon was aroused by the thought of making her pee. Samarkin's legs were draped to one side. When Sianon sat up she could see the reddened place where she had whipped her. The spot was small. When she touched it, Samarkin murmured and opened. Sianon told her that she would make her pee. She gave her more to drink while Sutrice pulled back the hood of Samarkin's clitoris and licked the knob, but not enough to bring her on.

Sutrice then opened Samarkin fully, putting both hands back to back between the girl's legs. All eight fingers went inside her, stretching her gently. There was a lush, deep, hollow pink space between Sutrice's hands. 'Masturbate her, while she is open,' Sutrice whispered.

When Samarkin was very near to pleasure, Sutrice allowed Sianon to take charge. 'Slowly – keep her on,' she said. 'I shall go and get her treatments.'

Once she was alone with her, Sianon allowed Samarkin to stand up. She let her walk around the room, then made her drink again. Sianon asked her if she wanted to pee. She cupped her vulva in her hand. The movement had helped it return to shape after the opening. Sianon pushed her fingers in, then lifted them and slowly pulled them out: the infolds of Samarkin's enlarged sex slid out, layer upon layer. The innermost lips pouted; Sianon played with them. They stayed out, swelling larger as the masturbation progressed. Sianon put her fingers in again and pressed the bladder. Samarkin gasped. Sianon asked her what she wanted; Samarkin asked if she could sit down. Sianon put her on a straight chair with her hands behind her back and her legs spread sideways. Then she put a cushion behind her to force her belly out. Her pushed-out infolds projected over the chair edge. Sianon fed her more liquid. She taught her to control her urination. Keeping her with her legs wide open, Sianon played with her or licked her then let her pee into Sianon's cupped hand, but only till the hand was full. She kept two fingers up inside Samarkin: when they pressed, Samarkin peed; when the finger-pressure eased she stopped. The liquid was not wasted; Sianon spread it over Samarkin's breasts and neck and under her arms. It evaporated quickly. She fed her liquid to keep apace with the loss through urination, so Samarkin's bladder stayed full, keeping the masturbation more effective. The weak wine, passing through her, became infused with her scent. Sianon taught her to associate the smell with the intense prolonged pleasuring she was feeling.

When Sutrice returned, Samarkin was again being masturbated standing, belly bowed, back hollowed, legs open, her swollen infolds out behind her. Her skin was silky with the sheath of evaporated pee. Sianon's breasts were hurting from the pressure of the milk inside.

And the pleasure in them hurt her when she had to crouch behind Samarkin and hold her labia open for the treatments. Sutrice had brought two plungers, one for each side. They were used upon each lip in turn. Funny feelings came to Sianon as the shivers ran down Samarkin's inside legs. Sianon's breasts leaked, then spurted as she felt Samarkin's sex lips swelling harder in her hands.

Sutrice wanted Samarkin caned in the place she had shown Sianon, at the point where the sex adjoined the anus. She wanted Samarkin to keep urinating during caning. She made her kneel on the floor, her bottom up, her sex thrust back between her legs. When Samarkin started to pee, Sianon whipped the cane across the place where her sex adjoined her anus. With the sudden stab of pain, Samarkin stopped peeing.

'Wait,' Sutrice ordered her. 'Kneel up. Lean back.' And for the transgression, she spanked her breasts with her bare hands, using two hands, one for each breast. Samarkin's belly arched, her breasts stood full and tight; Sutrice spanked them till she was gasping. Then keeping her with her head back, she masturbated her. The tightness kept coming in Samarkin's belly and in the muscles of her inside legs. Samarkin moaned: 'Please . . .?' Sutrice waited, made her drink, then began again, playing with the swollen pink folds, milking the clitoris. 'Ahh!' gasped Samarkin. Sutrice whispered: 'No. No urination during masturbation.' There were droplets of wet on Samarkin's legs. 'Save it for the caning.'

Again she made her kneel, head down, vulva thrust back below her buttocks and between her legs. There was a red mark where the cane had caught her. Sutrice waited. Samarkin held her breath, gasped gently then started peeing.

Sutrice nodded. Sianon whacked the cane against the red mark above the vulva. Samarkin stopped peeing. Sutrice sighed. Samarkin began to cry as she was lifted. 'Shh . . . Lift back, my darling. Hold her.' Sutrice waited until the belly was thrust out, the legs were splayed open, the breasts were pointing up and to the sides. Then she spanked them. As Samarkin shuddered and thrust, Sianon's excited fingers reached up between her buttocks and pinched her anus gently through the spanking. She held it too while Sutrice tongue-kissed Samarkin and while she masturbated her again, and when she was made to drink, Sianon slipped a finger in and rubbed it inside her bottom.

Then when Samarkin knelt down again – her breasts to the floor, her buttocks in the air, the thick folds of her vulva protruding behind her, and she began to pee and Sianon caned her – the flow did not stop. Each time the cane whacked down, she groaned, the stream was momentarily thinned by the contraction, but it was a gentle thinning, not a stoppage, not a refusal. And with each weak contraction a soft ripple of pleasure seemed to grip Samarkin's anus, as if Sianon were rimming it with her finger. Her pee had saturated her thighs, her sex, her belly, her upturned breasts and it kept coming, never stopping while Sianon caned that one sweet place until the girl was empty. Only then did Sutrice deem her trained to urination during caning.

It took a little while for her bladder to refill; she drank copiously of the watered wine. A ball of gold-sheathed lead was then put inside her sex; she was made to walk around with it inside her; then to deliver it into Sianon's hand. It came out coated with thick lubricant. Even though she was so tight from the swellings, this heavy liquid helped it slip back inside. The pressure of the ball inside her soon made her want to pee. Sianon allowed her to. She sat her down so her sex overhung the edge of the seat. But she made her do it slowly, made her control it to the barest trickle. She kept taking the ball out of her and slipping it back inside. As it went in, the vulva seemed so swollen, each lip a ridge quite separate from the rest. After each insertion, Sianon masturbated her nearly to climax, then made her expel the ball. The fourth time it entered, Samarkin began to climax, but it was a prolonged climax, extending over two more quick insertions and masturbation and heavy spurts of pee.

It was evening. The prolonged pleasuring of Samarkin progressed under Sianon's even more provocative touches. The box of thorns lay open on the floor. Samarkin's fingers were pinched about her own bulging nipples. She was moaning in the throes of pleasure. Her knees were up beside her breasts. Small red tubular lumps were now present in the stretched skin of her vulva, held open by the weighted clamps. The trickles of pee kept coming, crystal clear, like faintly perfumed water. And Sianon kept reaching for them with her mouth; each time her lips closed round the tip of the vulva, Samarkin would shiver, Sianon would swallow.

At length, Sutrice drew Sianon aside, took her into the next room and made her lie down. The scent of the girl – musk and sharpness intermixed – was on Sianon's mouth. Her heavy, full breasts slipped sideways. Her eyelids were languorous; she hunched her shoulders, gathering her breasts between her elbows, offering them, making them more swollen. Fine beads of yellow milk began to ooze from the tips.

'You want me to suck them?' Sutrice asked.

Sianon shivered.

'I cannot. I can but help prepare them. You know that you were chosen for your breasts? Soon they shall be used. Open your legs. Hold yourself open.'

Sutrice put her fingers up into Sianon, through the dense, soft, clear mucus; she examined the entrance to the womb. Then she took the small gold charm – a snake – and put it up inside her, inserting it through the mouth of the womb until the charm had disappeared and all that emerged was the thread. 'It will protect you.' Then as Sianon held herself open, Sutrice masturbated her gently, making the pleasure an aching pressure between Sianon's legs. When that pressure became unbearable, she made her get up quickly, stand rigidly still, and the climax was averted. 'Go to your toy,' Sutrice whispered. 'Play with her. Keep her liquid coming.'

Sutrice then looked out from the open window to the lake. In the distance was the ferry coming in. The time had come for Sutrice to leave the noviciate of Servulan to the mercy of the soldiers. She crept out quietly, on a different errand. As she moved through the stillness of the abbey, an excitement burgeoned within her. Her mind began to race as she thought about the instruments she might adapt to this new usage: she had never done it to a man, never explored the differences fully, never had the chance.

When the contingent from the ferry burst into the room, Sianon was asleep with Samarkin in her arms.

'Which of you gives milk?' The guards dragged Samarkin off the bed and began mauling her breasts. Sianon was terrified. The ferry-marshal approached her. 'Ah . . .' he said. Her nipples were turgid. He turned to the man beside him. 'Connar – lift her up.'

As the guard drew Sianon upwards by the arms, and her belly was stretched, it happened. Sianon cried out with the feeling – the shiver through her breasts, the sweet ache between her legs. The marshal moved swiftly, dropping to his knees. She gasped in pleasure; her labia opened round his gloved middle finger. 'Let it come,' he whispered, 'let it come.' He did not force his finger into her. The guard just held her suspended by her wrists. But it came again – the shiver and the sweet sexual ache. The guard gathered her bursting breasts. She cried out; powerful spurts of milk came out of her and splashed across his arm. When he lowered her, she swooned sideways to the floor, the gloved finger still inside her, her breasts and belly swathed in her sweet warm milk.

16

The Thrall

Josef was locked inside the very picture: that was how it felt – as if his mind had taken the vision of Iroise from the page and woven around it an elaborate dream. But all the events he was witnessing were real. The dream-like quality was simply this: he could do nothing to intervene.

He was in a room such as might be found in an ancient castle. A coat of arms overhung the fireplace. Tapestries adorned the walls. He was staring at a pompous, swag-bellied creature wearing a gold chain around his neck. Josef dubbed him 'The Baron'. His head was pear-shaped, heavy-jowled; his eyes bulged bloodshot. By degrees, Josef became aware of other parts of the room, because his perspective constantly changed, as in a dream.

There was a gallery; sometimes he was there – he glimpsed a figure on the stairs – at other times he was standing on the floor. Then he was looking down at Iroise's lovely face and shivering, for it was as if she could see him. In her eyes was desire, the same deep, shy, sexual desire that he remembered so well. Then with a shock, he sensed that he was seeing through the Baron's eyes, and that this awful creature was controlling her, just as the Warden had.

She was on a couch. He had her naked except for a man's lawn chemise which could not have been his because it was far too small. Leather bands were round her wrists and ankles. The chemise was open; she was making no attempt to fasten it. There was submissive languor in her pale limbs, her lips were moistly open, her eyes darkly wide. There was fear there, but more powerful seemed to be the longing. And there was no hint that she found her watcher unattractive.

The perspective suddenly altered and now Josef was

looking down at the two of them from the stairs. He thought: there were no sounds – when Iroise's lips had moved, no sound had emerged. And while he had watched her through the Baron's eyes, he had experienced none of the man's thoughts or feelings, only his own. But Josef himself had no control, either over his viewpoint or over his own body: there was a dullness in his muscles, as of constraint.

Looking up, he saw a woman, a lady, in the gallery. Then he understood what must be happening: each time his perspective changed, he was seeing through another's eyes. He tried to recall how many different viewpoints he had perceived since the beginning, then the view jumped back to the gallery and he saw the dark figure of a man descending the stairs.

Suddenly Josef was inside this figure and looking out, looking at the Baron's swollen face, his eager eyes, his thick wet lips flapping out words that Josef could not read. A cold, dreadful numbness descended over Josef as he watched helplessly through this other man's eyes – watched the black leather bag placed upon the table, and the bottles taken from it, then the needles. He watched Iroise shrink back from the stretching fingers, gasp then close her eyes.

A momentary blackness fell. The perspective jarred; he watched the lady walking down the stairs. In her eyes was fascination. She went to Iroise, whose legs lay open on the couch. Taking up her station beside her head, she whispered to her, kissed her, touched her wristbands and her exposed breasts. Whenever Iroise's soft mouth opened to a soundless moan, the lady's tongue explored it. The man rubbed liquid into Iroise, between her legs.

The perspective had shifted again; Josef was seeing with the lady's eyes. Her fingers slid down to where Iroise was holding herself open, the right pubic lip pulled out further than the left. Her clitoris was swollen. The needle rubbed it, made it jump, then returned to prick the inside of the lip, repeatedly and finely, where the dye had been painted, implanting the colour into her skin. It took some time. The skin was then wiped with balls of moistened wool. She was masturbated by the lady's fingers and by the shaft of the needle rubbing her clitoris. A new colour was applied inside her pubic lip, then came the rapid pricking, the silent moans, the masturbation. At one stage her knees were lifted while a shiny flared pipe of lubricated steel was introduced into her anus. Because its insertion almost made her climax, she was allowed to rest. But it remained inside her, keeping the muscle open, until the tattooing was complete.

When she was ready the Baron examined her, spoke gently to her and took her in his arms. Her lawn shirt was open, her pink-tipped breasts were against his barrel chest; his wet lips sucked upon her naked, flawless neck, depositing a purple stigma there. Peculiar feelings came to Josef watching this creature holding her, his hand cupping the place between her legs, one finger now slipped between her smooth pubic lips, stroking the motif tattooed inside her at his behest.

Then the lady put something up the steel pipe. Iroise began gasping. The lady smothered her with kisses and withdrew the pipe. But Iroise continued to writhe and gasp.

The scene faded to blackness for a timeless while, then reopened in a luxurious boudoir. Iroise was on the sumptuous bed. Her demeanour told she had been played with for a long time; she was drugged by arousal. Looking down, Josef again saw delicate hands – the lady's. In her fingers was a fine steel rod capped by a tiny ball. The hands moved towards Iroise. Iroise stared up at Josef; her eyes grew wider; her mouth opened; she shuddered. Then he was looking down. The fingers must have performed the insertion solely by touch; most of the rod protruded from the urethra; the ball was just inside the mouth. The fingers twirled it expertly, gently, until Iroise's legs reached open, her vulva lifted, her clitoris began to bulge and pulse. Then the scene faded.

In the next one, Iroise was with three men. The setting seemed to be a smoking-room. Josef glanced down: he saw fat hands rubbing together; the Baron was the watcher, moving round the room, sometimes closer to her, sometimes distancing himself, sometimes wrenching his gaze away. He had chosen young men to service her. Always there were at least two at once, sometimes three. The Baron never joined in, never intervened. Iroise was wet between the legs, wet on the breasts; her hair was tousled, matted. Fluid glistened there too, fluid that had escaped from her lovers too quickly or freely. The view moved closer, moved down, became intimate. Most of the time, her eyes were closed – not through fear – it was a languid closure, pleasure in excess, and waves of delicious tension sweeping her climax ever nearer. One shaft slid alongside her sex; her fingers closed around the balls, caressing them. Above her, the flow of near-transparent semen welled down the rigid purple stem. A hand came under Iroise's neck, forcing her to drink it; her mouth pouted against the penis just above the balls. The sensations started coming to Josef. He watched her being opened anally. Her sex was left untouched. It bulged from the pressure of the cock inside her bottom. She held the right lip open so the tattoo could be seen.

The Baron approached, his brown, silky cock distended. It rubbed up between her legs, up against her open labia, until his thick white ejaculate coated her tattoo. Then he sealed the lips, lifted her off the other cock and laid her on his lap. The view was down between her legs; his semen squeezed from inside her. He took the thin steel rod, put the semen-coated tip into her urethra and gently twirled it. Her legs stiffened then tried to close; she tried to sit up. He held her open, twirled the rod again and kept twirling until she screamed a silent scream of pleasure and her open mouth closed hungrily about the naked folds of flabby flesh festooned below his breast.

A deep-down ache was coming inside Josef; he could not move his arms. Then the scene opened again, in a very different place, with quite different players. The character he was inside was lying on the floor. There was a girl, dark and small, full-lipped, beautiful. Round her neck was a slave collar. And there was a woman in black leather. Josef's heart stopped: she was Quislan.

She dragged the girl across, seemingly offering her to the character Josef was inside. But then Quislan suddenly drew back as if scalded. Her tiny mouth fell open to an 'o'. Fine lines of puzzlement tainted her pure white brow. She hovered closer, staring, her black hypnotic pupils engulfing him.

'Is it you?' she whispered. And he could hear her voice. 'It is you!' And for the first time, he could move independently. He glanced down: and it was his own body; on his finger he could see the ring. The ring – the Talisur. Everything tumbled into place: the Talisur was responsible for these visions. But now it had taken him further – he was here in the flesh with Quislan. He saw her eyes glint.

'Quickly!' she cried. 'Restrain him. Don't let him take it off. And we have him!' Josef struggled to move. She fought him only with her eyes; his fingers were around the ring, but they felt heavy, so heavy. For a split second she was distracted by the girl's crying; and that was enough – the weight lifted from him, he wrenched the ring off and threw it down.

Quislan smiled like a cat. 'Welcome traveller . . .' And he knew then that he had been tricked into removing his one protection from her.

The vision faded. Josef woke; he was still in the study. The ring was on the floor. His hand shot out. The monk's foot trapped it. The Abbess picked up the Talisur. 'She wants him brought to her in the tower.'

'He has never had it, Sutrice – not this way. And oh – it is a discovery for him.' Josef's breathing quickened; his heartbeat raced; his buttocks burned. 'Look at me,' Quislan whispered, stroking the whip up his bursting penis. The guards had been dismissed; he was tied and at the mercy of the women. And he was staring at a sweet pale visage that was perfect – her skin flawless china, her eyes pools of liquid black. All the memories flooded back: the night at the manse, the sexuality she engendered in the women, the way she had left him for dead on the road. His body ached again now; the flesh felt seared from his buttocks, all because of her. He should have hated her.

215

'But you do not.'

Josef shivered. Her lips had never moved. She had spoken inside his mind. Quislan smiled at him; her lips brushed soft complicity over his naked skin.

Then she whispered: 'You saw her, Iroise with her new sponsor ...? No matter: Thuline has confessed. Even Reikz should never have had the Talisur. I am amazed you could use it.' Her fingers closed softly round his penis. Her lips were open. She licked them. He shuddered. 'Oh – not yet ...' she teased.

'Sutrice – you may practise your explorations further. Use nothing that might dull the senses. I want him to re-member this night.' So saying, she went back to the girl, taking her by the collar. Her pendulous breasts brushed Quislan's palm; the nipples stood down, erect. 'Go down,' Quislan commanded and the girl obediently pressed her lips to Quislan's booted feet. 'Down ...' Her nipples touched the floor; her breasts rolled as she twisted; her knickers had a dark patch between the legs. Quislan put her toe there, urging the fabric into the moist fleshy cup, leaving a circle of wetness round the toe of her boot.

Josef tried not to struggle this time, tried not to tighten, as Sutrice tied his legs wider. All was in vain. She knew what she was doing. The lash struck liquid fire across his buttocks. She kept it at arm's length to increase the power of the throw. She whipped only his buttocks, only the welts Quislan had already put there. And with each lash, his anus tightened, his erection ached. Then she folded the whip back on itself, opened him and pushed it inside. 'Oh ...' she murmured, kneeling in front of him, 'Mmmm ...' sucking his bulging penis as the whip sprang slowly open and elbowed out.

Unfastening him from the frame, she made him kneel with his penis between his legs and his wrists tied to a ring on the floor. Then she stood behind him and smacked him with a tawse. She never smacked the penis itself; she smacked his anus until the feeling came, that he would spend if she persisted. But she pressed her thumbs into the place Quislan had shown her, below the tip of the glans, and his erection subsided. Then she smacked his anus again. Each time he became erect, she squeezed him till his erection softened. But the feelings deep inside him never went away. Quislan left the girl and came to watch. There was talk of how this method – anal spanking, then squeezing the knob – was used on girls; comparisons were made with his reaction. Several times the feeling came, that he would spend, but his tormentors were always able to prevent it.

Quislan spoke to Sutrice of a special place inside a man, saying that when the man became sufficiently aroused, without relief, this place would become swollen and distorted. Sutrice put her fingers into Josef and found it. 'I have some metal tongs,' she said, 'that we could use to squeeze it.'

His wrists were fastened to a bar that ran below the ceiling. The jaws of the tongs were shaped. She put them up inside him. When she squeezed gently, he moaned, his penis leaked. She took out the tongs and slipped her fingers in. He felt the inner swelling move under the pressure of her fingers. Between his legs, his balls were bursting. Sutrice rubbed the place inside him and his yield increased to an oily runnel down his stem. And again he felt it move – the living growth inside him, like a slowly squirming creature under her fingers. The gland ached to empty – he felt its first involuntary pulse. Very gently, Sutrice took out her fingers and lapped up his leakage. The tip of her tongue against the base of his penis almost precipitated his climax. Then she applied the firm thumb-pressure that took his erection down.

The whole exercise had been one of exquisite agony for Josef. But it was not over.

'Open,' she whispered. He thought she wanted to put her fingers back inside. But she held his buttocks spread and spanked him back to erection. He hung, knees bent, back hollowed, buttocks pushing back. Then she led him, hands still fastened to the bar below the ceiling, to the corner where a heavy bowl rested on a plinth. Sutrice now repeatedly spanking him then made him squat with his balls

217

cupped in the bowl and the pressure of the thick rim underneath them. Each squat caused a small issue of clear liquid which trickled from his balls into the bottom of the bowl. Sutrice then masturbated him carefully with his weight resting on the rim. She found the rhythm that made his yield increase from trickles to a stream without the fluid either spurting or becoming milky. Then she angled into him an instrument which had a spring which pressed a pad against the gland. His yield was maintained by this pressure of squeezing. And in this state, Sutrice left Josef hanging, gasping softly, his fluid welling down his penis to the bowl.

'Time – the simplest and greatest aid to pleasure,' she whispered. 'Yet so often, it is ignored.' She began searching through her box of instruments. Her victim could only watch and wonder what excesses might be in store.

Sutrice seemed an ordinary woman, lacking any of the Perquisitor's powers. Josef looked at her sharp features, her lustreless black hair, coarse, stiff, cut without precision. Her skin was sallow. Tiny white pimples clustered on her cheekbones underneath her eyes. Her lips, though small, protruded, the upper one overshot. The skin above it was smooth and waxy. Her ears had at one time been ringed; one lobe had a tiny nick, a tear, long-healed. And yes, Josef felt sexual desire for her though she was doing these things to him – or perhaps because of that. He thought again of the time in the Training Cloister when she had asked him to lie across the table and had offered to put things into him. Had she known then – before he did – that he was capable of harbouring such feelings?

Her narrow fingers tested the smooth metal instruments. She moved coldly, without passion, but she must have been feeling passion. She glanced at him; he could see it in her eyes – the passion, not for him, but for what she was doing to him. Their eyes met again; the shiver ran through him – the complicity was there between them, the dominatrix and the submissive.

Her fingers kept returning to a long, thin, slightly curving, tubular instrument of gold. It tapered a little towards

218

the tip, which was shaped like a tiny nipple. Sutrice played with this tip. Josef's erection ached. She removed the pressure-pad and lifted him off the bowl. 'It must be down,' she said and while she waited, she fitted to the tip of the instrument a ball of resin.

After a long time, she was able to feed the tip with its ball of stimulant into him. His erection began while she was doing it. She kept the instrument in place and his penis swallowed it. He could feel the ball inside him, at the base of his stem, pressing against a constriction. She twisted it gently and the ball came free; it was left inside him when the rod was withdrawn. The pleasure was excruciating as she rubbed the base gently and the ball began to dissolve. She told him this would help him make more fluid. She made him turn around. Then she held his penis shut near the base. And she spanked his anus gently as the pressure of his fluid built. When he could take no more she put her fingers up inside and stimulated the gland directly. Then she fastened a harness tightly round his penis and scrotum.

He became aware of shouting outside in the yard below. Sutrice went to the window. 'They are into the cellars,' she said.

'No matter,' Quislan replied calmly. 'They serve us well. We would not deny them this amusement. But come here, Sutrice – she needs us both.'

The girl was belly-down on the bed. There came a subdued ache inside Josef as his stimulant continued working and her pleasuring progressed. His penis strained at its harness. Quislan parted the girl's legs, then her buttocks. She tried to probe her bottom with her fingers. 'She has not as yet been stretched,' she said. They used oil. Sutrice got three fingers in without hurting the girl. Quislan came to Josef and unleashed his straps. She massaged the furrows under his balls. Then she brought the oil, explaining that she would put her hand inside him – not just her fingers as Sutrice had done, but her hand. She played with him expertly, keeping him hard. She pulled his balls downwards, stretching the pouch, finding the stringy tubes inside him, holding them between her fingers while the girl writhed gently, face down on the bed. Then she showed him the polished ivory ball that her hand would grip as it went inside him.

The girl on the bed had been turned over. Sutrice took up a thin rod. The girl's legs began to close. Sutrice wrenched them open till her knees were flat to the mattress.

Quislan continued to masturbate Josef as Sutrice whipped the girl's labia with the small fine rod, whipping below the clitoris, where the labia had now swelled.

'Sutrice – he needs treatment,' Quislan said, lifting his scrotum.

He shuddered as the freezing tip of the plunger touched the firm pad of flesh behind his balls. A fine jet of ice seemed to connect through inside him to his anus. Sutrice, kneeling in front of him, continued squeezing the plunger. The icy numbness became warmth, the arousal spread upwards and his penis curved and touched his belly. Quislan held it there and with the rod whipped his balls. Sutrice started to suck him. Quislan oiled her fingers then bunched them. She told him to relax his anus. Then she pushed her hand, her slim small hand, inside. Sutrice had to stop sucking to prevent ejaculation; even then it almost came.

Sutrice went back to the girl. She made her kneel head-down and bottom in the air then placed between her legs a glass vase with a constricted neck. Her swollen labia had difficulty fitting inside the mouth. With Sutrice administering anilingus, the girl was made to fill the vase with pee. It took time, for her flow kept stopping through the ambivalence of impulse stimulated by the licking movements of the tongue. Sutrice eventually lifted the vase away and tasted. Then, putting it to Josef's lips, she made him drink. The arousal caused him to contract about Quislan's slender wrist. Taking her hand out, Quislan explained that there must be no contraction – that his semen, should it come, must spill not pump. The pleasure must be taken passively. Sutrice wrapped a length of narrow bandage once round the glans of his penis and held it by these ties.

Quislan took up the ivory ball, oiled it, then the fist holding it. She asked again that he relax his anus. Then she

220

pushed both fist and ball inside. When his climax came, he wanted to tighten, wanted to close around her wrist. She pulled; her slim cool fist came against his anus from inside. 'Shhh . . . Still . . .' she murmured. 'There . . . Just let it run . . . Oh, Sutrice – can you smell it?' The feeling of sinking went on and on. He hung there, doing nothing, not moving, letting everything take him, his fluid pouring out of him, streaming down the bandage and running from his balls.

Wiping her hand, Quislan returned to the bed and began peeling her leathers from her slimly muscled body. There was no colour in her, just the dense whiteness of her skin and the glossy jet blackness of her hair. She appeared as though lit by limelight. The only tint was in those lips of pale rose madder . . . black eyebrows, black irises, black nipples; small, cuspate, undeveloped, pure white breasts; no hips; white, tight labia splitting shiny black pubes. 'Sutrice – the double dildo . . .' The girl began shivering.

No straps or supports were used. Protruding from the crotch of Quislan's alabaster figure was now a shaft of shiny pink. She forced the girl to suck it, then turned her over and lubricated her sex and anus. Because the dildo was so long, it would reach only part way inside. The girl became very aroused by the depth of penetration. She remained open-mouthed while Quislan moved in turn inside her anus then her sex, then masturbated her, with the dildo inside her as far as it would go. 'Now him,' said Quislan. 'And I want him like a girl.'

They tied him across the bed. The potion was brought; the surrounds of his nipples were treated in several places, rubbed and pulled, then treated again. He felt tingling warmth there as they began to swell. Quislan pulled and slapped them. She let the girl play with them. His erection curved up like a bone. She said she wanted it down. 'A girl would never become erect so quickly.' Sutrice found the pressure-point with her thumb. His penis lolled. Quislan went into his mouth with the dildo. His penis came up. Sutrice squeezed it. He started to gag because the dildo was so long. The girl scratched and plucked the tender skin of

221

his breasts. Quislan's slim thighs gripped his head; he could smell her sex, feel its warmth as she worked the dildo deeper.

And while the three of them used him, it happened – a feeling so profoundly sexual, deep inside him, akin to drowning, of having no control. It stayed with him all the while that Quislan knelt astride him. His penis, rigid again, began weeping sexual fluid. She kept saying she wanted it down, but he could not make it do that.

She withdrew from his mouth. 'Untie him . . . Over,' she instructed him. He acquiesced. Her belly, cool as marble, touched the hollow of his back. The dildo, nudging, found the hotness. She took him from the side. She did not lubricate him. He started gasping. 'Is this not how a man expects it of a woman?' she mocked. Nothing touched his penis. All the feelings came inside. It was prolonged, exquisite pleasure. The girl sat spellbound, watching the ejaculate pumping over his belly, pouring over the sheets. The knob of the dildo kept rubbing up inside him, gently and without stopping, siphoning a steady stream of hot thin fluid from his deeply swollen gland.

Drawing herself off the dildo, leaving it in him, Quislan said: 'Now I want him pierced.' She pointed out the place, below the mouth of the penis.

The watching girl sat spread-legged, seeping arousal over Quislan's fingers. As the ball of the torc being pushed down the penis began emerging from the puncture, the involuntary expulsion of seminal fluid came again. Sutrice drew the ball back inside to block the exit from the tube itself, and the dense white fluid issued through the piercing-point like milk through a retracted nipple. Sutrice sucked it, drank it, licked the tiny aperture clean.

The door opened. Two women entered. They stood like well-trained soldiers. Their skin was weather-bronzed. They were tall and beautiful. Beneath their jerkins, their proud bare breasts were criss-crossed by leather thongs.

'Maran,' said Quislan to the taller one, 'tell the ferry-marshal you have another passenger. Put him through his paces. Ditch him if he fails to please.'

17

The Marshal and Maran

The guards took only Samarkin from the bedroom. Sianon was left kneeling on the floor. 'The ferry does not leave until the early hours,' the marshal whispered, walking round her, removing his gloves. The tip of one of the fingers was wet from inside her. 'It means we have some time.'

Sianon, looking up, swallowed softly. Fine bluish-white droplets of breast-milk still clung below her nipples. He wiped them gently away. 'Up, missy . . .' As he lifted her bodily off the floor, her generous breasts, replete with milk, pressed against his arm. The fullness came; the teats glutted. She gasped softly – with the pain of stretching came pleasure. If he were to touch them it would bring on a new emission. Lowering her on to his lap, her bare body against his clothing, he slipped a finger in between her legs. A subdued moan escaped her lips. Her thighs spread for him. It was the intimacy of the single naked finger that so aroused her. He asked her name then said:

'You have been opened, Sianon – like this?'

'Yes,' she whispered.

'Often?'

She nodded. The marshal raised her chin. 'Your tongue,' he demanded. While he licked it, his finger, moving inside her, pressed against the tail of the trinket protruding from her womb. Her thighs stiffened; her breath shuddered into his mouth.

'And you have been smacked?'

She shivered as the goose-pimples pricked her naked skin.

'Here? Lift up.' He rubbed her anus with his thumb. The skin wrinkled tightly, the access sealed. 'Has Madam Abbess failed to train you?' he taunted gently.

She heard the door open; the young guard had returned alone. Samarkin had been put to the soldiers. 'Turn over,' the marshal told her. Sianon glanced shyly at the guard standing with his arms folded. 'Over,' the marshal repeated.

Her breasts sank against the seat of the couch. He made her spread her bottom cheeks to expose her anus. He dripped spittle on to it. Then he smacked it with his fingers. The shame she experienced did not stop the pleasure. Her breathing became laboured. The skin dried. He dripped more spittle and smacked again. Then he made her sit up. Even the movement – the turning over – aroused her. He made her keep her legs open. The seat pressed to her enlarged anus. She saw the young guard's burgeoning erection.

Then she felt the marshal's finger sliding slowly into her. Her sex took suck upon it; her liquid oozed out. She gasped meekly, her legs opened fully to try to keep at bay the pleasure and her hand came down and very lightly touched his wrist – the wrist that did these things to her – in a soft pleading gesture, a stroke, a fingertip caress – and suddenly her tongue reached up and licked his mouth and she lifted so the tip of his little finger pressed againt her burning anus.

'Kneel up – face me,' he whispered thickly. 'I shall make your breast-milk come.'

He kept touching her between the legs – her sex lips and her anus. 'Lean back against the couch. Stretch your arms out, Sianon. There . . . Oh, God . . .' he murmured. Her breasts had moved apart and lifted, tight and fat, crowned by the dark, waxy, bulging nipples. He pushed her arms over the back of the couch. She moaned because her breasts were so full they hurt her; they stood out further as the tension in the skin increased. 'Oh, God . . .' he whispered again: tiny points of milk had appeared upon her nipples. He licked them. They moved like small eggs trapped under the skin. The tiny creamy points erupted again. He licked them clean. The flow abated. He plucked her nipples, rubbed gently under her arms, gently but surely, so her breasts lifted and fell. Her nipples gradually softened. He took them between thumb and finger and milked them. They fattened and extended. Her mouth moved open. She was on her knees, legs open – wanting him to touch there too. He encircled each breast with a hand and squeezed. She moaned. Then he pushed his thumbs under her protrusive thickening nipples and stroked the upper sides with his fingers. Sianon's breathing stopped. Sweet trickles of coldness seemed to come inside her, running down her breastbone. She felt her nipple being sucked into his mouth; she shivered then sobbed in pleasure. Her nipple bulged then squirted, hard at first, then steadily, in a fine warm spray against the back of his throat.

Smiling smugly, the marshal sat back. 'Connar,' he shouted to the young guard, 'help me get her to the bed.'

They carried her, legs open, breast-milk running, then sat her in the middle of the bed. Connar removed his trousers and knelt between her thighs. The marshal pinned her arms back; reaching round, he put two fingers into her. Her mouth enveloped Connar's cock. She started to move against the marshal's fingers; her bottom pressed against the bed; the cock pushed deeper into her throat. She groaned; her nostrils flared. The cock pulled out glistening.

'Go back – lean on your hands.'

'Ahh!' The fingers still rummaged inside her.

'Go on.'

'Mmm. Ahh! Mmm . . . Oh. Oh!'

'Keep breathing – slowly.'

She could not keep her legs still. 'Ahh! Oh – please. Nnnn.' Her bottom cheeks were spread, her anus rubbed against the bed. Her elbows began shaking. The marshal put an arm around her shoulders, spread her sex and held her clitoris. 'Go forward.'

'No – oh please!' she begged. But she was too far gone now. 'Oh! Ooooo!' Her wet was running through his fingers.

'Go on. Go down. Let it press against the sheet.' When her wetted labia spread under her weight, she started losing control – making open-mouthed cries and moans. It was as if her upper body was somehow filled with trembling liquid; amid the squirming, he could hardly hold it. But he lifted her again, then eased her down, until her sex wept through the sheet. She tried to lift to ease the pleasure. Her breasts shook. Connar's cock stood hard; he tried to slip it under her armpit. She collapsed forwards, her belly in the marshal's hands, Connar's balls against her breast, his cock under her chin, her anus peeping out behind her, pulsing in the split.

And as the marshal's fingers slowly opened out her bottom, Sianon's climax started. As they journeyed up inside her, her climax was prolonged and the soft, smacked mouth of her bottom kept on squeezing. When he drew out his fingers, the inner skin inverted, pouting through the entrance then slipping back inside.

'Shall we take her down?' Connar asked.

'Not yet – we are only starting.'

They lowered her backwards, hands trapped, knees doubled underneath her and played with her again, taking turns, working slowly, one man beside her, kissing her stroking her breasts, the other holding her labia open – fattening them, pinching them, rubbing the clitoris with his thumb.

Then she was carried back to the couch. The marshal slid his belt off. Connar stood behind her. 'Hold her still ...' She felt Connar's hands under her arms, drawing her back, exposing her. She felt Connar's rigid cock against her cheek. Shivers came between her legs as the shiny, brass-tipped tongue of leather touched her, tapping her labia from side to side. Then she felt it being pushed inside gradually, deeply. Her belly bulged to meet it. Connar released her. Her swollen labia, stretching round it, tried to swallow, tried to keep pace with the relentless pushing. 'Oh yes,' the marshal whispered. 'Yes ...'

And from his perfect vantage point between her legs, he kept feeding the stiff brown band of leather into her until it happened again, that ambiguous gesture, that sweet encapsulation of submission: the gasp, the hand coming down between her legs in a soft half-protest, caressing the

226

belt that pushed inside. He draped the remainder over her thigh, where it writhed slowly with the movements of her belly. Then he watched her sweet impassioned face while he milked one breast then the other until her milk ran copiously, soaking his fingers. He wiped the emissions around her teats and under her arms. He put his fingers between her legs again and played with her until her juices, warm from inside her, started running down the belt. He held her open and gently pushed the leather even deeper until she moaned and her hand came down again and touched the belt so pleadingly and submissively. Then her mouth slid round the cock that nudged against her cheek.

With his belt still within her, the marshal teased her teats – stroked them, pulled them, sucked them. And her climax started through her nipples while he was still drinking. She tried to hide it but could not. Quickly he released her nipple and made Connar withdraw from her mouth. Then he just watched.

'Tongue out. Oh, yessss . . . sweet creature,' the marshal whispered. 'Poke it.' He kept her legs open with his knees, the leather writhed like a living thing, and he held her breasts up, his fingers stretching back the skin, and he watched her nipples squirting freely. 'Only through your breasts,' he said. And he saw her eyes then, dark with sexuality, below her soft eyebrows.

'Connar – you want to try her?'

Ceding his place to his deputy, the marshal walked around the room. He examined the instruments of insertion, looked at the pictures. But he could not keep his gaze from the girl Sianon – every murmur, every moan, excited him. He came back and leant against the table. Connar was kneeling astride her, squeezing her breasts around his rigid shaft. They kept slipping from his fingers and bouncing as he rode them. Her thighs were trying to squeeze the belt – could it be happening again, so soon? Reaching back, Connar pulled them open then continued riding her breasts. Her knees were trembling with the need to close. Her gasps of pleasure turned to groans. Then her milk came; it came in spurts because her breasts were bouncing.

It sprayed upon Connar's fingers, upon his cock and it sprayed upon the seat. He kept her breasts jumping, slapping and spraying against him until the thick gluts of his semen splashed across her teats. He wouldn't let her close her legs. Then as he knelt beside her, massaging her breasts, her milk bubbling through the shiny film of thickened semen being plastered over her skin, the climax took her properly. Her belly lifted; her shoulders arched over the back of the couch; her beautiful, dripping breasts hung upside down.

Reaching over from behind, the marshal tugged the belt; her labia pouted, the wet leather slid gently out and the smooth brass tongue was yielded. He picked up a vest; whose it was, he didn't know. It didn't matter. He unrolled it over Sianon's head, pushing her malleably submissive fingers gently through the armholes, stretching the cloth over her spunk-wet breasts. It scarcely fitted; it must have been the other girl's; it stuck in patches to her teats. He could smell her – sweat and spunk and milk all mixed together.

'Get up.' They took Sianon out, hurrying her downstairs towards the music and laughter, pushing her in front of them along the narrow candlelit corridor, her naked legs and bottom bathed in pools of liquid light.

'Stop.'

Sianon half turned. The marshal did it to her standing, while Connar watched. He came in from behind. He pulled Samarkin's sticky vest up over her teats. He would not let her brace herself against the wall. She stood there, overbalancing, her breasts out before her, bouncing to his thrusts. He made her hold her bottom cheeks apart, so he could get deeper into her sex. He bottomed out. Her toes came off the floor; he had to hold her. Her breasts spilled up and out above his hands. He said that he could taste her – with his cock – the raw sweet honeydew inside her. When he pulled out and turned her, his cock was coated with it; he pressed it to her belly. She tried to climb him to get it back inside. Her breasts slipped upwards against his chest; he fingered her between her legs and she buckled. He hauled

228

her upright and made her run, with her vest rolled up to her armpits and her breasts bouncing up and down.

As Sianon stumbled through the doorway of the hall, the marshal caught her. She clung to him. 'We are late, it seems,' he laughed. 'The rut is well begun.'

Sianon's frightened eyes darted around the naked girls on the tables, on the floor, girls being apportioned between the wild-eyed drunken soldiers. Some girls were bound together in pairs; others were fastened to the wall. Above, on the balcony, a girl was being lifted over a makeshift swing. The marshal took Sianon by the chin. 'And now – your bottom, missy, if you please.'

Obediently Sianon faced the wall. 'Hold it open.' She spread herself. Her face and neck began to burn. Her anus was exposed; her sex was naked, pushed out behind her; they would see it make its moisture. They used their bare hands, taking turns again, smacking upwards, deep into her crack. Her arousal came on quickly. 'Get it open wider. Push it out.' She teetered, knees bent, legs opening ever wider. With so harsh a smacking, the mouth of her bottom swelled and burned. A moan of sexual submission escaped her lips. 'Oh, yes . . . Look at how she moves it. Keep it going. Slower. Just gently – slap it. Ohhh . . .'

Her knees trembled; she was near to coming. She felt as if a bulging hot fruit had been jammed into her bottom. They played with it, wetted it then turned her round. 'Vest up,' the marshal said. 'Legs spread.' He moved behind her. Connar was in front. She wanted to close her eyes. Sounds of ribaldry and pleasure issued from all around. The air was thick with the smell of smoke and wine. Then she saw staring at her a woman – not a nun or novice, but a woman, very tall, dressed like a soldier and wearing short-cropped, sun-streaked hair.

There was a trio next to her on the floor: a girl crouching over a soldier's face, another man fingering her. The woman was watching the girl, perhaps directing, but casting frequent glances at Sianon.

The girl leant forward: the small brown ring between her buttocks expanded and the soldier's fingers entered. The

229

man below her began to moan. Her thighs convulsed about his head. She started grinding downwards, open-legged now, driving her sex deeper, pushing for his throat. She shuddered, collapsed forward, her bottom contracting in spasms about the buried fingers. The man with his fingers inside her started slapping her breasts and taunting her because she was coming. And at that moment, the marshal began rubbing Sianon's breasts and drawing her nipples out for Connar to play with. Sianon gasped; the girl climaxed; Connar gently tugged Sianon's nipples. She slumped against the marshal, her nipples out on softening stalks. And the woman with short hair was watching her – taking charge of her from a distance with her gaze. Sianon moaned gently. Her breasts shuddered. 'Not yet,' the marshal whispered, pulling her vest completely off her, leaving her breasts wobbling. 'I want these bigger – you hear me? So full of milk, they hurt you all the time.'

They moved her on, passing a girl sitting spread-legged in a bowl of punch from which the men were drinking. Beside her was Samarkin, slumped on her back over a soldier's knee. Her head was to the floor, her legs in the air. A swan-necked drinking vessel sprayed a fine jet of wine upon her swollen sex and anus. The wine spilled down her belly and over her breasts. Willing tongues licked it from her skin. Her protruding labia were opened, the fine jet played inside. Samarkin jerked in pleasure when it brushed her clitoris. When the smooth glass tube was fed into her anus and the jet sprayed up inside, her body twisted and she climaxed, her wine-soaked breasts protruding, craving to be sucked.

Then they found Vernel. Thick loops of cloth were round her ankles. Her toes wriggled – she was on her back or rather, on her shoulders, for her legs were almost straight above her in the air; they had been fastened open. Her eyelids were heavy, sleepy with arousal. Her sex and bottom exuded cream.

As Connar took over the clystering of Vernel, the marshal worked Sianon's breasts. Her nipples were almost as thick as his thumb. He rolled them gently; she seeped little creamy seepage; he scolded her.

'Perhaps she needs them smacking,' said a soft voice. It was as if a bolt of pleasure went through Sianon.

'Maran!'

Sianon looked up and saw the woman who had been watching her. Her jerkin stood open. Her breasts were strapped with criss-cross leather. A beaded cord was round one wrist.

'Let me oil her,' she said, proffering a bottle.

'Where?'

'Where she needs it most.'

They put Sianon kneeling on one of the tables. Her head sank back. Her knees splayed for the oiling. Soft sucking sounds issued from between her legs, soft murmurs from her lips. The oil trickled from Sianon's sex down Maran's sun-bronzed wrist. As Maran's fingers probed her, Sianon's breathing deepened. Then Maran put the bottle down and used two oil-drenched hands on her, one between her legs, one on her breasts. Her breasts changed shape under the pressure of fluid being massaged down to the teats. She gasped in pleasure as the fingers inside her, curling down, pressed against her bottom from within.

The fingers pulled out; her sex stayed open, hot. Maran unbuckled her trousers and lifted Sianon up against her, breast to burnished breast, sex to sun-blonde sex. 'Gently,' she whispered. 'Slowly . . .' Sianon whimpered in pleasure. The stiff ridge of female flesh slid between her oily pubic lips. The slim, bronze female fingers probed her swollen bottom. 'More oil here,' Maran said. When the nozzle touched her bottom, Sianon's mouth reached for Maran's nipple pushing through the strands of leather. The oil glugged and bubbled into Sianon's bottom. Maran sucked her tongue and clawed her softly, deep inside her bottom. When she moaned out loud, Maran pushed her gently away.

More oil was poured into her sex and bottom; thicker fingers followed. Maran watched. Sianon began gurgling, moaning, twisting, bucking against the fingering. The maral began briskly to slap her teats. She sagged forwards, breasts slipping, wobbling.

'She's coming on,' Maran said.

'Quickly – help me carry her.'

Her climax came as she was being lifted; her breast-milk arced across the air. It kept pumping as she was carried down the back stairs. With no fingers now inside her, and no slaps against her teats, the pleasure came to her diffusely. 'She's still hard,' he said. Her clitoris was poking up. Her sex was swollen.

'Don't touch it. Just hold her steady.' Maran pushed Sianon's knees back. Her belly arched, her naked labia protruded from between her legs. Maran fed the beaded cord slowly up Sianon's bottom. Then she put her finger through the loop and pulled. Sianon's belly bulged; her anus pouted. The cord shed pleasure bead by bead. She shivered as the cord came free.

'She's still on,' said the marshal. 'Her knob – still hard. Oh, God . . .'

'Then keep her still,' Maran said. 'Relax the muscle,' she told Sianon. 'Let it open.' Sianon's feet were held trembling in the air. 'Wrap her breasts up. Make a sling.' They used her vest. When the marshal drew it tight and then the beaded cord was drawn out through her bottom, she started pumping properly. Twin pools of warmth soaked right through the cloth and dripped to the floor.

'We need somewhere quieter,' said the marshal, 'where we can –'

He was interrupted by a soldier: 'Marshal – this girl. Have a look at her.' She was physically small, small breasted. Her cheeks were wet with tears.

'She was hiding on the stairs. She keeps asking for the Abbess.' Then the soldier displayed her. Her sex was unused. But her anus was enlarged and tender and her labia were fastened by a tiny, ruby-studded chain.

The marshal watched the lights of the abbey recede across the lake. The first glow of cloudless dawn was already in the sky: the departure had been late. But his cargo of precious flesh was safely stowed below deck – all except for one sweet creature, who languished nude in his arms. He name was Leah. She had been kept as concubine to the Abbess. But the Abbess had tired of her.

Leah's breasts were small and unblemished; her anus was not. Her tiny chain tinkled as her naked legs stretched open for his thumb to slip inside it. Leah moaned with sexual arousal: already, he had played with her long. Her hand came down and cupped her sex.

'You have it now, this feeling?' he whispered.

She gasped softly: 'Between my legs, where I am chained.'

'And in your bottom?'

'Burning.'

'And this burning makes your sweetness come?'

Leah shuddered as the soft thick muscle of her bottom moved with his thumb. Her fingertips cupped her sex but could not stem the flow of young warm honey from inside her.

In the garden he had given her a kerchief with which to cover her sex while the soldiers took pleasure with her mouth and bottom. And oh, how Leah liked to suck cock. Afterwards the smell of come was strong upon her lips. When he had drawn her open by the ankle and smacked her anus, she came to climax – a prolonged, diffuse and beautiful one. When he took her cloth away, her little sex began dripping honey past its chain.

The marshal carried her to the prow of the ferry. She became frightened by the sounds of whipping. When he put her down near the lamp, she clung to him. It was a sexual whipping – buttocks, inner thighs, around the sex, the nipples. The marshal tickled Leah's chain. She stood stock-still, breathless in arousal.

It was the domain of the boat-women. One whipped, the other fingered, wetted, kissed, inserted. The victim was upright, facing away, spread-eagled, naked, fastened by the wrists, feet and anus. The marshal looked at Leah. She did not understand how the taut emergent cord was secured to the post. He spoke to the women; they let her touch it. And then they touched her: they lifted her belly over the rail, opened the eye of her bottom and put the stock of the whip

233

just inside. Because of the way her body reacted, they did not want to return her. The marshal lifted Leah down and put her where she could see the prisoner's face. Her eyes widened then she gasped.

'You know him?' the marshal asked.

'The Commissioner –' Leah whispered.

The marshal laughed. 'Is that what he told you?'

Leah's expression changed; her gaze slid down the body to the swollen balls, the standing cock, so unnaturally distended, pierced by the heavy ring. 'Let Shenta show you what to do,' he said.

Innocence empowered knows how to take its pleasure. Leah required scant guidance. She liked to touch cock, liked to kiss it. Shenta did the punishing, Leah the masturbation and the kissing. She seemed fascinated by the ring through the head of the shaft; she kept licking it and pushing her tongue through it. Her small breasts rubbed the prisoner's thigh; her fingers explored the place where the cord went inside him. Leah's nervously sexual suckings brought the prisoner on. Shenta pulled her away and whipped the cock as it climaxed. Strings and flecks of semen squirted past the ring and twisted in the air. Witnessing this while she was prevented from licking so aroused Leah that the marshal had to take her aside.

He suspended her from a punishment ring. Her body dangled, toes above the deck. Her fingers clasped the ring. Despite her virginity, Leah's sexuality was acute. But throughout the things he did to her, he was unsure if her climax ever fully came. He loved the little cries of pleasure she made. Her clitoris stayed hot and fiercely erect; he touched it minimally; he wanted her to experience the feelings through her anus.

Shenta asked to be allowed again to touch Leah while she was in this state. Few pleasures ran deeper for the marshal than to support a highly aroused girl while she was being masturbated or sucked by an experienced woman. It put a bone in his cock that hurt him. Leah's full young bottom jutted out, her ruby chain tinkling in Shenta's fingers. 'I want her,' said Shenta. 'Sweet cut that she is – how I want her.'

Making a fist, the marshal pinched the velvet areola under Leah's nipple between the knuckles of his fingers. She dangled like a fruit ripe for plucking. And like a fruit that you would squeeze the sweet juice out of, Leah was now lifted high in the air, overbalancing, open-legged, her little jewelled sex inside the marshal's open mouth, pumping its heavy nectar round his stiffly poking tongue.

'Where's Maran?' he asked Shenta as he set the gasping Leah down.

They found her in a cabin with the girl Sianon. Maran had her nude astride a stool bolted to the floor. A rope dangled below it from the centre. A tube snaked up from between her legs to a bag hooked to the ceiling, but the tube was very fine and it came from the front. Maran was preparing to re-insert it. Looking up, she said:

'I asked her to whip him. She refused. Now she must take her medicine.' She greased the gold tip of the catheter.

'Maran is filling her,' the marshal whispered to Leah. 'It will come on quickly.' He put Leah down – and again she was inquisitive. Sianon's legs moved restlessly; the action stirred her breasts. Lifting her tousled hair from her face the marshal touched her waxy nipples. Her breasts looked fit to overflow again. The tube trembled with the pressure of liquid. Sianon started making small groans of pleasure and trying to move against Maran's fingers, which kept pinching the tube to stay the flow. 'Watch,' said Maran, reaching down. As soon as she took hold of the dangling rope beneath her, Sianon began moaning. Leah's eyes widened; her breathing quickened; the marshal rubbed her small breasts. Sianon's arms became uneasy. Shenta poured more liquid into the bag. Sianon gasped. Maran, crouching, pulled the rope gently downwards. Sianon cried on the verge of pleasure. Maran wrapped the dangling end of the rope around a stick and began twisting it. The more the rope tightened the more Sianon moaned. 'Leave her now, a little while,' the marshal said. The twisted rope remained in place. He brought Leah closer.

'There is a hole through the stool. The rope goes up her bottom. It is attached to this . . .' He showed her one of the devices. 'This part – when it is inside you – look . . .' He twisted the base and it opened like a flower-bud. 'Open, like this, it cannot be withdrawn. While she is being filled or played with, her fixing is tightened – slowly – till it brings on the feelings.'

Maran showed Leah the tiny strap that could be used gently to smack the erect clitoris. And she showed her how the pleasure of insertion of the greased tube between Sianon's legs caused Sianon's breasts to bulge. As the bag was topped up with liquid and Sianon murmured and moaned her responses to the toyings and her bladder progressively filled, the marshal explored those things short of climax that made Sianon's let-down come about – stroking, pressing with his fingers, stripping gently downwards to her teats, and most effectively of all, slapping. Slapping made her milk come quickly. Her breasts would tighten, then shiver – like the build up to a sneeze, but the sneeze would not happen; instead her milk came in warm spurts, wetting the fingers that still slapped her, so the spurts splashed back. And then the wetness of the smacking made the spurts become a flood. Her shoulders sank back and her luscious breasts pushed out for smacking. He asked her to control her let-down while he played with her nipples. She moaned, for the flow of milk kept up inside her; the ends of her breasts swelled visibly. He saw Maran looking at Leah and exchanging glances with Shenta.

'Take her,' he finally said. Leah stared pleadingly at Maran, who approached her with one of the instruments of attachment on a cord. Maran turned her around; Leah stood between the two women as Maran slowly introduced the shiny bulb into her anus. When Leah's ring muscle was partly open, with Shenta pinching her breasts, it seemed Leah might come. Maran's slim, bronzed arms enfolded Leah's body until the moment had passed. Then the metal bulb was twisted until it opened out inside her. 'Lift up.' Leah could hardly stand.

An upright post was chosen and Leah's bottom was put against it with the rope drawn through a hole. When the rope was tied-in, Leah's heels lifted from the deck. Then

Maran masturbated her. Leah's belly sagged because of the way she was fastened. She gasped and shuddered; her legs moved open. As she buckled, Maran moved away and Leah hung doubled from the waist, moaning softly, her climax incomplete. Maran lifted her shoulders up and back against the post. She fingered Leah again; Leah again buckled; her moans were louder. Maran lifted her up. She set her legs wider apart. Leah was on tiptoes. 'Tighten her,' Maran said. Shenta did it. Then Maran began to slip things under the chain of Leah's sex until her thighs cramped and she teetered on the verge of coming.

The marshal stood in front of Sianon. He took the tube very gently out of her. He could feel how full she was. Every movement made her murmur sweet protests. He opened his shirt, put his arms around her and held her beautiful body to him, her hot breasts deforming softly and moistly to his chest. And he kissed her. Then he asked her to lean back. He put his fingers in between her legs and into her. He slapped her sex with the tiny strap. And he applied a gentle half twist to the stick fastened to the rope up her bottom, keeping it in this state of tightness. And because the tension remained there, her climax was drawn out, all the while her urine spurted and splashed into his hand.

He unfastened her from the stool but left the rope dangling from inside her and laid her on her back on the table, where Maran was waiting to minister to her breasts. She wetted them then fitted a small bulbous glass over each nipple. 'Bring me a taper'. She lifted the glass and held the taper under it until the air was consumed, then fitted it over the nipple. The wetness sealed it and the suction began; the glass remained in place. She did the same with the other breast. As the thin air in the glasses cooled, the suction deepened. 'Look . . .' Sianon's bursting nipples were being drawn into the glasses. Her milk was coming in tiny pinpricks welling from the tips. Sianon moaned. Her breasts rolled outwards, stiffly bulging, erect, capped by the milk-blotched glasses. Maran drew Sianon's arms away from them. She fingered her in the armpits. The marshal

237

opened her labia and smacked bare-handed inside her legs. He did not smack her sex, but because he had opened it the pleasure was focused there. Maran kissed her like a lover through the smacking. Sianon gasped and moaned and put her tongue out; Maran sucked it. The marshal tugged the rope in Sianon's bottom until her let-down came on fully and Sianon creamed into the glasses. They turned her gently on to her side and detached them. Then they fed her milk to Leah.

Drawing Sianon to her knees, Maran fastened her wrists to the ceiling then played with her breasts, squeezing them individually between her hands. 'Let it come,' she whispered. As she pulled the rope between Sianon's legs and the weight was drawn against Sianon's anus from inside, Sianon tried to open. Sianon moaned. Maran's lips pushed hungrily about her nipple and Sianon milked into her mouth. When the marshal spoke of smacking inside Sianon's sex, her milk came even through the breast that was not being sucked. He held it squeezed upwards and pointed to one side, and kept whispering, 'Good,' and that he was pleased. Her milk trickled down between his fingers.

Maran pulled away from Sianon's breast. 'Shenta – the crop.' Shenta left the trembling Leah fastened to the post.

Sianon hung there, a circle of wetness around one glutted nipple, a runnel of milk snaking down her other side. Maran took the crop to her and whipped her underarms, not hard nor long, but precisely and deliberately. A small deluge of milk issued from her nipples.

'Do it again,' the marshal said. But he was watching Leah.

Red lines appeared under Sianon's arms; her breasts stood milky-white, her nipples bulging brown. Maran whipped until the deluge was repeated.

'Again ...' This time he held Sianon by the nipples; Maran whipped beneath them. 'Oh God,' he whispered. He could feel it pumping between his fingers. Her head fell back; her breast-milk squirted inside his wrist. The dangling rope moved snake-like over the table. Leah stood, legs open, bottom squirming against the post. Leaving Sianon to the women, he detached Leah's tether, released her clamp then tugged the cord; the closed weight slid through the cup of Leah's anus. The skin was pulled; he put his fingers there.

'She milks too freely,' Maran was saying of Sianon. It seemed she wanted to block the flow – not stop the build-up but only prevent expulsion. They fitted clamps to her nipples. Thereafter, the only leakage came between her legs. He felt Leah's anus tighten round his searching fingers while Sianon's open sex was being smacked. Leah's mouth fell open; her warm breath caressed his neck; her chain tinkled; her little teats engorged; he squeezed them gently in his fingers. Keeping her legs open he spread her labia as far as her chain would allow. She started leaking. Maran was smacking Sianon at a steady pace, smacking her while she was wet; smacking the insides of her labia, not touching her clitoris. Splashes of her wetness sprinkled her thighs. Her breasts splayed sideways. Shenta started to stroke her clamped nipples then to lift them back and smack the undersides. Sianon's breasts pulsed unleaking, her warm lubricant pouring out of her to wet the table.

The marshal touched Leah's small, jellied breasts, softly pinched the tender nipples. Her belly bulged, so sexually, so sweetly. Sianon was moaning. Leah's shaking legs bowed open, wanting him to touch her up there, where Sianon was being penetrated by Maran's hand. He slid his arm under hers and across her shoulder-blades. His hand was in her moist armpit. When he lifted, she moaned, her back arched, her breasts thrust out. The marshal smacked them – gently – while Sianon's legs were lifted open in the air and the women took the small strap to her sex, her anus and her breasts, which began lactating through the clamps, wetting the strap. When the marshal put his fingers between Leah's legs, her lubricant came in tiny spurts like the milk from Sianon's constricted nipples. When the milk-wet strap smacked down on Sianon's anus, her climax came. The marshal quickly slipped his thumb up Leah's bottom and Leah nearly climaxed too. He carried her on his hand to Maran's bed then leant her shoulders to the wall. He tucked her knees up underneath her breasts. Her labia were swollen, nipped by the ends of their chain. He took a long, curved white feather to her clitoris and whispered, 'Tuck them – tuck your knees.' It made her sex project so beautifully moistly. There were tiny red marks where the gold pierced her skin. The small knob of her clitoris pouted out above her chain. The feather-tip kissed it, stroked it, moistly smacked it. Soft, wet, sticky, dabbing smacks of lightweight feather smote Leah's shiny sexual knob. Her chain stretched taut. Her gathered belly was reaching up. Her anus was exposed.

Maran appeared behind him. 'Let me taste her.'

Yielding his place, the marshal watched the way Maran dealt pleasure to Leah and how Leah responded – how she was able to take it, layer upon layer yet remain aroused, desiring ever more. Maran's tongue laved Leah's anus, licked the flesh there sticky-clean, lapped the honey that Leah yielded. She spread Leah's knees as if she were a specimen on a surgeon's table. Leah's thigh muscles bulged; her sex opened, like a full-lipped oyster, to the limits of its chain. Maran's middle finger slipped along the lippy furrow, stroked the shiny sexual pearl. Leah's legs jerked open. Maran slapped them. The middle finger pushed inside the pouted anus. Leah moaned. Her sex gaped sweetly. Her belly puffed as if she were pregnant. Her knees came off the bed. Maran slapped her thighs back down. Mouth to sex, Maran took Leah. Leah's small fingers clawed the pillow. Her tongue poked out. Her head rolled. Maran leant back and smacked the wet chained lips of her sex and the bloated, pink, sticky-clean anus.

The marshal opened the box and removed the jewel-studded Tormunite sheath. It was appropriate Leah should receive this now, on the eve of her arrival. He placed her face down on the sheets. And he examined her bottom intimately. Then he put the sheath on. She moaned when this aid to perverse opulent pleasure opened out her anal ring. But her bottom came up to meet it. The jewel-sheathed shaft pushed gently through her folds of tender skin. Her ear was burning brighter than her bottom. He

240

took the lobe between his lips. She tried to bring her legs together. He turned her on her side, exposing her sex. Carefully, he drew a tubular fold of the sheet up between her labia, up under her chain, up against her clitoris. The fold turned wet as she lubricated. When he drew the fold out, her bottom tightened; the pleasure was exquisite. He thrust gently deeper; but as he pulled back, she went so tight that his cock slipped from the sheath. And she was starting to climax. He tried to get his cock back in; it slipped underneath; the tip lodged in the mouth of her sex then slid along her pubic lips and snagged under the chain. The sudden tightness caused a premature squirt of hot semen over her clitoris. She moaned; he held her legs open, held her gently, held her still and withdrew his glans from under her chain. And her pleasure was for now averted.

He turned her on her belly with her legs wide open. Maran gently pulled the jewelled sheath from inside her. Then she licked her anus softly until the tension came, the nearness of pleasure.

He took Sianon in his arms. He let her watch as the women made a toy of Leah, kissed her, lay between her legs. They opened her sex and introduced the round quill of the feather into her tiny pee-hole while they rubbed her clitoris. The feather jumped; Maran stroked it; Leah's nipples came up to fervent points. Maran spread Leah's legs. Shenta held the glass: thick creamy droplets of Sianon's breast-milk fell on Leah's warm, pink, naked sex. Shenta licked them. Leah struggled to keep the feelings at bay. The tip of her feather shook circles in the air. When Maran showed her the thick, shiny dildo, Leah's legs tucked up in wanton readiness, her anus pouted and her small labia stood out redly, linked by their shiny chain. Shenta continued to finger-paint Leah's labia with Sianon's milk while the sturdy girth of polished wood was inserted up Leah's bottom. As the base of the dildo spread her fully, Leah's climax came. The women had to hold her down; the dildo was expelled by her contractions.

Leah's shudders of pleasure seemed to echo through Sianon's bulging breasts. The marshal pulled the clamps off with his teeth then cupped his hands beneath them as her breast-milk overflowed. 'What will they not do with you when they get you in the palace?' he sighed.

For one thing was certain: that in all his years of plying this lake, he had never known creatures more sweetly sexual than Leah and Sianon. And no practice or perversion the Tormunite masters might have in store for them could ever surpass these simple pleasures – a full breast pumping warm milk gently through your fingers, a warm, chained sex taking suck upon your glans.

He went with Leah one more time – one last time – cock-naked, just to feel it that way, in her bottom, her hot moist sticky inner body kissing his tightly drawn-back foreskin; her back hollowing so deeply it felt his knob in-side her was rubbing noses with the bumps along her spine; and between her legs, her fingers pressing the honey-cloth against her partly open sex to gather her every drip.

The women were brought on deck into a sun-warmed early day. The water was still and shallow. All was silent in the cove. The ferry stood off a hundred yards from shore yet still the huge walls of the palace-fortress loomed above it, dwarfing it to a tiny boat.

'What of the male one?' Maran asked coldly.

'If he no longer amuses . . .' The marshal threw a glance far out into the lake.

Sianon cried out, falling to her knees.

The marshal walked over to her. 'He means something to you?'

'Yes – oh, yes,' she pleaded. 'Yes.' The tears filled her eyes. 'He only thought to save me –'

'But you were not lost . . .' he whispered, shaking his head, stroking Sianon's tresses. 'What has gone before counts for nought here, Sianon.' But Sianon's clear brown eyes remained uplifted, pleading. There is something about beauty and gentleness, that speaks to the soul.

Maran stepped forward. 'Then let him take his chance now – with the others.' Sianon closed her eyes.

Suddenly there came a booming sound like thunder. Sh

looked up. The tranquillity of the scene was broken: the great gates were opening.

'You shall be first, Sianon.' He gathered her gently, as you would a precious, special thing, carried her to the side and lowered her naked and open-legged into the water. She gasped with the cold; her breasts tightened, submerged then floated, expressing milk in cloudy drifts into the clear blue, freezing water.

NEW BOOKS

Coming up from Nexus, Sapphire and Black Lace

Nexus

The Pleasure Chamber by Brigitte Markham
July 1999   Price £5.99   ISBN: 0 352 33371 5

After an unsuccessful attempt at seduction by her friend Laura, Mary escapes to the French chateau where her flatmate, Philippe, is spending a holiday. The Count at the chateau has some curious ways of entertaining his guests, however, and the naive Mary and Philippe are soon initiated into new and perverse ways of loving. Laura, worried about Mary, follows her to France and joins in the bizarre games at the chateau. But what they don't realise is that the Count harbours a terrible secret, which puts all their lives in danger. By the author of *Chains of Shame*.

The Black Masque by Lisette Ashton
July 1999   Price £5.99   ISBN: 0 352 33372 3

The ceremonies of the black masque are magnificent events steeped in an erotic blend of myth and fantasy. The depravity of these rituals is boundless and each rite culminates in orgiastic excess. As they move towards their greatest ceremony yet passions run high among the perverse members. Eager virgins are prepared and the sacrificial altar is readied as the masque anticipates its finest night. Unwittingly entangled in the twisted ceremony, private investigator Jo Valentine is drawn into their dark world of pleasure and pain.

Obsession by Maria del Rey
July 1999   Price £5.99   ISBN: 0 352 33375 8

A mysterious woman phones Jonathan de Molay late one night. A wrong number. A mistake. He should forget her, and the bizarre world of which she accidentally revealed a glimpse. But Jonathan can't get her out of his mind. He searches for her, and finds himself among people who are masters, mistresses and slaves. His personal odyssey is a story of the discovery of pleasure – through submission and pain. By the author of *The Institute*. This is the sixth in a series of Nexus Classics.

A Dozen Strokes Various
August 1999   Price £5.99   ISBN: 0 352 33423 1
This, the first in a series of themed collections from Nexus, is a paean to the delights of discipline. Mixing extracts from hard-to-find genre classics with new material, this is the definitive CP compilation, and an indispensable guide to the joys of a freshly birched bottom.

The Master of Castleleigh by Jacqueline Bellevois
August 1999   Price £5.99   ISBN: 0 352 33424 X
When Richard Buxton is forced to leave the delights of 19th century London, marry and run a country estate, he assumes that the pleasures of the whip are no longer his to be had. Both the estate, and his new wife Clarissa, however, provide unexpectedly perverse opportunities, and he is diligent in making imaginative use of them.

His Mistress's Voice by G. C. Scott
August 1999   Price £5.99   ISBN: 0 352 33425 8
Sensing a powerful, animal drive within Tom that echoes her own, Beth decides to make Tom's initiation into bondage a swift one. His hesitant first steps soon quicken as he is drawn further into her dark and intimate web. Just when their relationship seems to have reached its peak, Beth introduces him to Harriet – and the games suddenly become even kinkier and more convoluted. This is the seventh in a series of Nexus Classics.

A new imprint of lesbian fiction

Millennium Fever by Julia Wood
July 1999   Price £6.99   ISBN: 0 352 33368 5
The millennium is approaching and so is Nikki's fortieth birthday.
Married for twenty years, she's grown tired of playing the trophy
wife. Previously, her sapphic adventures have all been conducted in
secret, but her attraction to other women is growing stronger by the
day. In contrast, young writer Georgie has always been out and
proud. But there's one thing they have in common – in the midst of
millennial fever, they both want action and satisfaction.

All That Glitters by Franca Nera
August 1999   Price £6.99   ISBN: 0 352 33426 6
Marta Broderick is an art dealer with a difference. She has inherited
the art empire of her Austrian uncle, and has been entrusted with
continuing his mission of retrieving art treasures lost in the Second
World War. When an investigation is set up into Marta's activities,
the chief investigator discovers to her horror that Marta is a former
lover, and one with especially kinky tastes. When another of Marta's
innocent lovers appears on the scene, can the investigator keep her
mind on the job in hand?

NEXUS BACKLIST

All books are priced £5.99 unless another price is given. If a date is supplied, the book in question will not be available until that month in 1999.

CONTEMPORARY EROTICA

AMAZON SLAVE	Lisette Ashton		
BAD PENNY	Penny Birch		Feb
THE BLACK GARTER	Lisette Ashton		
THE BLACK WIDOW	Lisette Ashton		Mar
BOUND TO OBEY	Amanda Ware		
BRAT	Penny Birch		May
CHAINS OF SHAME	Brigitte Markham		
DARK DELIGHTS	Maria del Rey		
DARLINE DOMINANT	Tania d'Alanis		
A DEGREE OF DISCIPLINE	Zoe Templeton	£4.99	
DISCIPLES OF SHAME	Stephanie Calvin		Apr
THE DISCIPLINE OF NURSE RIDING	Yolanda Celbridge		
DISPLAYS OF INNOCENTS	Lucy Golden		Apr
EDUCATING ELLA	Stephen Ferris	£4.99	
EMMA'S SECRET DOMINATION	Hilary James	£4.99	
EXPOSING LOUISA	Jean Aveline		Jan
FAIRGROUND ATTRACTIONS	Lisette Ashton		
JULIE AT THE REFORMATORY	Angela Elgar	£4.99	
LINGERING LESSONS	Sarah Veitch		Jan
MASTER OF DISCIPLINE	Zoe Templeton		
THE MISTRESS OF STERNWOOD GRANGE	Arabella Knight		

SAMPLERS & COLLECTIONS

EROTICON 4	Various		
THE FIESTA LETTERS	ed. Chris Lloyd	£4.99	
NEW EROTICA 4			

NEXUS CLASSICS

A new imprint dedicated to putting the finest works of erotic fiction back in print

THE IMAGE	Jean de Berg	Feb
CHOOSING LOVERS FOR JUSTINE	Aran Ashe	Mar
THE INSTITUTE	Maria del Rey	Apr
AGONY AUNT	G. C. Scott	May
THE HANDMAIDENS	Aran Ashe	Jun

- -

Please send me the books I have ticked above.

Name   ....

Address   ....

            ....

            ....

            .... Post code........................

Send to: **Cash Sales, Nexus Books, Thames Wharf Studios, Rainville Road, London W6 9HT**

Please enclose a cheque or postal order, made payable to **Nexus Books**, to the value of the books you have ordered plus postage and packing costs as follows:

UK and BFPO – £1.00 for the first book, 50p for the second book and 30p for each subsequent book to a maximum of £3.00;

Overseas (including Republic of Ireland) – £2.00 for the first book, £1.00 for the second book and 50p for each subsequent book.

If you would prefer to pay by VISA or ACCESS/MASTER-CARD, please write your card number and expiry date here:

....

Please allow up to 28 days for delivery.

Signature ....

- -